MANTIS

MANTIS

WARRIOR WOMAN OF THE SAMURAI
BOOK TWO

INDIA MILLAR

Red Empress Publishing
www.RedEmpressPublishing.com

Copyright © India Millar
www.IndiaMillar.co.uk

Cover Design by Cherith Vaughan
www.CoversbyCherith.com

All rights reserved. No part of this publication may be reproduced, stored in a retrieval system, or transmitted in any form or by any means, electronic, mechanical, photocopying, recoding, or otherwise, without the prior written consent of the author.

ALSO BY INDIA MILLAR

Secrets from the Hidden House

The Geisha with the Green Eyes

The Geisha Who Could Feel No Pain

The Dragon Geisha

The Geisha Who Ran Away

The Song of the Wild Geese

The Red Thread of Fate

This World is Ours

Warrior Woman of the Samurai

Firefly

Mantis

Chameleon

Spider

Dragonfly

Scorpion

Cricket

Moth

Daughter of the Yakuza

Wild Iris

Midnight Sakura

Haiku Collections

Dreams from the Hidden House

Song of the Samurai

*This book is humbly dedicated to Baizenten, th[e]
Goddess of writers and geisha. May both you and
words written herein!*

MANTIS

WARRIOR WOMAN OF THE SAMURAI
BOOK TWO

INDIA MILLAR

Red Empress Publishing
www.RedEmpressPublishing.com

Copyright © India Millar
www.IndiaMillar.co.uk

Cover Design by Cherith Vaughan
www.CoversbyCherith.com

All rights reserved. No part of this publication may be reproduced, stored in a retrieval system, or transmitted in any form or by any means, electronic, mechanical, photocopying, recoding, or otherwise, without the prior written consent of the author.

ALSO BY INDIA MILLAR

Secrets from the Hidden House

The Geisha with the Green Eyes

The Geisha Who Could Feel No Pain

The Dragon Geisha

The Geisha Who Ran Away

The Song of the Wild Geese

The Red Thread of Fate

This World is Ours

Warrior Woman of the Samurai

Firefly

Mantis

Chameleon

Spider

Dragonfly

Scorpion

Cricket

Moth

Daughter of the Yakuza

Wild Iris

Midnight Sakura

Haiku Collections

Dreams from the Hidden House

Song of the Samurai

This book is humbly dedicated to Baizenten, the Japanese Goddess of writers and geisha. May both you and she enjoy the words written herein!

PREFACE

*Though the sex to which I belong is considered weak you will
nevertheless find me a rock that bends to no wind.*
Queen Elizabeth I of England, 1558—1603

PROLOGUE

Yo sifted through the wood ash with me. When we had enough, I smeared it on my hands, feet, and face. I loosed my hair and allowed it to fall lank and unlovely around my shoulders. I had not washed it for over a week and it looked dirty and unkempt. To make sure the effect was properly noticeable—for I expected to be viewed only from a distance—I rubbed more ash into my scalp, combing it through to the tips of my hair.

"Will I do?" I asked Yo. He looked me over carefully and nodded.

"Apart from your kimono, you look like a petitioner. Just remember to behave like one as well."

"Of course I will." I smiled at him, but then a thought occurred to me and I paused. "Do you think he might find it strange that my hair is so short?" I asked.

Yo shrugged. "I doubt it. From all I've heard of Akafumu, he's not greatly interested in anything that doesn't concern his own comfort. Even if he did notice, he would probably think you had cut it as a mark of respect for your position."

I nodded in agreement. My kimono was white cotton,

the color of mourning. Not silk, as that would shine inappropriately. My obi, also, was white. Perfectly plain. I held my grimy hands out in front of me and was pleased. Just right, I thought. After all, I was a petitioner, one who begged for my lord's mercy. It was only correct that I should look the part.

"Ready?" Yo asked. I nodded and stepped forward briskly. He left me at the great door leading into Lord Akafumu's audience chamber. He could not come in with me. I glanced down at my hands and feet, and when I raised my head, he had gone. I wasn't surprised. After all, he was shinobi—what superstitious peasants called a ninja. It was his stock in trade to move silently, to vanish like a ghost. And to kill like one, if necessary.

But now, my lover had gone, and I was alone.

It was down to me to ask for what I wanted. If I failed, then I had no one to blame but myself. The thought gave me courage.

ONE

There is nothing in
This world that I cannot face
If you are with me

*M*y neck ached. I turned to punch my sobagara—the buckwheat-hull filled pillow that was usually so very good at supporting my spine and neck—and winced as my closed fist met something much harder. I dismissed the minor discomfort with a shrug of irritation. I was still tired. More than tired, my body craved oblivion.

"Keiko-chan." The man's voice was soft and very tender. I didn't care. I wanted him to go away and leave me in peace. Almost as annoying, a breeze must have come through my open shoji and disturbed the covering I had drawn over my face. The light was in my eyes and the sound of fluttering close by.

"Go away," I sighed wearily.

Matsuo growled softly, sounding oddly uncertain. I put

my arm around his neck and the akita leaned against me. As I moved, my back became cold and I reached around to tug my kakebuton closer. My groping fingers found only empty air.

"Keiko-chan, you must wake up."

Yo. My lover. I was confused. What was he doing in my bedroom, in what appeared to be full daylight? Shinobi he might be, but even he could not hope to get out of our house during the day without being discovered. And if it were either my father or my brother, who saw him, then his blood would inevitably be spilled in the name of honor.

Blood. Although my eyes remained tightly shut, I could smell blood, and no small amount. With the nauseating reek came memories I did not want.

"Go away," I said again, but this time my voice was a whisper. "Go away and leave me alone. I want to be here, with my dead. It's where I deserve to be."

I reached out, groping for my brother's sword. Not his katana. That would be too long for my purpose. I wanted his shorter, second sword. Isamu's wakizashi, the sword he wore thrust through his obi during battle. It was close by, I knew. I had seen it yesterday.

I took a deep breath, holding it for a long time to steady myself. Less than a day ago, I had been gloriously happy, looking forward to my future with little concern for the past. My family honor was safe. I was free and about to begin a new life with Yo. I knew my brother would be horrified by my decision, but I would not let that lessen my happiness. My life was my own, and I would use it as I saw fit.

I had been away from home for over a month, held a prisoner in the Floating Word, yet I doubted that Father even noticed I had been absent. Even my sister, Emiko—the beauty of the family who had always held a place in Father's heart; a place that eluded me entirely—had to ask for an appointment to see him if she had something she needed to discuss with him. No, Father would not have noticed I was missing. Even if he had noticed, I doubted he would have cared greatly. But it had amused Isamu to teach me the way of the code of bushido. It was he who had set my feet on the road to becoming onna-bugeisha, a legendary warrior woman of the samurai. Isamu would surely have missed me. While I had been held captive, I had consoled myself with the idea that he would think I had run away to taste more of the delights of Edo's Floating World. The world he had introduced me to. But even then, I was sure that he would have worried about me.

The same as I worried about him when upon my return I found not a living soul in our family home. Even the servants were missing. I knew something was very wrong, but I was so bewildered I had no idea what to do, still less where to begin my search. Matsuo had far more sense than I did. He had been shut up in the stables, and when I released him, he had immediately led me to the dry riverbed.

And there my search had ended. I found my father and brother, both dead. Fallen to the arquebuses of our own villagers. Conquered by the weapon that Isamu had dismissed with contempt. How the villagers had ever managed to obtain an arquebus, I had no idea. The guns were not common and were expensive. Perhaps the head man had one, used to hunt ducks and rabbits in better times when there had been enough cash available to buy balls to fire from the muskets. Neither Father nor Isamu would tolerate the use of a gun in battle. Guns were not the way of the samurai; there was no honor in being able to kill from a distance with no need for either skill or courage.

And now that same scorned weapon had killed them both, piercing their armor as if it were no more than paper. True, they had dealt death to many of the villagers. Terribly thin, ragged bodies lay all around my menfolk. But what was the point? Death was death, no matter how it arrived.

I could hardly believe I had slept amid such horror. Had my mind simply given way and I had been unconscious rather than asleep? Either way, unlike my father and brother, I had awoken. The knowledge added to my guilt. I had arrived too late, but only just. If I had come home a few hours earlier, I could have fought alongside my men. Died with them, surely, but at least I would have died with honor. Instead, I had spent the time they were fighting and dying in pleasuring myself with Yo.

There was only one option open to me. I was glad Yo was at my side to help me leave this world in an honorable fashion. I frowned as I saw that he was holding Isamu's wakizashi firmly in his grip. I held out my hand for it, demanding what was now mine.

"No." Yo put the sword behind his back, as if he thought I might snatch for it. I stared at him in astonishment but spoke reasonably.

"I must. You know that. Please, give me the sword. I'm sure I've got the courage to make the first cut, but I don't know if I can manage the final slash. Will you truly be my lover and do it for me? Finish me before I can wish I hadn't done it? Put an end to my pain?"

"You are not going to commit seppuku. I won't allow you to."

I laughed, my heart suddenly light. Yo was speaking

nonsense. Seppuku was the traditional way for a samurai to atone when he had brought dishonor to his family. I was onna-bugeisha, and I should have died fighting with my men. As I had not, seppuku was the only way to atone for my actions. Yo knew that perfectly well. It was only for love of me that he denied my wish. That pleased me greatly.

"Yo, I have no option. Give me Isamu's sword, please."

A noise close to Father's body startled me. Yo turned quickly, Isamu's sword held in a two-handed grip waist-high, ready to strike. He relaxed as I called out to him.

"No, don't hurt him. It's Father's golden eagle. The one I stole from the nest with Isamu. His name is Soru. Father always took him with him when he went hunting. He couldn't have foretold how this hunt would turn out."

Yo lowered his arm, watching Soru intently as he smoothed down some ruffled feathers with his wickedly-curved beak. It seemed the two had reached an understanding. Yo finally put the sword back on the ground, slowly, so as not to alarm Soru.

"He was lying next to you when I got here," he said quietly. "He had his wing stretched out over your head. I nearly killed him. I thought you were dead and that he was pecking at your body. Even eagles will eat carrion if they're hungry."

"He was protecting me," I marveled. "Even though I took his freedom away, he still guarded me." Tears smeared my eyes and I blinked them away, reluctant to allow even Yo to see my weakness. I held out my arm and Soru immediately took wing, circling down cautiously to land on my wrist. Beneath Father's armor, I could see the leather wrist guard he used when he was hunting with Soru. For a moment, I wished I was wearing it. My wrist was naked and the pain was very great when Soru perched himself on my arm and dug his talons in deeply, rocking to find his balance. Blood ran down my arm. I ignored it. What was my pain compared to that my men had suffered?

"You had little to fear with Soru and Matsuo at your side." Yo put the sword on the ground but kept his foot on it. I shrugged. A moment more or less on this earth wouldn't matter. Besides, before I took my own life, there was something I had to do.

I raised my arm, holding it far away from my body to give Soru room. "I took your life from you, Soru, but you kept me safe." The beautiful bird cocked his head to one side, as if he was truly listening and understanding. "In return, I give your freedom back to you. Go back to your mountain. Find yourself a mate and raise a family in peace and safety. Go!"

I raised my arm at the last word and threw Soru toward the sky. He flapped his wings, beating the air. For a moment, he seemed to be poised on the wings of the wind, and then he was rising. He went so high, he was barely more than a dot, and then he turned and winged away from me.

"You are generous to the eagle. But what about me? And Matsuo?" Yo added as Matsuo whimpered, deep in his throat. "Are you going to give us our freedom as well?"

I was suddenly tired of all this discussion. I was ready to die. I *should* die. What was the point of discussing it any longer?

"I would be grateful if you took care of Matsuo," I said politely. "He has more sense than many humans, and you will find him an excellent companion. Now, will you give me that sword?"

Yo glanced down at the *wakizashi*. I noticed that the blade was discolored, and the edge not as sharp as I remembered it. I swallowed; my death would be painful. I closed my eyes, almost feeling the jagged blade entering my belly, and Yo grabbed his chance.

He kicked the sword away and leaped fluidly toward me. The last time we had fought, I had been naked and my oiled body difficult for him to grip. Now, we were equal. Matsuo rose and walked away from us without a backward glance. I glared at him. He was supposed to be my dog! Surely, he should be leaping to my defense?

"This is not your day to die, Keiko." Yo circled me cautiously. "If the gods had wanted to take you, they would have sent you home earlier so that you could fight and die alongside your men. They did not. You were meant to live. Meant to get vengeance for your family."

He had barely finished speaking when he feinted to the left and lunged. But I was no longer there. I turned quickly and thrust my foot out, tripping him. But Yo righted his balance with the grace of a dancer and grabbed my robe, trying to throw me. I moved with his force, slipping away from him before he could secure his grip.

"I am samurai, *shinobi*," I taunted him. "You would never understand. It's a matter of honor."

"Better to be alive than to die an honorable death," he mocked me back. I glanced past him and my eyes widened in horror. I thought the trick had worked when Yo seemed to follow my gaze, but I was wrong. I was so busy planning my next move that I slowed for an indiscernible moment and Yo took full advantage. He bent so quickly, his body was blurred as he scooped up a handful of sand, throwing it in my face. I was quick, but not quite quick enough. I avoided most of the sand, but a little went into my eyes, effectively blinding me.

No matter. I closed my eyes against the sting and existed in my other senses. Yo was holding his breath, so I couldn't track him that way. I ordered my ears to be deaf. When he moved, I knew where he was by the push of displaced air. He had gone low, intending to grab me around the waist. I let him almost touch me, then dived under his grip and slid away, reaching for the wakizashi. It was in my hand in far less than the time it took for my heart to make a single beat. I held it in front of me, the point resting beneath my left breast.

"Enough, Yo. I win."

The blade may have been well used, but it was still wickedly sharp. Isamu had always boasted it was sharp enough to part a hair down its length. I had no reason to doubt my brother's words.

"And killing yourself is winning?" Yo spoke very quietly, barely out of breath in spite of our violent activity. I did not move to face his voice, but kept very still, ready to move in case he tried to take the sword away from me. "If that is really what you want, then I will give you the finishing stroke. I love you, Keiko. And I could never see you suffer."

His voice carried the bitter ring of truth, and I relaxed slightly.

"Thank you. I am very glad the gods allowed us to meet, my shinobi. A great pity we didn't have longer together, but one must be grateful for any mercy."

I slid to my knees, making myself comfortable on the bare riverbed. I wriggled, assessing carefully the best place to make the first incision. Yo spoke again and I frowned in irritation as his words disturbed my concentration.

"Keiko, listen to me. If you're still determined to go ahead when I've finished, then I'll help you pass into the next world. But listen to me first."

I bowed my head and shrugged. He was right. Another minute wouldn't hurt. The sun had risen above the horizon now, warming me. I felt a great surge of sorrow at knowing I would soon be cold forever. As cold as Isamu and Father, I thought. I was angered by my own cowardice.

"Hurry, Yo. I can feel my menfolk's souls here still. The spirits of those who leave this life violently often stay behind for a while. Perhaps they're waiting for me. If they are, I don't want to disappoint them again."

He squatted down in front of me. I had blinked the sand out of my eyes and smiled at his face. It had become dear to me so very quickly. I was glad that Yo was the last thing I would see in this life.

"Keiko, this is not the only way." I shook my head, and he held up his hand quickly. "I know. I'm not samurai. I don't follow the code of bushido. But I understand that you think you have brought great dishonor to your family. You have not. Believe me."

"I was with you when they died, Yo," I said softly. "I should have been here with them. Then I would have died with honor at their side. As I was not here, it's up to me to restore that honor by dying courageously by my own hand."

Yo squatted back on his heels. He lowered his head, his expression suddenly unreadable.

"If you had been here when the villagers attacked, do you really think either Isamu or your father would have let you fight alongside them?"

I flinched at his words with the same pain I would have felt if he had struck me. "Of course they would have. Isamu trained me to become onna-bugeisha. He would have made Father let me fight with them."

"No, he wouldn't," Yo said brutally. "If you had been here, he would have insisted that you go as far away as you could at the first sign of trouble. I know Isamu trained you to be a true warrior woman of the samurai, but in spite of that, your brother would never, ever have let you go into battle with him."

"He would!" I protested angrily. "He was the one who told me about my ancestor, the great onna-bugeisha Tomoe Gozen. The thing he treasured most was a book that showed her fighting alongside her samurai husband as his equal. He would have been proud that I had become a warrior like her."

"He would have died by his own hand rather than let you die beside him," Yo said bluntly. "The legend of a warrior woman is one thing. Having your own sister fight alongside you is another."

I shook my head, refusing to believe him. I would have made Isamu—and Father, at the very last—proud of me. Yo was lying to try and stop me from killing myself. I knew at that moment how much he loved me, and the knowledge filled me with joy.

"You're wrong." I smiled at him gently. Yo closed his eyes and spoke slowly, as if I was some stupid gaijin who could understand Japanese only at half speed.

"It amused Isamu to teach you to be onna-bugeisha. Was it part of the code of bushido when he dressed you up as a boy and took you to the Floating World for his own entertainment?" Doubt made a hollow behind my breasts. But still, I shook my head stubbornly. "I'm right, you know I am. If you had been here, and your men had somehow survived the battle with you at their side, do you think either of them would have been so proud of you that they would have boasted about it to their comrades? Would they really have told them how a mere girl child had helped them win?"

"You're twisting things," I said. The hollow behind my breasts made it difficult to breathe. "If we had survived, I would never have expected them to speak of my part in the battle. They couldn't. It would be unthinkable to have a woman fighting alongside her men."

Even as I said it, I cursed my foolish tongue for falling into Yo's trap. I spoke rapidly to hide my error.

"It doesn't matter. It's *my* honor that's at stake. I can't live with their deaths on my conscience. I would rather die now than wake every morning and curse myself for being alive when they are dead."

"It doesn't have to be that way. The gods wanted you to live. Use the life they've given you to honor your family."

"Do you mean I should take revenge on the villagers who killed them? I don't blame them, poor souls. They were driven to this from desperation. If I had known they were starving, I would have gone to Father and begged him to release some rice for them. Once the rains came and there was a good harvest, they could have paid him back then. Something else for me to regret."

"That's not true. Your father wouldn't have listened to you," Yo said with quiet authority. "Isamu asked him to let the villagers have some rice time after time, but he wouldn't budge."

I stared at Yo in shock that he could have known that when I did not. Then I remembered he had bribed one of our servants to allow him to take his place when he had first become interested in me. He had heard the gossip then, no doubt. There was no magic in it.

"None of that matters now," I said wearily. "I should have been here. If I had been, I would have fought by Father's and Isamu's sides whether they wanted me to or not. I've had enough of talking. Give me that sword, Yo. Let me ease my burden."

"So, you think you're wiser than Tomoe Gozen, do you?"

I stared at Yo in shock. What did he know about the legendary onna-bugeisha? "She didn't die at the side of her man, did she? He sent her away from him so she could live. Do you really think you're more courageous than she was?"

I licked my lips, lost for an argument to throw back at him. Worse than anything else was the knowledge that Yo had kept me lingering for too long. My courage had shriveled. I no longer wanted to die. I wanted to be persuaded by him. I was torn in two. I glanced at Isamu's lifeless body and prayed that he would send me a message from the next world. I strained to hear his voice, but there was nothing.

"Leave me alone," I whispered.

Yo stood and stretched. "Come with me," he said. I shook my head. "Come with me. Leave the dead here. Killing yourself won't bring them back. All that will do is cause me pain. Come with me and live the life the gods want you to live."

"I don't want to live. I've nothing left." I gestured around me sadly. "My spirit died here with them. I have nothing at all to offer anybody, especially a man who lives by his wits like you do. My sad heart would slow you down, Yo, and eventually you would come to resent me. Let me go. Do both of us a favor."

"You're alive, Keiko. I will not leave you, nor will I allow you to die. If you were to die, then you would take my soul with you. Do you want *that* on your conscience in the next life?"

He sounded so serious I began to smile.

"No. My conscience is burdened enough as it is," I said. The sun rose fully and glinted in the many shards of my father's and brother's armor. Life was suddenly very precious again. A thought began to unwind in my mind. I put my head on one side, thinking carefully. It was a chance. A very slim chance, but a chance none the less.

"You may be right," I said. "Perhaps there is a reason that I was spared. It may be that the gods have shown me a way to redeem my honor and, more importantly, carry on the family name."

TWO

Appearances mean
Nothing. If you don't know my
Mind, you don't know me

I knocked on the door and waited for the call to enter. It would be a few moments in coming, I knew. One did not enter the court of a great daimyo—a true aristocrat such as Lord Akafumu—casually. The supplicant had to be kept waiting, if only to ensure a proper state of nervous apprehension. I used my waiting time to prepare myself. I lowered my head humbly and hunched my shoulders. I clasped my hands tightly, my fingers entwined in front of me. And above all, I instructed my mind to forget, at least for the moment, that I was onna-bugeisha, a warrior woman of the samurai. For the next—moment? Half a day? Even more? I had no idea how long my wait would last—I was to be a lowly petitioner, desperate for the favor of my lord.

The doors swung open as I was taking a deep breath. I hunched a little further into myself and walked forward with a teetering, hesitant tread. I took great care to plant each foot in front of the other, walking like an old woman rather than a young and vigorous girl. I heard someone fall in behind me, and after a few steps, his voice hissed at me.

"Stop, that's far enough. Prostrate yourself."

His peremptory tone raised the short hairs on the back of my neck. Immediately, I wanted to go against his command and carry on walking, but brain won out over instinct and I obeyed his words. I fell to my knees and bowed deeply, then kowtowed, my hands stretched in front of me and my head banging on the floor. Unsure of what to do next, I stayed where I was, waiting for further instructions. I was surprised when the words came from in front of me rather than from my escort.

"Keiko-san, you may rise."

I was about to get to my feet when the voice behind me hissed, "To your knees. No further."

I sensed my escort walking away on silent silk-slippered feet. This was it, then. There would be no second chance. I kept my head bowed respectfully but peered through the matted hair that covered my face.

Courtiers were arranged on each side of me. All of them were men, and all of them were staring at me with avid interest. I felt like some freak who was kept in a cage and taken around the villages to milk coins from gullible peasants. No, worse than that. Surely a caged human being would arouse a little pity. I could sense only amusement from this audience. No doubt they were delighted to have their daily routine interrupted.

I knew I had to wait until Akafumu decided to notice me. I took a deep, silent breath, ordering myself to relax, to remember my role. I was a beggar before my lord, waiting on his word. My future was in his hands.

Lord Akafumu ignored me. He chatted to the men who stood at each side of him. He was perhaps twenty paces in front of me. I closed my eyes and concentrated all my senses on my hearing. He was talking about some member of the shogun's court, laughing slyly about a joke that had been played on the man. I longed to raise my head, to call out that I could hear him. That I was not prepared to wait in this submissive posture until it suited him to pay me some attention.

Of course, I did no such thing. I waited silently, beginning to feel an ache in my shoulders as I kept them hunched. No matter. The end result would be well worth it. I hoped.

"Ah, Keiko-san." *At last!* Lord Akafumu sounded startled to find me still there. Suddenly, I realized that this was all a game to him. A bit of novelty to break up the aristocratic routine of his noble court. He knew I was there. *Why* I was there. He was simply stretching out the fun.

I kowtowed again. The gesture was an automatic response to his voice, which made me angry with myself. Still, it could do no harm.

"Lord Akafumu." I pitched my voice at what I hoped was the right level. Loud enough to be heard over the background buzz of the courtiers, but still profoundly submissive. "I beg your indulgence, my lord."

"Yes, I'm sure you do." Akafumu laughed at his own wit. The courtiers followed suit, tittering obediently. "Well, I'm pleased to see that at least you're following the proper traditions, Keiko-san. There's so much civil disobedience these days, sometimes I wonder if people still understand their proper place in life."

The breath caught in my throat with shock. Didn't he know why I was here? Surely, even if he was above listening to gossip, his chamberlain must instruct him in daily business. He must know that my father and brother had been slaughtered by peasants whose hunger had finally tipped them into desperation. And that being so, could he be so heartless, so insensitive, that he joked about knowing one's place in life? My daimyo answered my unasked question himself.

"I blame all these gaijin that are about Edo these days. Striding about as if they own the place. Refusing to dress properly. I don't believe any of them even bother to learn Japanese. When the lower classes see such men flaunting disrespect and appear to prosper, then they get ideas above their station in life."

His tone was pettish, but my sensitive instincts caught an undercurrent of fear beneath the words. He knew what had happened to my menfolk. And it terrified him. I was pleased; this great aristocrat was not invulnerable. And even better, he knew that himself.

"My lord." I spoke quietly, and I realized at once that he had not heard me. I tried again. "My lord, you see everything clearly. You are as all-seeing as you are benevolent, and I am beyond grateful that the gods have seen fit to give me such a daimyo as you."

I thought perhaps I had laid the flattery on too thickly, but I had not. I stared at Akafumu from beneath my screen of hair and saw him preen. He was far younger than I had expected, perhaps no older than his mid-thirties. I thought he would be a tall man when he stood, but already I could see that the good life he had led was beginning to ruin him. His robe was a rice bowl over the mound of his belly, and as I watched, he frowned and rubbed his chest as if to dislodge a spasm of pain.

"Keiko-san, I am sorry for your loss. A terrible thing to

happen in my domain." He did know, then. And his tactlessness was all the more astounding. "But I am pleased to give you some good news. I have ensured that those peasants who escaped from the bravery of your father and brother have already been dealt with. The men have been executed and their women sold into slavery."

Akafumu obviously expected me to be pleased. I gripped my hands together so tightly my nails broke the flesh on my palms. My whole body shuddered with the effort of staying still. That was not what I wanted. Not what I had come here for. Even through my grief, I understood that the villagers had acted out of desperation. They were starving, their children dying for want of the rice that Father had in abundance. They had known that they were signing their own death warrants when they broke into our rice stores. For them, it was face death one way or another.

I knew that and found it in my heart to weep for them. Also did I understand that the villagers were part of our family, that we were responsible for them. If Father had not been so mean that he refused to let them have enough rice for this one season, if he had seen fit to give what they had been forced to take, then both he and my brother would be alive. And I would not be on my knees, humbling myself before this arrogant, over-fed man.

"My lord, your words are those of a great man." I could not bring myself to thank him, but he seemed not to notice.

"It was essential," Akafumu said crisply. "There is too much of this sort of impertinence going on. Although, I doubt we will see any more of it in my domain. You may not be aware that a number of your maidservants threw their lot in with the villagers. When my men went to round up the ringleaders, they found them with the peasants. They have been suitably punished, also sold as slaves. I will ensure that the money that was obtained for them is handed over to you at the time of the next accounts."

"Too gracious, my lord," I said. My heart cried out. My own maid must have been amongst them. She was a nice girl who would never harm a living thing.

I choked back my distress and waited. After a moment, I felt Akafumu's growing impatience with my silence.

"Well, Keiko-san? We have been pleased to accept your petition. I have told you that the cash that is due to you will be paid. What else do you want?"

"I want my home. My land." The words burst out of me. I added quickly, "If my lord would be kind enough to listen to a mere woman, I would be grateful for your favor toward me."

The silence went on and on. Even the courtiers had stopped murmuring amongst themselves to listen, for I was turning out to be even more entertaining than they had expected.

"You want *your* home? *Your* land?" I had expected Akafumu to sound astonished. Offended, perhaps. My hopes began to blister and burn as I heard the amusement in his voice.

"My lord." I clenched my hands together, enlacing my fingers in a gesture of supplication. "I am the last to bear the name of our great family. My father and brother are dead. I have no more male relatives. My only sister is married and bears the name of her husband's family. There is no one else to carry on our great samurai tradition. I beg of you, bestow my father's title upon me. If you do not, then the great house of Hakuseki will die."

I ran out of breath and became silent. I thought the noise was Akafumu's seating platform creaking, then I realized he was laughing. At me. The rest of the court followed his example until I was in the middle of a great swell of glee, all of it malicious. All of it aimed at me. By an effort of will so deep it caused pain to clench my guts, I stayed still and silent.

"You, Keiko-san?" Akafumu wiped tears from his cheek before he went on. "You want me to make you a samurai? You may well be the last of your family's line, but you seem to have forgotten that you're also a woman."

I am onna-bugeisha! I shouted in my head. *I am a warrior woman of the samurai. Give me a chance. Just one chance! Pit me against your best warrior, and when I win, then tell me that I am just a woman.*

"My lord." I paused, trying to form my thoughts into words that could persuade Akafumu. He didn't give me the chance.

"We admire your loyalty to the spirit of your ancestors, Keiko-san," he said indulgently. "And we must also applaud your spirit. It must have taken a great deal of courage to come before the court. And I daresay, being a woman, you could not appreciate how ludicrous your request is. The title of samurai can only rest on a man and your family appears to have run out of menfolk." The courtiers tittered at his misplaced witticism. I was surprised that my daimyo didn't burst into flames under the intensity of my hatred.

"No, it's impossible. But we would not see you without a suitable place. You are obviously your father's daughter and a woman of true samurai spirit. I have been told that not long before his untimely death, your father entered into negotiations to betroth you to Tadatomo-san?"

My mouth opened and closed, but no words came from between my lips. I had rehearsed my audience with Akafumu over and over again in my mind until I was sure I had an answer for anything he might ask me. But I had never considered this.

"Nothing was actually agreed, my lord," I said quickly.

"I understand. No matter. As your daimyo, it is my duty to stand in place of your father," Akafumu said graciously. "We are aware of his intentions and I have already spoken to Tadatomo-san. In addition to the money raised by the sale of the wretched female insurgents, which I have no doubt you will want to spend on clothes and fripperies for your wedding ceremony, I have agreed to provide a dowry for you."

I found my voice at last, but it was no more than a strangled yelp. In his grandeur, Akafumu interpreted it as delight. He waved his hand as if bestowing a blessing upon me.

"You may go, Keiko-san. I shall attend your wedding if it doesn't conflict with anything I already have arranged, and always supposing the shogun doesn't call me to his presence."

I was dismissed. Akafumu called for one of his courtiers to come forward as if I was suddenly invisible.

I rose and bowed deeply, backing away from his presence in the correct manner.

I was shaking with fury. I wanted to throw myself at Akafumu. He was well guarded, but I had no doubt at all that my hands could squeeze the life out of his kintama before anybody could stop me. I could feel them squeaking together between my finger and thumb and then realized my fingers were clenched tightly and it was my own palm that I was holding so firmly it had swollen.

I heard the doors open behind me and I knew I had lost my desperate gamble. Once the doors were closed in my face, I shook myself like Matsuo coming out of water, throwing my head back and standing straight.

"How did it go?" Yo was suddenly at my side, unseen and unheard until he chose to make his presence felt.

"It went as well as could be expected, I suppose." I smiled wryly.

"He turned you down," Yo said quietly.

I shrugged and rubbed my arm absently. The ashes itched. I wanted nothing more than to be clean. To throw off my disguise of mourning and to return to my life.

Whatever it held for me.

THREE

> Watch! Frost melts at my
> Touch. If only winter could
> Be lost so quickly

We stepped aside as a man—reasonably well off by his dress—approached the doors that had just closed behind me. He glared at me, obviously expecting me to move aside. I stood my ground until Yo grabbed my arm and tugged me away.

"I am so sorry, master. We did not intend to get in your way." He bowed his head courteously. "My lady is in mourning, as you can see. She has just left Lord Akafumu's presence and is overwhelmed with joy by our lord's generosity."

"Really? He's in a good mood, then?" Yo nodded and the man grinned widely. "Excellent." He pushed through the doors jauntily before they were even fully open.

"Why did you lie to that person?"

Yo had hold of my elbow and was turning me away as I spoke. His face was serious, but I could feel the suppressed laughter vibrating in his body.

"I didn't like the way he pushed past you." He smiled sweetly. "It struck me that if he was willing to treat a poor woman in deep mourning that way, it was entirely possible that with a little encouragement he might not treat Lord Akafumu with the respect he normally receives."

A smile crept across my face.

Once outside the court, we were suddenly invisible. The courtyard was crowded with servants and Akafumu's retainers, all bustling about briskly. I wondered cynically how much of it was real urgency and how much was just for show to impress anybody who might be watching them. Yo obviously didn't care. He pushed his way through to a well and filled a bucket with sweet, cold water. I accepted the dipper gratefully, pouring water over my hair repeatedly, and then my hands and wrists, and finally my face and feet. It took a long time to wash away the last of the ashes, and even then, my skin itched as it was still filthy. Yo filled the dipper again, and this time I took a long drink.

I sat, watching the court fuss around us, my feet and hands stretched out to dry in the cold winter sun. Even though Yo was my lover, and had proved himself to be a rock I could depend on, I was oddly reluctant to speak to him. I had done my best, but I had failed. I felt intensely foolish that I had even hoped to get what I wanted from Akafumu. I could imagine Yo shrugging, asking if I had really hoped for anything better? I flinched from the thought and stayed silent, pretending to be absorbed in the activity around us.

Yo perched beside me without speaking. I was puzzled. I expected somebody to challenge us, to ask what business we had there. Nobody paid us any attention at all.

"It's as if we're invisible," I marveled. "Is this what it feels like to be shinobi?"

"Yes," Yo said simply. "Do you like the feeling?"

"You know what? I think I do."

I grabbed Yo's arm and nodded as the man who had pushed past us earlier strode across the courtyard. His face was stone, but it was evident from the rigid set of his body that his mission had not prospered. I expected him to stop and vent his anger on Yo, but it seemed that we were invisible to him as well.

"He didn't notice us," I said in surprise.

"We don't exist." He nodded at the man's retreating back. "He's too full of the affront to his dignity to notice anything else. Everybody at Akafumu's court is used to seeing petitioners. We come, we go. We have no part in their routine, so they don't bother taking any notice, understand?"

"I think so. Is that what you do when you are shinobi? Make yourself ordinary? Is that the secret of it?"

"That's part of it." Yo stared at me, and I knew his patience had worn thin. He wanted to be told what Lord Akafumu had said to me. I sighed; no point in putting it off any longer.

"Lord Akafumu was very sympathetic. The surviving villagers who killed Father and Isamu have already been executed. Their women—along with our maidservants—have been sold off as slaves. Our poor maidservants had taken refuge with the villagers. Where else was there for them to go? Akafumu seemed to think it would please me that they had all been suitably punished."

"That was it?" There was a curious note in Yo's voice. I kept my eyes on the ground. I did not want to see his expression when I told him the rest of it.

"No. My daimyo has given great thought to my predicament. He has decided in his wisdom that the gods would be pleased if I followed my father's plans for me. He is going to give me a dowry, and I'm to marry Tadatomo. He's the elderly widower Father finally chose for me. Such is the benevolence of Lord Akafumu that he's also going to let me have the money he raised from selling our servants. I suppose it's a sort of wedding present. He told me I could spend it on anything I fancied for my wedding."

My throat was suddenly dry. I had run out of words. I stared at the floor, waiting for Yo to speak. If he laughed at me, lover or not, I would tip him backward into the well and leave him for the court servants to fish out.

Luckily for both of us, he did not laugh.

"And your family estate? What about that?"

"He laughed at the idea that a mere woman might take the title of samurai," I said sourly. Shame at the way I had been dismissed by Akafumu turned into blazing fury. I wanted to force my way back into the audience chamber and demand that he listen to me. That he give me what was rightfully mine.

I half rose, but Yo grabbed my wrist and held on to me. "No," he said sharply. I tugged away from his grasp, infuriated by his response. Who was he, or any other man, to tell me what to do? "Please, Keiko-chan. Listen to me."

I sat down slowly, my temper ebbing as quickly as it had risen. I felt empty and dull. He was right, I supposed. Akafumu had insulted me once already today, why give him the chance to taunt me again?

"That didn't come as a surprise to you, did it?" I asked.

Yo shook his head. "No. None of it did," he said simply.

"If you were so sure of the way it was going to go, why did you encourage me to humble myself in front of Akafumu?" I stared at him incredulously.

"You had to try. According to your own samurai code, it

was the right thing to do. Besides, if you hadn't tried, you would have tortured yourself for the rest of your life, worrying and wondering if something might have come of it. And there was always the slightest chance that you might have caught him in a really good mood and got something out of it. It didn't work, but now your conscience is clear and you can move on."

"I suppose so," I said ungraciously. "But I still want to know what's going to happen to the family estate. It should be mine, Yo."

"It should. But the only way you're going to get it is by marrying your old man. And even then, it would not be truly yours."

I stared at him and licked my lips. For once, I waited before I spoke and found the answer to my unasked question myself.

"Akafumu would give my land to Tadatomo if I married him?"

Yo said calmly, "I think it's possible. I seem to remember that Tadatomo's lands adjoin your family estate?" I nodded. "That was probably one of the reasons your father thought he was so suitable for you. No doubt your daimyo thinks the same way. Of course, it's essential that land be kept in the hands of the aristocracy." He grimaced as he spoke and I almost smiled as I understood what he really thought of that idea. "You told me that Tadatomo has no children by any of his wives or concubines, and he has outlived all the other men in his family. He's a very old man now; how likely is it that you would bear him male children under the circumstances? If he died without male heirs, then Akafumu would be allowed to claim your joint lands for himself. All he has to do is wait a while."

I took another dipper of water; my hands were shaking

so hard a great deal of it spilled. I drank deeply from what remained. I was aware that Yo was watching me carefully. I turned my head and looked at him. His face—just like mine—gave nothing of his true thoughts away.

"I see. I had hoped that the gods spared me for a reason. And now I believe I know what it is. Akafumu is a selfish and greedy man. He intends to wipe out my entire heritage as if it never existed without thinking twice about it." I paused as my emotions threatened to overcome me. "I see now that is why I was spared. I may have lost my chance to claim our estate, but as long as I walk this earth, the name of Hakuseki will live on in honor and our heritage will not become dust. And I will make sure that my menfolk are avenged for what he tried to do to us. Will you help me do that, Yo?"

"And if I say no? Will you bring down the great daimyo on your own?"

I wondered if he was mocking me and looked at him very closely. His face was open to me, but still I wondered. He was shinobi, deception was bred into his very bones.

"Yes. Or at least I will die trying. If you can't bring yourself to help me fight to put right the wrongs that have been done to my family, then walk away from me now. There'll be no ill feelings. It's different for me. I'm onna-bugeisha. It's up to me to carry on the samurai tradition of my family. I wouldn't expect you to understand that."

"I see. But would you miss me, onna-bugeisha?"

"Yes," I said simply.

"Then, I'll stay."

I put my hand to my face to hide my pleasure from Yo. I wished the weight of my samurai heritage did not lay so heavy on my shoulders. But at that moment, I felt a great urge to be free of everything. Had I not been samurai, I could have put my arms around him. Accepted his embrace and shown my delight that he had agreed to share my burden and my future. But centuries of tradition lay between us and I sat stiffly, wordless.

"Thank you," I said with absurd politeness.

"Think nothing of it." Yo's voice was so cheerful, he startled me. When I turned to look at him, he was grinning broadly. "Fortunately for both of us, I am not samurai. I am shinobi. I am less than nothing. As you once told me, I'm nothing but a mercenary who's happy to be paid to do the dirty work of the highest bidder. No code of bushido for the likes of me!"

I was speechless. I blushed deeply, shrugging my shoulders with embarrassment. "I'm sorry," I mumbled.

"No, you're not." Yo's grin faded to a wry smile. "You meant it. But do you understand the irony of it, Keiko? You're now exactly the same as me. You have nothing except what you can gather by your wits. I suppose you can think of yourself as an honorable ronin if it makes you any happier, but it doesn't make any difference. You have no lord; you gave the right to his protection away when you decided you were not going to obey Akafumu and marry old man Tadatomo. You have no family left. Even Emiko bears the name of her husband. The day she married him, she left your family for his. You are left with me—a mercenary shinobi with neither family name nor an honor you would understand. But I tell you now that I will be at your side until the day comes that you tell me to leave you and you mean it."

He seemed to have run out of both breath and words and stopped abruptly. It was the longest speech he had ever made, and I loved him all the more for the honesty that rang in it. But still, an imp of mischief made me want the last word.

"If I am ronin, then I still have my honor, Yo."

He shrugged sulkily, and I knew I had hit home. Every child knows the true story of *The Forty-Seven Ronin*. When I had been much younger, Isamu had made me enact out the story with him. Isamu began, of course, as Asano, the samurai who was forced to commit seppuku unjustly. Once that bit of drama was out of the way—with Isamu suffering most nobly before he died—he immediately resurrected himself as Oishi, the leader of the men who became ronin and put themselves outside of society in their search for justice for their dead lord.

Isamu always made me play the villain, Kira. Much against her will, Emiko was often rounded up to play one of the other ronin, together with any servants Isamu could find. Emiko resented being made to play alongside servants. In any event, just as in history, Isamu in his new role as a defiant ronin finally took his revenge on me—on Kira—and murdered me. At which point Isamu and the rest of the ronin had to commit seppuku yet again to atone for his dishonor in killing Kira. No matter how Isamu rolled his eyes at her, Emiko always refused to sit on the ground to do it, in case she got her kimono dusty. I often thought that the part of the play he relished most was the chance to die an honorable samurai's death not once, but twice.

My nostalgia died as quickly as it had come as I thought of the death Isamu had actually suffered. Truly, he would have committed seppuku a hundred times over rather than die dishonorably at the hands of a peasant wielding a musket.

"I'm sorry," I said again, and meant it. "I forgot myself. Forgive me, Yo. It must seem to you as if I'm just hanging onto a past that has no meaning at all for me. I can't help it. I was raised in the knowledge that I was samurai. When Isamu trained me to become onna-bugeisha, I felt as if I had found something I had been searching for all my life. Everything else that mattered has been taken away from me. I can't let that go as well."

"I understand. We are what we are. If it pleases you to think of us as ronin, then that is what we shall be."

A little of the frost around my heart began to melt. I put my finger to Yo's face and stroked his cheek. We smiled at each other in perfect understanding until our peace was shattered by a servant, shouldering his way to the well.

"You two might have all day, but I haven't. Move, will you?" he snapped. We stood up abruptly, moving out of his way as he splashed the bucket down into the well, cursing under his breath all the time. I stared at him in amazement. How could it be possible that the world was going on in the same way as always when everything that mattered to me had been destroyed with a few words? Yo put his hand on my arm and I felt a little comfort in his touch.

Whether it was enough was another matter entirely.

FOUR

Bats are silent to
Our ears. Would I could fly with
Such quiet intent

"**W**hat?" I realized that Yo had said something, but I was so lost in my thoughts, I hadn't heard him.

"I said, have you seen the state of this place?" Yo sounded bone-weary. I was bewildered, both by the comment and his obvious annoyance. I glanced around and shrugged.

"You're right," I agreed in surprise. "It could do with a really good clean." I patted the cushion I was sitting on briskly and a cloud of dust made me cough. Glancing at Yo, I was amazed to see him shaking his head incredulously.

"Don't you see the dirt? The mess this place is in? You're so wrapped up in thoughts of getting revenge on Akafumu that nothing else matters to you."

I thought about his words and found myself bewildered. He was right, but why should he find it surprising?

"You think a bit of dust is more important than restoring my family's honor?" I asked calmly.

"It's not just the dust. It's you. You don't care about anything at all except your *honor*." He almost spat the word at me. "The house is filthy. We've never eaten a meal here because you don't cook. Our clothes need washing. Even Matsuo could do with a good brushing. I sometimes wonder if you'd notice if I just walked out and never came back."

Ah, that was it, then. It wasn't my neglect of the housework that was infuriating Yo, it was my neglect of him, and I suppose he was right. My thoughts were pulled toward Akafumu constantly. I had thought of—and discarded—a hundred schemes to get my revenge on him. And with each failure, I became angrier with myself. He was my last thought at night and my first waking thought in the morning. I found it impossible to concentrate on anything else. But surely Yo, of all people, would understand that.

I smothered my irritation and answered his question. "I agree, the house is certainly in need of a good clean." Yo's face was smug at my response. "If it bothers you that much, there's a broom in the corner. I suggest you pick it up and start on the tatami."

I was about to add, "And while you do that, I'll shake out the futons," but the astonished fury in Yo's expression stopped me dead.

"Me? You expect me to do housework?"

I had no time to reply, he carried on at once. He was almost shouting, and I put my hand on Matsuo's head as I heard him growl. His coat was a little rough.

"I'm shinobi, woman. Not some sort of household skivvy. I suppose I should have known you would have no idea about cleaning and cooking. What samurai *lady* would ever demean herself so far as to even think about such lowly things?"

I tilted my head, considering his question as if it mattered. Yo was almost panting with fury. I knew instinctively that he wanted me to defend myself so he could tear down anything I said. I had been right from the start; I saw the hurt in his eyes and understood what all this was about. Yo's fury had nothing to do with my lack of household skills —which I was the first to agree were lamentable. It was all to do with the fact that I was excluding him from all that mattered in my life. He was hurt, and this big, strong man had no way of showing it except by trying to pick an argument about nothing.

It had been six days since my visit to Lord Akafumu, and we had not made love since. In fact, I realized guiltily, I had barely spoken to Yo in all that time. Nothing mattered to me but my revenge on Akafumu. Yo obviously understood that, but still he was hurt by what he saw as my rejection of him.

"I'm sorry. You're quite right, of course. Samurai ladies are taught the arts of flower arranging, of singing and dancing. I can play the samisen beautifully, and I excel at the tea ceremony. But housework is beyond my capability." I spoke lightly, hoping to defuse the situation. When Yo was calmer, then I would try and explain that I had not forgotten him. That I was sorry for my neglect of him. But he had to understand that until Akafumu had been punished, I couldn't live a normal life.

"It's not just the state of the house. It's Akafumu. You're obsessed with him," Yo snarled. Ah, so we were coming to it at last.

"Yes," I said simply. "You know how I feel about him. He insulted me by the way he treated me when I humbled myself before him. But far worse than that, when he denied me my birthright, he destroyed my family. Half a millennium and more gone in a few cruel words. He destroyed the honor of my brother and father and all of my ancestors back down the centuries. And he did it casually, as if it was nothing. But he forgot that I am samurai too. I can neither forget nor forgive what he has done. I will not rest until I—and all of my family—have been avenged."

I took a deep breath, feeling as if I had a heavy weight pressing on my chest. Yo's lips were pursed, his expression unreadable.

"I understand you feel you need to punish Akafumu."

I wanted to explain that *punish* was the wrong word. I needed revenge, a different thing entirely. I stayed quiet, sensing that Yo needed to bring his thoughts into the light.

"But you don't have to do it yourself. I can help. Just say the word and I'll gather together a band of my brother shinobi and we'll visit Akafumu in the night. Nobody will ever know we've been there, I promise you. If you want him left dead in his own palace, then that will be done. If you want him to disappear, then we'll remove him silently and deal with him elsewhere. You will have your revenge and we can begin to live again."

Yo sat back, smiling. He was obviously delighted by his simple solution. I stared at the tatami in appalled silence. How could he possibly misunderstand my motives, misunderstand *me* so very badly? I was horrified. Yo was not only my lover, he insisted he loved me. I had always thought that our minds were in perfect tune until this moment.

"Thank you," I said blandly. "If I wanted Akafumu dead, then I would no doubt be pleased to accept your offer. But I don't want him to die. That would be far too quick and easy for him. I want him alive, but for each day to be a torment for him. I want to destroy everything dear to him, just as he destroyed everything that matters to me. And any revenge that is visited on him has to be by my hand and no other. It's a matter of honor."

"Honor?" Yo snapped impatiently. "The precious samurai code."

I nodded. That is what it came down to. Couldn't he understand that?

"And I suppose you feel leaving Akafumu to rot in what sounds like a living death is more honorable than giving him a quick, clean death? How do you think you're going to achieve that?"

"You don't understand," I said wearily. I would achieve it. If I died trying to restore the honor of my ancestors, it would be worth it. Yo's idea of a quick, clean death for Akafumu was not enough. As I thought that, an idea began to take form in my mind. Yo was shouting again, but I barely heard him.

"You and your code of bushido. Can't you understand that all that's behind you? You're not playing at being a samurai warrior woman any longer. This is what matters, Keiko." He waved his hand at the room around us. "Having a clean, sweet-smelling home. Food on the table. A comfortable futon. Those are the important things in life. As long as I'm earning cash, I can provide us with all that. If your pride won't let me deal with him for you, then forget about Akafumu, I beg of you. The gods will deal with him in their own good time. Think about us, not following your dreams."

I smiled at him pityingly. Such a shame he clearly couldn't understand how wrong he was. Especially about me "playing" at being a samurai warrior woman. I was onna-bugeisha, and I would never leave that behind me.

"I need to go out for a while," I said. My mind was

working furiously, and I was pleased that my voice sounded calm and steady. Yo's face was blank with astonishment as I rose and clicked my fingers at Matsuo. "I may be gone a while."

It was only when I was outside in the street that I wondered if he would be there when I got back. The sweet words he sang to me by the fountain about being by my side no matter what turned out to be only that—words.

I hoped he would stay, but I shrugged the thought away quickly. If we were so far apart in understanding each other, then I decided I wasn't greatly worried.

FIVE

Why do I bother
To scold my cat? She listens
But never hears me!

That being so, why then was I pleased to find Yo exactly where I had left him when I returned? Matsuo annoyed me immensely by immediately rushing over to him and fawning around his legs. I ignored Yo. I would not speak first; the quarrel had been none of my doing. Fortunately, Yo spoke first.

"I'm sorry, Keiko-chan. I spoke hastily, and I'm very pleased to see you back safely. The kettle is boiling. Would you like some tea?"

"I'll make it," I said hurriedly. I was not being in the least bit conciliatory with the offer. I had tasted Yo's tea once before. He made it so strong it was undrinkable, and I was very thirsty.

We sat opposite each other and sipped our tea politely.

"You had no need to worry about me," I said stiffly.

"Even without Matsuo to protect me, I would have been perfectly safe."

"Of course you would," Yo said promptly. I was immediately annoyed with him for not being at least a little worried about me. He must have read my expression as he sighed deeply. "Whatever I say, it's going to be wrong, isn't it?"

He sounded so very weary I stared at him and frowned, wondering if this was some sort of trick to get beneath my guard.

"I don't know what you mean," I said honestly. Yo surprised me by smiling and shaking his head with obvious amusement.

"You really don't, do you? Any other woman would be ready and eager to play the game of blame. To go around in circles until little by little we come to a compromise and admit that there were faults on both sides. But not you, Keiko. You see everything in black and white, with not a shade between."

I stared at him as if I might understand his words better if I could see his expression. Yet still I did not comprehend. Yo had mocked my life's quest. He had treated me like a silly little girl. On a much lower—but still intensely irritating—level he had blamed me for the house being dirty and untidy when he knew perfectly well I had never had to raise a finger in the house in my life. And anyway, at least half the mess was his!

"You mocked me," I said finally. "You know what Akafumu has done to me and my family. You know I've sworn to get revenge on him. And yet you still laughed at me. You of all people!"

I wanted to say so much more. To explain how I had thought he understood me. That I had believed he was the one man in the whole of my world who would stand by me no matter what. He had betrayed that trust. I stayed silent. I knew that if I tried to speak, my anger would overcome me and I would begin to argue with him again. And if I did, I thought that Yo would see my frustration as arrogance. When he spoke again, he surprised me.

"I was angry myself. If I spoke out of turn, then I apologize," he said gently. "You must see that your obsession with Akafumu is taking over your life. You think about nothing else. Didn't you understand that was the real reason I was furious with you?"

"No," I said simply.

"Did you never argue with Emiko? Or with your brother?" Yo sounded amazed, and I stared at him in confusion. What was he talking about? I would never have dreamed of contradicting anything Isamu said. And if I had dared to disagree with Emiko, she would have told me to leave her presence. I thought about Yo's words carefully and realized with amazement that I had never argued with anybody ever, until today.

"No," I said. "This was the first time I've ever really argued with anybody. I suppose that's why I...misunderstood."

"There are two sides to every...discussion, Keiko." He really was laughing at me this time. I looked at him curiously, wondering both why he was amused and also why I wasn't angry with him for it. "Next time you don't understand what I'm talking about, don't just walk away from me. Shout back. It's impossible to have an argument on your own."

"I'm sorry I offended you, Yo-san," I said stiffly. It was as far as I was prepared to go in terms of an apology. He could take it or leave it.

"Oh, stop being so prickly." Yo was having none of my

affronted dignity. He leaned toward me and stroked my nose with his finger. I refused to respond. "I wasn't laughing at you or anything you said. I know you've felt intensely frustrated all this time, trying to find a way to get your revenge on Akafumu. I've been waiting for you to ask me for help. You should have known that I would be willing to help in any way I could. I meant it when I said I would be delighted to do the job for you."

I stiffened at once. "Thank you. But I have no need of any help from a shinobi. Your way is not my way. I will deal with him myself, even if I die trying."

"And that is what worries me." Yo was suddenly no longer smiling. "The wretched man deserves to be punished, I agree. But the thought that you might get caught trying to harm him terrifies me. He is powerful, Keiko, and very well protected. If you make one mistake, it will be your last. I know your pride stops you asking for my help, but it's yours anyway."

"No," I said firmly.

Yo rubbed his forehead as if he had a headache. "I said I would help, not take your vengeance for you. I know you're a samurai warrior woman. I know you can beat most men—me included—in a fair fight. But you're too much a slave to the code of bushido. If something does not seem honorable to you, then you will disdain it. And that is why I'm worried. Akafumu might be a daimyo, but he has less honor than I do. Less honor than a mere shinobi, think of that!

"He will not hesitate to kill you without even thinking about it if you cause him the slightest problem. *He* fills *your* thoughts to the exclusion of all else. To him, you are less than nothing. I don't suppose he has spared a thought for you since you left his presence. Accept my help, Keiko. I promise you, without it, you will die trying to hurt him and

Akafumu will live a long and no doubt happy life. Is that what you want?"

"I would die an honorable death. Nothing matters more," I said. I was deeply annoyed to hear the tremor in my voice.

"You would surely die, but it would be a death without any point." Yo persisted. "And besides, if Akafumu hurt you, then I would be forced to kill him myself. So, either way, you will have my help whether you want it or not."

Yo's argument was seriously flawed, I knew that, but in spite of it, I began to smile.

"I think I have a lot to learn," I said ruefully. "And not just about housework." It was a major concession on my part, and I was pleased when Yo looked surprised. "But I didn't waste my time while I was out just now. I have been thinking. I need an anma, Yo."

His mouth opened and closed. His expression was so astonished, I almost laughed out loud. "An anma? We are both perfectly healthy. What do you want an anma for?"

"Not just any anma," I explained eagerly. "A very special anma. I know Akafumu uses the same trusted woman for all of his massages. I want you to find her and bring her here to me."

Yo surprised me. Instead of questioning my plan, he asked another set of questions entirely.

"How do you know Akafumu has need of an anma regularly? And how do you know it's always the same woman? And how am I going to find the right one? There must be hundreds of anma in Edo."

"Isamu mentioned it once, after he had been hunting with Akafumu on our estate. Our daimyo complained he was full of aches and pains from his time on horseback. Isamu offered to get an anma for him from the nearest village, but Akafumu refused. He insisted he had to have his own masseuse. He said that she knew his body. Knew how to bring him relief. If it had been anybody but our daimyo, Isamu would have laughed at him. As it was, he had to take it seriously. He had Akafumu's anma brought to our house from the Floating World just to please him.

"I remember her because she gave me nightmares for months after I saw her. She was an elderly woman and didn't cover her eyes like most anma do. They were strange, all white. It was obvious that she couldn't possibly see, but she had a strange trick of looking at you as if she could not only see you, but see inside you, see what you were thinking. And—I know the poor woman couldn't help it—she was ugly. She terrified me."

I waited for Yo to ask why I wanted this anma, but he did not. That annoyed me to the extent that I almost blurted out the whole of my plan to make him understand how serious I was, but I held my tongue. He was shinobi. If he was as skilled as the legends said, then he should have the intuition to guess what I wanted the anma for. It was petty, but he shouldn't have laughed at me. Instead, I simply answered the question he asked.

"Do you remember her name?"

"I never heard it. But even amongst the many anma in Edo, she must stand out. If she serves Lord Akafumu, she will be well known."

I stared at Yo, certain he was going to refuse, to tell me he needed more information. He stared into space for a moment and then smiled at me.

"If I find her, will you tell me what you're planning to do?" he asked.

"But of course. *When* you find her, I'll tell you everything."

I was torn between annoyance that he had succeeded—apparently effortlessly—and excitement that my plans were suddenly coming to life when he announced the next day that we were to go to visit Akafumu's anma.

"Why can't she come here? I want to speak to her privately."

"Because it's safer if we go to her. Reiki may be blind, but she finds her way about Edo with nobody to guide her. If she can do that, she could find her way here again easily. If things go wrong, it will be better if she has no idea where we are."

Reiki. As soon as Yo spoke the name, I knew it must be her. In Japanese, the name means one who practices the spirit of healing. I wondered if Yo was waiting for me to ask how he had found Reiki. I did not, but nodded calmly as if I had always expected him to succeed.

"I imagine she must be busy. When can we see her?" I asked.

"She's waiting for us," he said simply.

I insisted we take Matsuo with us. Reiki lived in the poorest part of the Floating World, and I was apprehensive. I felt we needed to appear prosperous, but that was an invitation to be robbed. I explained carefully to Yo that I was not at all frightened of would-be robbers, but neither did I want to attract attention to us.

He nodded. "I think that's very wise," he said. He was laughing at me again. I inclined my head graciously and ignored him.

I almost regretted my haste as I gaped at the filthy hut Yo was indicating. It leaned against a wall at a jaunty angle. There were no shoji, just reed mats to form the outer walls and the roof. The door was another reed mat, hung on cords. A good shove and the whole lot would collapse. This couldn't be the home of a woman who was the favorite of a daimyo. Nor could I believe that a noble as fastidious as Lord Akafumu could bear a woman who lived in this hovel to be in intimate contact with his body. I was ashamed of my thoughts as soon as they passed through my mind. This anma worked—and no doubt, very hard—for every coin she possessed. I had no right at all to feel superior to her.

"Here?" I mouthed silently.

Yo nodded. "Reiki-san. May we come in?" he called courteously. I remembered her voice at once. It was as sweet as honey and made her terrible appearance all the worse.

"Shinobu-san. Please, come in. Mind your head, the door is low."

I put my hand to my mouth to hide a smile. The name Shinobu means "endurance," no doubt a reference to Yo's training; that, and the less than subtle pun on his profession. Matsuo looked at me with troubled eyes and I held my finger up to him, instructing him to sit and wait. He obeyed me at once. If only all men were so dependable!

The inside of the shack was no better than I expected. I hoped Reiki would not ask us to sit, but she did. Even though I knew she couldn't see me, I kept my expression neutral as I lowered myself to the filthy tatami matting. As soon as I sat, my body itched.

"Welcome back, Shinobu-san. And this is the lady you spoke of? The one who wanted to see me?" She stared at me with her white eyes, and immediately I was a child again, sure Isamu had invited a witch into our house. "Do I know you, lady?"

I was so startled, I jumped with surprise. I had my body under control almost at once, but I guessed that Reiki had felt my shock.

"I don't think so, Reiki-san," I said politely.

"Is that so? If you're not sure we've met, then we certainly don't know each other." She smiled cynically, and I realized she couldn't be as old as I had thought. Her teeth were all there and good. And an old woman would never have been able to sit cross-legged so comfortably. "If you have already met me, you would never forget me. But *I* don't know *you*. I don't recollect your voice. Or your smell. No matter. What do you need so badly that you found your way to me? I doubt it's problems with your man here. He strikes me as being extremely vigorous. Has he already got a troublesome wife that you want made barren so he has an excuse to get rid of her for you? Or is it you that can't bear him children?" She sniffed the air noisily. "No. Not you either. You smell all right to me."

"How do you know?" Was she pretending wisdom she didn't have to impress us?

"You sound like a young woman, and you move as if you're used to exercise and enjoy it. And I would guess from the smell of your skin that you're nearly due for your moon phase." I nodded, awestruck. She could really tell all that without even being able to see me? Embarrassed, I realized I needed to speak as she couldn't see me, but Reiki cut me off. "There's something else about you, child. Something I can't pin down. There's much anger in you that's nothing to do with him." She nodded curtly at Yo. "Is it that anger that's brought you to see me? I hope it is. I like anger. It warms my old bones."

"You're not old," I interrupted. "Or at least, not as old as you pretend to be."

"Who is she, Shinobu?" She stared at me, but spoke to Yo. "She's trouble, this one. Why have you brought her to me? I might like the anger that burns inside her, but I don't want to be the one that suffers for it. What do you want from me, girl?"

"I want you to teach me the skills of an anma," I said. "I need to be as good as you are."

Yo turned his head to look at me, his eyebrows raised in surprise. I was pleased; he had not guessed what I planned after all. Reiki's head jerked from me to him and then came back and rested on me. I met those blind, white eyes firmly. Even though I knew she could not see me, still they worried me. I would have to get used to that. She was going to help me whether she—or Yo—liked it or not.

"Why?" she asked. I had expected her to sneer at me. To tell me it took years to learn to be an anma. That all anma were blind, so my request was hopeless. She might even have taken offense at my request, thinking that I had come here to tease her to amuse myself. The single word threw me off balance. Those dreadful eyes stared into my mind and I knew that nothing but the truth would suffice.

"You're Lord Akafumu's anma." I hesitated even then; was it safe to speak honestly to Reiki? Yo lifted his hand in warning, but I ignored him. This was my one chance. If I did not take it, then I might as well admit I was defeated now, before I had even begun. I stared at Reiki and saw the slightest hunch of her shoulders as she heard the daimyo's name. It was enough. I sensed her hatred and relaxed. We stared at each other for a moment, the sightless anma and I, and finally she nodded. Her next words surprised me.

"Give me your hand," she instructed. She ran her nail along my fingers, swirling it in the middle of my palm. I noticed that her hands were immaculately clean, and in contrast to her face, they were smooth and white. Finished, she clasped my hand in her fingers, stroking it as if I was a child in need of comfort. "Not a working woman's hand. A lady's hand. But strong. Very strong. You have great power in that hand. I feel that same power inside you. What do you want with the daimyo?"

"I intend to crush him. To take away everything precious to him. To leave his body alive but his spirit only living enough to know what he has lost."

The words came out with no thought at all. Reiki put her head to one side and smiled.

"Such hatred. I wonder what he's done to you to deserve that? No matter. You're not going to tell me. And you think I can help you, do you? How is teaching you to become a masseuse going to do that?"

I surprised myself by speaking the absolute truth. Somehow, I felt that this sightless woman would see straight through anything else I tried to tell her.

"It's the only way I can think of that will allow me to gain Akafumu's trust so that he allows me to get close to him."

"He's happy about this, is he?" She jerked her head toward Yo.

"If it puts my lady in danger, I'm not happy at all," Yo said quietly. "But she'll do what she feels is right, no matter how much I dislike it. That being the case, it is surely better to help her than try and hinder her. Whatever she wants to do, I will be there for her."

"You're a fine pair together," Reiki said. I caught sadness beneath her sneering tone, but it vanished abruptly. I guessed she was aware of her moment of weakness and angry with herself for showing it. "What else do you want from me, samurai woman?"

Was that a wild guess, or did Reiki truly see far more than those who were gifted with sight? I smiled, hoping the smile would sound in my voice.

"You can get closer to Akafumu than anybody. I want to be able to do that. I want to stand at his side and see him naked and helpless. I need you to teach me all the arts of taking pain away from a man's body. And of putting pain where there was none before. My senses have been well trained already, I promise you. I can find my way about as well with my eyes shut as when they are open. Blindfold me, close up my ears, pinch my nostrils shut, and I will find my way about almost as well as you can. I know I can learn the crafts of an anma. And..." I paused, choosing my words carefully. "When I've learned all you can teach me, I want to take your place as Akafumu's masseuse."

Reiki was silent for a long time. Yo and I were very still as we waited for her to speak.

"I believe you could learn," Reiki said finally. "Most people can't endure silence. They would have been tempted to speak, or at least shuffle about. But not you two. You both have the gift of stillness. You're dangerous, the pair of you. If I had any sense, I would throw you out now and pretend I had never come within touching distance of you." She paused and we waited again. "I have no reason to love Lord Akafumu. He pays me when he thinks of it. Leaves me to starve if he forgets. Calls me to him at any time of the day or night if he has so much as a twinge in his toe. I've lost many good patrons because of him."

Her voice was very cold. There was something else, I felt it.

"What else does he do to you, Reiki-san?" I asked softly. She moved very slightly, and I sensed she was about to speak and say something meaningful. Yo's growing anger made him break his silence, and the moment was lost.

"Akafumu is not fit to be a daimyo," he said. "A peasant would show more mercy to his mule than that man does to those he should be protecting. I hope the gods allow him to be punished as he should be."

"We can but hope so, Shinobu," Reiki said. "If I can help the gods in this matter, I shall die a happy woman. But in the meantime, I am very much alive. I assume you will make it worth my while to take such a huge risk?"

"Of course," Yo said.

Reiki stared at me and said nothing.

SIX

> The mantis scissors
> And death follows. Why does her
> Prey not dodge away?

I almost gave up in the first few weeks. I had thought it difficult enough to learn the skills of onna-bugeisha, but that had been nothing compared to this. I was deeply disheartened, sure that I would never gain the expertise I needed to become a decent masseuse. I was clumsy, inept; the whole thing had been a mistake. I would never succeed. I moaned to Yo about it, barely admitting to myself that if he agreed with me and told me to stop, then I would accept his advice. Reluctantly, of course.

He stared at me for a moment, his face unreadable.

"It's up to you. If you don't feel you can go through with it, then stop. Nobody is forcing you to go on with it. We'll think of something else." He shrugged. I sensed he was surprised, and I was deeply ashamed of myself. I knew I should be grateful to Yo for his understanding. Was there any other man in Japan who would be as supportive as he was? I doubted it. I should, undoubtedly, be grateful to him. But I had spent the whole of my life being thankful for any scrap that was thrown to me, and I was deeply weary of it. My mixed emotions spilled out as anger. I spoke far more sharply than I intended.

"It's all right for you. All you have to do is sit there and watch me fail. I suppose you'd be happy if I did give up so you could go off and practice your trade as a highly paid mercenary, available for hire to anybody who had your price in their purse?"

I wished I had bitten my tongue and kept my words to myself as soon as I spoke. Yo turned a stone face to me and then stood up and left without saying a word. I sat stiffly when he had gone, staring into space. I thought wryly that Reiki had given me the right name when—after my first few lessons—she had cackled with amusement and said that from now on, she intended to call me "Kamakiri." Mantis. Even without eyes, she could see how angular I was. How my legs and arms were too long to be graceful. How skinny I was. How even my cheekbones were sharp enough to cut any man who touched my face. And equally clearly, she could see inside me. See that my character was the same as my outward appearance, prickly and quick to take offense. I shrugged to myself. At least I had the virtue of honesty. Nobody could ever accuse me of trying to be something I was not.

"You're too hard on yourself."

Yo had come back in without me seeing or hearing him.

"I'm sorry," I apologized reluctantly. "I shouldn't have said that. I didn't mean it."

"Yes, you did," Yo said. "You meant every word of it. And you're right, of course. That's what I do. It's what any shinobi does. We're mercenaries. We work for the highest bidder and walk away afterward. It's all I know, Keiko. I can't change. And for that matter, I don't want to change. It's the tradition of my family, just as yours is the code of bushido. We're not so different, you and I. You would do the same as me if you felt it was the right thing to do. That's the only difference between us. You look upon yourself as honorable. I have no honor."

Yo sounded hurt, and I understood that this was important to him. I took a deep breath and for once thought carefully before I spoke.

"You're right. I'm sorry. I was angry with myself and took it out on you."

"Just because Reiki calls you Kamakiri doesn't mean you need to act like one. I'd like to be able to sleep after making love to you without worrying I might wake up to find myself being eaten."

It took me a moment to realize that Yo was teasing me. I smiled and he smiled with me, and we were right together again. But I thought about what he had said and grudgingly decided that he was right. Perhaps more so than he realized. I chose to justify my actions by relying on the code of the samurai. Yo was honest about what he did. It was a profoundly uncomfortable insight.

We didn't speak of it again. But the knowledge that there was a chance that I might fail made me stubborn and I returned to Reiki with a new determination.

"That hurt you," Reiki stated. She had no need to tell me, I had felt the pain. I exhaled deeply and nodded.

The anma had told me that the only way to learn her

craft was for her to demonstrate it to me. On my body. That way, she said, I would learn quickly and not forget.

"The body cannot remember pain. If it did, then no woman would ever have more than one child," she instructed me. "Because of that, it is necessary to repeat the lesson."

Reiki caused me pain every time I went to learn from her. But today was different. I moaned as she pressed on my ribs. She did not press hard, but the pain caused by her fingers was extraordinary. I thought my heart was about to burst between my ribs. Only the slightest increase in pressure and I was sure I would be dead. She took her hand away and I was appalled to find the pain hardly lessened. Before, whenever she had taken her hand away from my body, the pain had stopped at once.

I lifted my head and looked at her, entreating her to stop the hurt. I had long ago ceased to worry that she couldn't see me. Reiki's other senses were, if anything, even more acute than mine. Just as I could, she would feel the displacement of air at the slightest movement. But far more than that, I had become sure that she could read thoughts that I left unspoken. I teased Yo that even he would never be able to surprise Reiki, and he agreed with me.

"Thank the gods she isn't shinobi," he said. "With her talents and the fact that I doubt she has any conscience at all, she could assassinate the shogun himself and not be caught."

I smiled with him, but his words pleased me more than he knew. Nobody would ever worry about an anma. A blind masseuse could go anywhere unnoticed and unchallenged.

"Still hurts, does it?" I heard satisfaction in Reiki's voice and replied shortly.

"You know it does." I gasped.

"Good. Now, you tell me how to stop it. Or even better, show me."

I could barely breathe. I was sure she had broken one of my ribs and that it was pressing on my lung. My heart was racing so fast with the intense pain, I thought it was going to explode at any moment. Reiki had inflicted this agony on me. How was I supposed to be able to put right her wrongs? I couldn't speak. I reached out and scrabbled for her robe, wordlessly begging her to put an end to my suffering. She slapped my hand away briskly and stood with all the fluid grace of a young woman. If I had not been sure I was about to die, I would have appreciated her poise. My mouth fell open in horror as she moved away from me.

She was not going to help me. I was going to die in agony lying on filthy tatami matting in a hut that was still damp from yesterday's rain. I hated Reiki for doing this to me. I hated Yo for not making me give up. And above all else, I hated myself for failing.

I bared my teeth in a silent howl of pain. My hand felt dead, but I found with an enormous effort that I could move my arm. I forced it up to my ribs, a jerk at a time. Because I couldn't feel my fingers, I pressed too hard at first and, unbelievably, my agony intensified. I found an odd kind of satisfaction in the increase in pain; if it could get worse, then I was not about to die. Or at least, not yet. I tried again, searching for the exact spot where Reiki had pressed. There! I was beginning to be able to feel my fingers, and I pressed with very great care this time. Immediately, the pain lessened to a dull ache. I gasped in relief.

"It still hurts, does it?" Reiki asked.

"No. Not at all," I said quickly, terrified that if I admitted my ribs felt as if they had been squeezed by a sumo wrestler, she would cause me yet more pain.

"You're lying," she said calmly. "Move your thumb a hair's width to the left. That's it. Press there."

Suddenly, not only had the pain gone completely, but I felt rested, as if I had awoken refreshed from a deep sleep.

"Thank you," I said from my very heart.

"Thank yourself," Reiki snapped. "You healed yourself. Not me."

She sat down again, crossing her legs. I sat up and faced her. She was silent for so long I thought the tough old woman had fallen asleep where she sat. I was so relaxed I almost slipped into sleep myself and shook myself awake. Reiki was grinning at me, and I knew I had misjudged her. She was alert, as always.

"How does it work, Reiki?" I asked curiously. "How can a simple touch either cause great pain or bring relief?"

"Have you ever watched an acupuncture master at work?" Reiki demanded. I nodded, puzzled. I had seen it done, but only once, when Isamu dislocated his shoulder after falling from his horse. He had been in agony, but the acupuncture master had reduced his pain almost miraculously. Emiko and I had peeped through the shoji, watching and cringing as needle after needle was pushed into Isamu's skin, some near his shoulder and others down his side and in his leg. We drew in our breath sharply as the acupuncture master tweaked each needle in turn, causing them to vibrate.

Emiko pointed to her leg and raised her eyebrows. I shrugged, as puzzled as she was as to how a needle in his leg could possibly cure pain in Isamu's shoulder. But it did. Not long after the needles were extracted, Isamu could rotate his shoulder with no pain at all.

"Then you understand. What I do is a little similar to acupuncture."

"But you don't use needles," I protested.

"My art is far older than acupuncture. And better. Anma were healing long before needles were ever thought of. But just like acupuncture, I use the channels of energy that flow through the body to heal. It doesn't matter if the body belongs to a man or a horse, the principle is the same. But unlike the acupuncture masters, as long as I have my hands and my feet, I can practice my art anywhere, with no need for any other materials."

I winced as I recalled Reiki walking on my back. It felt as if my spine was broken at first, and it was only when I stood up that I understood I was more flexible than usual, and that an annoying crick in my lower back had gone for the first time in months.

"Will I ever be as skilled as you are?" I was sure I knew what her answer would be, but I was curious. I had been coming each day for lessons for almost six months, and in all that time, Reiki had never commented on my progress.

"I have a headache," she snapped abruptly, and I stared at her in amazement. Reiki was as tough as teak. Even when the winter wind had blown through her hut so fiercely my fingers turned blue with cold and my knees creaked as if they were frozen, she had never complained. *She* had a headache? "Cure it for me."

I gathered my startled wits. I was about to stroke her head gently when I recalled an early lesson. *Never assume you know your patron's pain. Ask. Find out what the pain is like. Where it is. How long it has been there. Only touch when you are sure you know what you are curing. If you are careless, you can make things much worse.* Instead of touching Reiki's head, I pushed an imaginary strand of loose hair behind my ear with my raised hand.

"I'm sorry to hear that, Reiki," I said courteously. "Where is the pain, exactly?"

She pointed silently to the very center of her forehead.

"I see." Not the most tactful thing to say! I winced at my own ineptness. "And is it a sharp pain or an ache?"

"An ache. It bothers me greatly."

I had decided I knew enough when a sudden thought came to me.

"And do you have any pain elsewhere?"

I was sure I saw a flicker of a smile on her lips.

"My ear aches."

Ah! Now that was a different matter entirely. I took Reiki's head in my hands and then slid my fingers down her neck, placing my thumb just below her ears. Rather than pressing, I massaged the area very gently.

"Enough." I gave the line of her jaw one last rub before removing my hands. "I no longer have any pain." I wondered cynically if she had had any pain in the first place, and then I realized that this was Reiki's way of bestowing praise. I glowed with pleasure.

"I am delighted that I have been able to help," I said modestly. My pleasure turned to worry as Reiki spoke.

"There's no more I can teach you, Kamakiri. I thought you were chasing dreams when I agreed to take you on, but now I'm glad I did. I have no daughter to learn my art and take my place when I'm gone. But at least I know now that my small talent will not die with me."

It was the kindest thing Reiki had ever said to me, and I was touched. But suddenly I was also very unsure. I stared at my hands, wondering if I would be brave enough to use the skills I had learned when it really mattered.

"Thank you."

"No need to thank me, Kamakiri. Your man has paid me

very well for instructing you." Had he? I had never even thought to question how much Yo had paid her. I closed my eyes in annoyance at my own indifference. I would pay him back, I promised myself. I had no idea how, but I would not be in debt to him or anybody else, for that matter. "In fact, he's given me enough so I can leave the Floating World for good when you take my place."

I frowned. She was going to leave? Why? I felt foolish as I answered my own question. Lord Akafumu was her longtime patron. He trusted her and would never accept me as her replacement if she was still there.

"Where will you go, Reiki-san?" I asked humbly.

"To Nikko. My son lives there with his family. I understand the place has many *onsen*. I shall enjoy myself bathing in a different hot spring each day. Ah, but it will be good to feel clean! He's asked me often over the years to go and live with him. I never have because he has a large family and I don't want to be a burden on him. Now I have enough money that I can pay my way, so I shall go to him happily."

I nodded, hiding my astonishment. This humble anma had her pride, then. A different pride to that of the samurai code, but pride all the same. I was humbled; Reiki had taught me a lesson that had nothing to do with either inflicting hurt or healing it.

"You're too quick to lash out, Kamakiri." I shrugged. She was right, I knew. "Too much like your namesake. You think because you're samurai that you're better than the rest of us."

"Not at all," I protested quickly, but Reiki was having none of it.

"Of course you do. It's understandable. It's the way you've been raised. All your life you've had it hammered into you that you're noble. That you're superior to most other people. Perhaps you are, in some ways. But that doesn't mean to say you're always better than the rest of us. It wouldn't hurt you to remember that the next time that man of yours does something you don't understand. He's just as honorable as you are, but in a different way."

I looked down. I had no words to argue with. She was right. I just hoped I would remember it. I stared at her, for once forgetting that she would sense I was looking. Something else Reiki had said had startled me. She had a son? Somebody, at some point in her life, had found this wrinkled, smelly old woman attractive enough to want to make love to her? To have married her?

Reiki smiled serenely at me, and I knew that she really had guessed what I was thinking. I smiled back. She hadn't named me Kamakiri without thought. Perhaps we were more alike than I had wanted to acknowledge, this blind anma and I. Her voice took my smile away.

"When I'm gone, and you take my place with Lord Akafumu, be careful."

"Of course I will. He'll never know what I've done to him," I said. I expected Reiki to be smiling with me, but she was not.

"Take every precaution to make sure that is so, Kamakiri. I would be very angry if I thought I had wasted my precious time on you." She gripped my hand tightly and I felt the affection behind her rough words.

I was almost as surprised as I was touched.

SEVEN

Sand runs through my hands.
I hear the whisper of your
Words as each grain falls

I had agreed with Reiki that she would send a messenger to me when Akafumu next sent for her. I would take her place, and she would immediately leave the Floating World to go to her son.

"Better you keep away from me, now," she instructed. "There's nothing else I can teach you. In any event, no point in tempting the gods by you coming back here any longer."

I would miss her. I had gotten used to her caustic wit and determination that I would do things as she wished. I could not tell her that and simply wished her luck for her journey and the future. I gave her my jade and gold bracelet as a farewell present. She fingered it before slipping it on her thin wrist.

"Now there's a pretty thing for an old woman." She chuckled. "My daughter-in-law will envy me this. She's a discontented, lazy young thing. I don't like her, and she doesn't like me. I shall enjoy making her life a misery when I get to Nikko."

I tried to feel sorry for the unknown daughter-in-law, but Reiko's cackle was infectious and I smiled inside. I hoped that she might say she would have been happy if her son's wife had been more like me, but she did not. Still, her voice was gentle when she said her final goodbye.

"Take care, Kamakiri. If you could lose your anger, you would find life could be very good. Don't worry about Akafumu. You can deal with him."

We hugged and she walked away from me.

In spite of Reiki's confidence in me, I was trembling as I got ready for my first visit to Lord Akafumu.

I worried about my eyes above all else. I was supposed to be a blind anma. I was confident enough in my skills as a masseuse, but I became convinced that my eyes would give me away. I had tried practicing keeping them closed all the time, but as soon as I relaxed, they popped open on their own. And when they did, it was instinctual to glance around me. I couldn't help it, no matter how I tried. Keeping them wide open was even worse. I asked Yo how I looked and he shrugged.

"You don't look blind with your eyes open. It's obvious that you can see, even when you stare straight ahead. You have too much expression in them," he said honestly. "Do you want to try wrapping a bandage around your face?"

I could do that, I thought eagerly. It had worked when I had escaped from Hana, when she had kept me a prisoner in the Hidden House. But I had forgotten entirely that then, even after less than half a day, my eyes had become inflamed and very sore. Still, it was worth a try. As if my eyes remembered their darkness and resented it, they started to run and become painful after only a few minutes, and I found myself longing to rub them fiercely. When I tore the bandage off, both my eyes were bright red and felt raw. That wouldn't do either.

Becoming desperate, I stuck my eyelids closed with a dab of rice starch glue. That was even worse than the bandage. As soon as my eyes understood they could not blink, my eyelids seemed to take on a life of their own. They itched constantly, and I had to ball my hands into fists to stop myself scratching. In the end they tore themselves free anyway.

"Oh, this is hopeless," I moaned to Yo. "Why didn't we think about this earlier? How can I pass as an anma if it's clear I can see?"

"You kept your eyes closed well enough when Riku-san was teaching you to fight," he pointed out.

I shrugged in annoyance. "I know. But that was different. I could open my eyes if I wanted to. That's what the problem is now. Because I know I can't open them, I want to."

Yo rolled his own eyes in amusement. I glared at him.

"I might have an answer. Matsuo, do you want to go for a walk?"

He was doing it to irritate me, I was sure of it. I said nothing as he and Matsuo went out. It looked to me as if it might rain. Yo had not put a coat on. I hoped he got wet.

It didn't rain. And I was forced to be grateful yet again when he came back with a small, neatly wrapped package in his hand. He tore the wrapping off and displayed a tiny, stoppered glass vial.

"Put your head back and keep your eyes wide open." He instructed. I tried, but the liquid he dripped into my eye stung, and I closed my eyes automatically. "Didn't I tell you not to blink?" he scolded. I apologized, and he put another cold, stinging drop in each eye.

"What is it?" I stared around the room and found that everything had gone curiously misty. I could see, but nothing looked at all right.

"It's a distillation of a certain flower. The geisha and yujo use it a lot. The tiniest amount makes the pupils expand greatly, and the eye to appear glowing and very beautiful. But even one drop makes it difficult to see. A little more and everything becomes misty." I nodded; he was right about that! "But it also makes your eyes look so brilliant they seem very odd. With the amount I've put in for you, anybody would think your eyes were strange and take you for a blind woman. I know you can't see properly, but for you that doesn't matter. In fact, it's probably a good thing. It should make you use your other senses to compensate."

"Thank you," I said sincerely. And then, becoming worried, I added, "It will wear off?"

"It will, and should leave no ill effects. One drop lasts for hours, so two or three should be enough to make you into a true anma for as long as you need to be disguised."

I thought about that, and I was suddenly intensely jealous.

"How do you know? And how do you know yujo use it a lot?"

"Everybody knows that," he said easily. But it still bothered me.

I rolled the glass bottle in my hand. Even with my impaired vision, the contents looked beautiful. The liquid caught the light and shone like the inside of a wet seashell.

"It's very pretty," I commented.

Yo took the bottle from me. "It is, but it can be deadly as

well. I heard a certain very beautiful geisha, whose lover betrayed her, actually drank it instead of putting it in her eyes. Apparently, her lover had always greatly admired her eyes, and she felt it was a fitting way to die. She was wrong. She died not only in agony, but rolling in her own shit. This stuff is not nice at all, and there's no cure if you drink it."

I nodded seriously. Beauty was a double-edged sword, to be sure. Perhaps, after all, I was better off without it. The thought amazed me.

Yo gave a silver coin to the urchin who had brought Reiki's message. The child stared at it with huge eyes and ran off before Yo could change his mind and demand it back.

"Ready?" Yo asked. I nodded. I lied.

It was too late to turn back. Akafumu's chamberlain had his hand out, preventing me from going any further. I had anticipated this. I kept my head lowered humbly, my shoulders hunched. I had no need to pretend to be anxious; my heart was beating so fast I was sure the man next to me must be able to hear it.

"Who are you? My lord sent for the anma Reiki. What are you doing here?"

"My lord, Reiki-san is dead." I spoke softly, great sadness in my voice. "Her home was very damp and cold. When it rained for many days last week, her lungs became congested and she could not breathe. I did all I could for her, but neither I nor the apothecary I called in could help her. She was very old, lord, and I think she was ready to die. If the spirit is ready to go to the next world, no amount of skill can keep it chained to the earthly body."

"Aye?" I lifted my eyes and peered at a spot just beyond his shoulder. He was staring at me carefully, his face so close to me that even with my misty vision I could make out his features. He nodded finally and I sent up a quick prayer of thankfulness for Yo's potion. "And who are you, then?"

"Lord, my name is Kamakiri." He glanced down at my body and grinned, obviously finding my name appropriate. "I was Reiki's apprentice. She taught me her skills well, I promise you. Even when she lay dying, she was worried about the welfare of Lord Akafumu. She told me I must come here and take her place. So, I am here," I said simply.

"I see. Lord Akafumu is in great discomfort, so I suppose we must give you a try. But before I let you anywhere near my lord, I want to be certain you're harmless."

I held out my hands quickly in supplication.

"I am an anma, lord," I said. "I give relief from pain. What harm could I cause?"

If only he knew my plans! I exulted inside, but only for a moment. Truly, even monkeys can fall from trees.

"Take your robe off." The gloating note was clear in his voice. "Now, anma. I haven't got time to waste on you. I need to make sure you're not hiding any weapons. My lord is a powerful man. Like any powerful man, he has enemies. I'm not going to let a complete stranger in to see him, blind woman or not."

"Lord!" I put my fists to my mouth, miming distress. "I have no weapon. I bring nothing but my hands!" *And I could kill you silently before you could take a breath with these hands.*

"So you say. Take your clothes off or get out of here."

I was trembling with anger. I suppose he took it as shame and fear, as he grunted with satisfaction as I undid my obi and held my robe wide open. I was naked underneath; I was supposed to be a poor anma. I doubted I would be able to afford underclothes.

"See, my lord? I carry nothing with me at all."

"Drop the robe." I did as he instructed, shrugging it off

my shoulders silently. He walked around me, inspecting me from every angle.

"Lord, there is nothing in there but me!" I protested. He seemed to find my words amusing.

"So I see. I can't say I find you at all enticing myself, but there's no accounting for different tastes."

When I had begun my training as onna-bugeisha, Riku had knocked me to the ground time after time. He had caused me great pain and never once apologized. My brother had seen me naked in the bath often. Yo's hands had explored my body far more deeply than this man, and I had cried out loud for more. None of that had caused me any shame at all. Yet the impersonal actions of this strange man were rousing such humiliation that I almost forgot my mission.

At that moment, I wanted nothing more than to reach back to him, to pinch a certain point in his hamstring that would have him rolling on the floor in agony. Once he was down, it would take only a moment to push one finger between his ribs and find the exact point that would stop his heart immediately. Once he was dead, all I had to do was stand up and scream. No one would suspect that a naked blind woman could kill a man a head taller than she with her bare hands. The thought that it would surely appear as if he had had a seizure from excitement would only add to his humiliation. I smiled with anticipation, almost feeling his leg beneath my hand.

"Nothing there." He sounded almost disappointed and I took a deep breath.

"Lord," I whispered. "May I put my robe on now?"

"Of course." He was watching me intently as I stooped and scrabbled for my kimono.

I was shaking with relief as much as revulsion. Yo had

been right. If I hadn't listened to his wise words, I would surely have been on my way to the execution ground by now.

"I have no intention of killing Akafumu," I had explained to him. "I want him alive, but as incapable as a newborn baby. A ruined mind in a healthy body that could live for years. I want his sons to fight over his position. For them to go to the shogun on their knees, just as I did to their father. When that happens, I'll be avenged for what he did to me and all my family."

Yo stared at me as if I were a stranger to him. "So what do you need from me? It seems as if you have all your plans in place."

"I need you to get a certain drug for me," I explained. "Without it, all my plans are nothing. Reiki told me there were potions that could ruin a man's mind, but leave his body untouched. Do you know about such things?"

"I've heard of them, certainly. And I know a certain apothecary who would supply me with the right drug without asking too many questions. But how are you going to get Akafumu to take it? It sounds terribly risky to me."

"I've thought of that," I said quickly. "I'll dissolve it in my massage oil. Reiki said the drug would work if it were absorbed through the skin." I was pleased with myself, and annoyed when Yo shook his head.

"His guards would never let you take anything in with you."

"You think so? In that case, I'll put a little in the smallest bottle I can find, and smuggle it in."

"Where would you hide it? You're unknown to Akafumu's court. They'll search you." Yo sounded worried. I was becoming angry with him.

"I'll find somewhere to hide it," I snapped.

"You think so? I promise, they'll search in every opening of your body. Even if they didn't find it, it's not going to work." Yo spoke slowly, stressing each word. "Have you thought about the effect it would have on you? If it can be absorbed via the skin, then you would take it into your body through your hands when you gave him his massage."

My mouth dropped open. I had thought my plan was perfect! How could I have overlooked something so obvious?

"Perhaps if I coated my palms with wax?" Even as I said it, I knew I was beaten.

"No," Yo said firmly. "If you waxed your palms, you wouldn't be able to feel his skin and your massage wouldn't be right. He would be sure to notice the difference and would be suspicious at once. Besides, it's too dangerous. The oil could get smeared on to your own skin. You have the heart of a dragon, Keiko. But you're not naturally devious. Unlike me. Forget it. We'll think of something else, I promise."

And Yo had thought of something, of course. Although at this precise moment, I could think of nothing but how wise I had been to take his advice. I kept my head lowered submissively and did my best to tremble slightly as if I was in awe of this majestic place. I spoke humbly.

"Can I go through to Lord Akafumu now, sir?" A demon of mischief made me add, "Will you go before me so that the lord is not surprised by my presence?"

The chamberlain frowned and took his hand away from his tree slowly.

"Yes. Of course. Follow behind me, at a respectful distance."

He paused at the great entrance doors, squaring his shoulders and clearing his throat. I moved close enough to him to allow my breath to touch his neck, hoping to cause him even greater discomfort. He jumped and I swallowed laughter. I noticed he hobbled through with his hands clasped in front of his robe. What fools these men were!

If Lord Akafumu was as stupid as his chamberlain, then my task would be far easier than I had expected.

EIGHT

When I was a child,
Small things pleased me. Ah, how I
Wish for such ease now!

*R*eiki had told me cynically that when they were naked, all men were the same.

"It doesn't matter if they're a peasant or the shogun himself, once you get them beneath your hands wearing only their skin, you can't tell them apart. Treat them all the same and don't worry about it. Pain can't tell a noble from a beggar."

In spite of her wise words, I was jittering with nerves by the time the chamberlain forgot his own lusts and finally ushered me into Akafumu's presence. The chamberlain made me stand by the door as he had a whispered conversation with his lord. I kept my head bowed, my hands tucked in my sleeves. They needn't have whispered, I heard them clearly enough.

"Reiki dead, is she? Nothing contagious, was it?" Akafumu asked sharply.

"I think not, lord. This one says she died of a congestion of the lungs. She was Reiki's apprentice, and the old woman instructed her to take her place."

"Oh, well, I suppose she's a bit younger than Reiki, if nothing else. Anma, what's your name?"

"Kamakiri, Lord Akafumu." I spoke to the tatami.

"Well, that suits you, right enough." He huffed with laughter at his own wit. I smiled as if his insult had delighted me. "If Reiki sent you, I suppose I had better give you a try. I have the most terrible ache in my belly. Goes right through to my back. Reiki always managed to soothe it a bit for me. Think you can do the same?"

"I will do my best, lord." I held my head low and whispered my answer reverently. I waited until the chamberlain had gone—he made sure he brushed against me as he passed me by—before shuffling forward to my patron. Reiki had told me that I had to go on my knees before Akafumu and kowtow while I waited for his instructions. I thought cynically that I had done it once, I could manage it again.

Akafumu patted me on the head as if I were a pet dog. I took it as a mark of favor and sighed deeply, a sound that he might take for awed pleasure. It was actually fear leaving my body. As soon as I had stepped inside his grand mansion, I had begun to worry that he might recognize me. I told myself constantly that he would not. He had seen me only once before, from a distance, and I had looked different then, my hair loose and hanging over my face, my skin smeared with wood ash. Now, my hair was pulled back from my face and twisted tightly in a knot at the back of my head. So tightly, it was pulling my face into a grimace. My face and hands were spotlessly clean, my kimono old and threadbare. Yo had done his best to reassure me, pointing out that Akafumu would hardly associate a blind anma with a noblewoman come to his court to beg a favor.

"That's half of the art of being an invisible shinobi," he told me. "If I dress like a rich merchant and act like one, nobody at all associates me with the half-naked peasant they saw working in the fields the day before. Even you, who have more perception than anybody I know, wouldn't think about it."

He was right, but I worried until the moment Akafumu shed his clothes, throwing them to the ground with the carelessness of a man who simply expects a servant to pick them up. Naked, he flopped gracelessly to his divan, awaiting my attentions impatiently.

Reiki had trained me well. I knew as soon as I saw his naked body that I could treat his belly and backache effortlessly. When he took off his clothes, I could see clearly enough that his bones were well padded with fat, which had settled particularly in his belly. There was nothing at all wrong with him that less food and more exercise wouldn't solve quickly. But I made sure I took my time over the massage, grunting as if it was causing me great effort.

"Would my lord do me the favor of turning over?" I hid a grin at the sight of his buttocks, rearing at me like an overripe peach. Reiki had been right, it was impossible to feel fear when a man was trusting—and foolish—enough to present his naked rear to you. My fingers itched to reach for the nerve that ran from the base of the spine down each leg. Reiki had demonstrated to me—in fact, on me—how agonizing the pain any malfunction in this nerve could be. I could paralyze Lord Akafumu with one pinch. I contented myself with giving a light press in just the right place, and I was immediately rewarded with a squeal of agony.

"Ah, but that is painful! You're supposed to be healing

me, Kamakiri, not causing me hurt. You're even clumsier than Reiki was."

Lord Akafumu squirmed beneath my hands. I thought that he sounded exactly like a small child who had fallen and not taken any great hurt, but who still cries for his mother to comfort him. I pressed a little harder and schooled my expression to be deeply concerned as he yelped.

"I am so sorry, lord," I said quickly. "But until I can find where the pain originates from and what is causing it, I cannot help to take it away from you. Reiki told me how serious the problem was."

"I suppose you're right," he said. His mouth was set in a sulky pout. I longed to give him a good smack on his naked buttocks. "Have you finished? Reiki never caused me as much hurt as you do."

"Reiki was an old woman, lord. She did not have my strength."

"To be sure, you are certainly a strong young thing." He sounded appreciative, and I took a swift, cautious step away from the table where he lay, rolling my neck as if to ease a crick out of it.

"If you will allow me, lord?" I knew perfectly well why the wretched man had a backache. His pendulous belly would cause him to walk hunched over, putting a strain on the small of his back. I pursed my lips and blew out air with a concerned sound.

"What is it?" Where his own well-being was concerned, Akafumu was instantly alert.

"Reiki told me how your back made you suffer, lord." I made sure my voice was deeply concerned. "I know you also have pain in your stomach, but I think that is coming from your back. And now I understand what causes it. There are very many nerves, just here." I couldn't resist, I gave him a pinch and nodded wisely when he howled with pain. "You see? I barely touched you and your body protested."

"Can you heal it? Reiki never could, or at least not permanently. The pain always came back after a while."

Of course Reiki hadn't helped him too much. She depended for every grain of rice in her bowl on what Akafumu paid her. When he actually paid her, that was. She could have cured him quickly enough with a deep massage and hints about his diet, but she needed to keep him in pain. But then, so did I.

For a different reason.

"I hope that I can help, lord. But it will not be easy. I believe the nerves at the base of your spine are beginning to knot together. If it's not possible to treat them properly, the pain will become a great deal worse. Much worse," I added seriously. "Eventually, it may be that they are impossible to heal and you will find it difficult even to walk."

Akafumu whimpered. "Then do something about it, anma."

"Yes, lord," I said obediently. "I can most certainly ease the condition for a while."

"Reiki could do that. What I want is a cure," he snapped.

I set my lips in a straight line. I had to; I was longing to break into a grin. What a fool this great daimyo was! He was suffering from nothing more than the results of his own greed, yet he was persuaded he was enduring the most malignant pain the gods could inflict. Perhaps this was going to be easier than I had hoped.

"Of course, lord. May I ask, do you smoke opium? It can help relieve pain," I said earnestly. "Especially in cases like yours, where I believe the nerves are knotted because you cannot relax. That is a condition that is nearly always found in men of great power. Because you are constantly thinking of affairs of state, your body takes its cue from your mind and refuses to be eased."

"I see." I had appealed to his vanity; Akafumu nodded. "There may be something in what you say. I have so many calls on my time, I do find it very difficult to relax. But I already take opium occasionally. Of course I do. Even my good friend the shogun takes a pipe. If it hasn't done me any good so far, it's not going to help, is it?"

"My lord is very wise." I stroked the muscles of his lower back smooth and felt his body relax beneath my hands. I reminded myself to tread very carefully. Akafumu was a fool, but where his health was concerned, he was alert enough. "May I ask what sort of opium you use?"

"How should I know? The servants prepare me a pipe, and I smoke it. Ah. Now that feels a little better." He sat up and stretched. "But the pain will come back, you say?"

"It will," I spoke regretfully. "The body is linked to the mind in ways that are little understood, lord."

"So, you're as useless as Reiki was. In that case, get out and don't come back."

He had worked himself into a fury. I had a moment of panic. This was the most dangerous time. I spoke rapidly before he could clap his hands to have his servants throw me out.

"My lord, I beg your indulgence for a moment longer. Surely it will be worth it if I can find something that will ease your terrible pain?" I knew it! Mention of his pain had Akafumu deflating. He nodded and then, remembering I was blind, sighed.

"I suppose you might as well have your say. You have one moment longer. If I don't like what you're saying, you're going to regret it."

"I understand, lord." He shifted uncomfortably, and I spoke in an urgent murmur. "My lord, I understand that a noble such as you would find it difficult to relax. That your mind is always occupied with higher things." He was beginning to preen. I relaxed a little. "Because of that, you must make your body calm in spite of the powerful action of your mind. I believe that opium will help with that."

"I've already told you I take a pipe occasionally," he said sulkily. "Is that the best you can do?"

"No, lord. There is more, I promise you. Because your mind is so alert and agile, it is obvious to me that normal opium is not strong enough to make any impression on your character. To be truly relaxed, you need to take only the strongest and purest paste that is available. And not just occasionally, you must take a pipe regularly. At least twice a day. More often than that if your pain comes back. And of course, you will still need regular massages to ensure that the nerves do not knot themselves again."

I stopped. I sensed that if I pushed my "remedy" any further, Akafumu would begin to question my words. I let him think about it in silence.

"I notice that you think I would still need your services regularly." He sneered. I hunched my shoulders and tried to look terrified. "Well, I'll give it a try. An opium pipe never hurt anybody. I'll tell my chamberlain to procure some of the really good stuff for me. You may come back in seven days from now. And I hope for your sake that I feel better for following your advice. If I don't, you'll be sorry."

That was it. He stared at his fingernails as if they were far more important than I was. I bowed my way out of the presence-chamber backward, bowing deeply. My heart was beating so hard it almost deafened me. I would surely return as often as I could persuade Akafumu I was needed.

And I hoped that each time I would find that the daimyo was more and more in thrall to the opium I had prescribed for him. I had a sudden vision of Yo's earnest face as he explained his plan to me, and I sighed deeply as I remembered our discussions.

"It will take time," he admitted. "But the more you can persuade him to take, the quicker he will be enslaved."

"You're sure?" I asked doubtfully. I was not happy; so much depended on things that were out of my control. What if Akafumu didn't become addicted? If he did, what if his wives realized what was happening to him and persuaded him to stop? And above all else, was Yo really sure the opium would have the desired effect? So much could go wrong, and the longer the process took, the greater the danger became.

"If he takes the superior opium, it will enthrall him," Yo reassured me. "It would take a man of very great strength of mind to withstand it for long, and I don't believe Akafumu is at all strong. Eventually, he will care for nothing at all but his pipe. He will forget he's a great daimyo. Forget he has a position in life. He will be just as you want him. Alive and healthy but with no mind to call his own."

I had taken the first step and survived. I was deeply relieved, but my good humor melted away quickly. It was a minor thing, but I wanted my fee. The thought that a man as wealthy as Akafumu could cheat a poor anma out of her few coins annoyed me greatly. The chamberlain was nowhere to be found. I asked any passing servant I could find if they had seen him, but they shrugged my question away. Finally, I sat in the middle of the corridor leading to Akafumu's apartment and refused to be budged. It didn't take long at all for the scurrying servants to weary of walking around me, and the chamberlain arrived in an annoyed bustle.

"Anma. What do you think you're doing? If the daimyo has finished with you, go away."

"Lord Akafumu said you would pay me." My voice was a beggar's whine

"Of course I will. Reiki was paid at the end of each full moon. If my lord is happy with you, you will be paid then."

"I shall starve!" I moaned. "If you don't give me money now, I shall be dead before I can come back!" I grabbed blindly for the hem of his robe and clutched it. "I promise you, Lord Akafumu was happy with my services. He wants me to come back in seven days, so he must have been happy. Give me some money and I will go now."

The chamberlain gave in gracelessly. He threw some coins on the floor and I pattered around with my hands eagerly, pretending to search for them. He was gone before I retrieved the last one.

"May the gods bless you, my lord!" I shouted loudly.

Matsuo was waiting exactly where I had left him by the main gate. I would have liked to have taken my protector inside, but caution stopped me. I had doubted that Akafumu would recognize me, but I thought it all too likely that he, or one of his courtiers, would remember Isamu's magnificent akita and no doubt wonder what a poor anma was doing with him.

NINE

Everything made by
The hand of man must die. The
Gods alone survive

I put my miserable fee into Yo's hands proudly. It was nothing more than a pittance, but I was delighted to be contributing something for us to live on.

"It isn't much, but it's all they gave me." I washed my face, splashing water in my eyes. Oh, but it was good to be able to see clearly again!

"It went well?" Yo turned the coins over in his hands and smiled.

"As well as I could ever have hoped. He trusted me enough to allow me to massage his back, and he didn't recognize me at all." I had decided on the way home that I would not mention the chamberlain's behavior to Yo. He may have been right about the likelihood of me being searched, but I wasn't going to tell him that. "The man's a coward when it comes to the slightest pain. And he's vain, as well. He was eager to accept all the rubbish I told him about how such a great man as he would always find it difficult to relax and that was why his nerves were knotted."

"You're sure there's nothing really wrong with him?" Yo asked.

"The only thing wrong with Lord Akafumu is the fact that he eats too much rich food and drinks too much and sits all day. I could cure him in a day or two by putting him on a diet and making him take some exercise." Laughter welled in my throat. "Perhaps I should have suggested that! The shock would probably have overturned his mind!"

Yo smiled with me, but I sensed there was something wrong. His body was tense. There was something he was not sharing with me.

"What?" I demanded bluntly. "What's the matter?"

"You're going to see Akafumu again?" he asked.

"Yes, in seven days. Do you think there'll be any change in him by then?"

"I don't know. And that's the problem."

Problem? I stared at my lover in disbelief. This was *his* plan. He had convinced me that it was going to work. I had taken the first step on the road to ensuring Akafumu's ruin and *now* he was talking about problems?

"Why is it a problem? It is going to work, isn't it?"

"I'm sure it will." I lifted my hands out, palms up, in a gesture of bewilderment. Yo shrugged and refused to meet my gaze. "If he starts to take very strong opium every day, I have no doubt at all that Lord Akafumu will become a hopeless addict, crying for his pipe like a hungry child demanding his mother's breast.

"We know that Akafumu is an associate of the shogun. Before long, even the shogun will see that Akafumu is no longer the man he knew and trusted. Akafumu will twist and turn and lie of course, but the shogun will hear the truth from his courtiers, all men who would be delighted to see Akafumu shaken from his place at the shogun's right hand. That would be the real start of Akafumu's downfall. Once he's lost the favor of the shogun, he'll turn to his habit for comfort. His fate will be sealed with no way back. By that time, his court will have disintegrated around him. His friends will have deserted him. His wives will curse the day they married him. It's entirely possible that he might even have to sell off his concubines to pay for his habitual pleasure. Everything he once held dear will be gone."

"So?" I demanded suspiciously. "That's exactly what we planned. What's changed?"

"I have," Yo said quietly. "I think you must have bewitched me, onna-bugeisha. Just like Akafumu is going to be, I've forgotten everything that used to be important to me. Except for you."

I almost made a joke about the power of love, but I realized Yo was deadly serious.

"I don't understand," I said instead.

"I'm shinobi," he said patiently. "I live by my wits, and I am very good at what I do. I didn't tell you, but I've already turned down several commissions that would have taken me away from Edo. I felt I needed to be here, with you. If I turn down any more, my patrons will think I've turned away from my trade and they'll look elsewhere. Once my reputation's lost, I'm lost. The problem is that I don't know how long it will take Akafumu to become hopelessly addicted. If it takes many months longer, I will no longer have any value as a shinobi. I don't know anything else. Will you still want me as your lover when I'm penniless with nothing in my future?"

A well of tenderness made my eyes prickle with unshed tears. Yo had known all this when he put his plan to me. Yet he had been willing to let me go ahead. I wished that he could have brought himself to discuss his worries with me earlier.

"I understand what you're saying," I said quickly. "But it doesn't have to be like that. You could leave me here. I'm sure I'll be safe. If a commission is offered, then you should take it."

Even as I said it, I was distracted by his earlier words. It could take many months to enslave Akafumu to his opium? Did I have the patience to wait so long? Deeply frustrated, I pushed the thought aside and concentrated on what Yo was saying.

"I could do that," he said reluctantly. "But I don't want to. This is still dangerous for you. I know it's something you feel you have to do, and I understand that. But if I accept a commission, I will have no idea how long I'll be away from you. And I have to be able to concentrate on the job in hand. If I'm worried about you, I can't do that. And that makes it dangerous for me."

We stared at each other bleakly. Yo was right. I was right. If he stayed, he would throw away everything that had been his life. If I gave up my plans for Akafumu, I would lose my honor. And what was the point of a samurai without honor?

His face was expressionless, but I sensed he was hoping I would give in and agree to forget about Akafumu. Follow his wishes as any good woman surely would. But I could never forget the way Akafumu had treated me when I had kneeled before him as a proud samurai woman. He had humiliated me then. He had used my friend Reiki and not cared if she starved to death for the sake of a few coins. He had sold my servants into slavery. He had executed my villagers without once wondering why they had been driven to take what my father was too mean to give.

And not once when I had humbled myself before him had he spoken one word of sorrow for the deaths of my father and my brother. Men who had been proud to serve him as their lord. In fact, he had wiped away my entire family's proud samurai tradition as casually as a peasant might swat an annoying fly.

I thought bitterly that I should have killed Akafumu when I had the chance. If I had—assuming I had survived, of course—then both Yo and I could have walked away and lived our lives together without his shadow over us. I sighed; I hadn't done it. Spilled water cannot be coaxed back into the tray; there was no point in wishing for what might have been.

"All we can do is wait," I said finally. "Perhaps things will resolve themselves. It may be that Akafumu takes such a liking to his opium that things move quicker than you think. And it might be a while before you get word of a commission and have to leave. But if you're needed, then go. I would hate myself if I kept you here. I promise you that I can look after myself."

Of course I could. Had Yo forgotten that I was onna-bugeisha? That in both bodily and mental strength, I was at least the equal of any well-trained soldier? Besides, there were other things I was determined to do, apart from bringing about the downfall of Akafumu. And those things would be a great deal easier to achieve if Yo was not here.

I smiled at him and hoped that this time he could not read my thoughts.

TEN

> We are all flesh and
> Blood. Why then is each of us
> Made so differently?

I knew the gods had finally decided to smile on me when unbelievably one of the despised foreign barbarians solved my problem without even knowing he had done so.

I was following Matsuo home. It had become habit with me to play the part of an anma whenever I was out of the house on my own. Yo agreed that it was an excellent thing to do. If it became instinct, I was less likely to betray myself when it mattered.

"Anma, a word, if you please."

I stopped, staring straight ahead. Although the words were Japanese, the intonation was odd and the quality of the voice was very strange indeed.

"What do you want?" I was so surprised, I forgot to be polite. No wonder the voice sounded strange. The man who had spoken to me was a gaijin.

I had to work very hard not to show my surprise. I had never been so close to a gaijin before and was deeply suspicious of him. He was dressed in decent robes, not the strange clothes so many of the gaijin wore. But that wasn't in the least reassuring; I thought he looked uncomfortable, as though the robes didn't belong on his back.

"I am in need of your services, anma."

His Japanese wasn't bad, apart from the strange rhythm of his voice. He spoke very slowly, as if he had to mentally translate every word before he spoke. At least that made it easier for me to understand him. I found myself speaking slowly in return. He looked relieved, and I almost smiled, forgetting for a moment that I was blind. I reached down and patted Matsuo; I wanted to read his reaction to this foreign barbarian. If there was any danger, Matsuo would be tense, his hackles rising. I was surprised to find he was relaxed. Very well, I would trust both our instincts.

"Do you have pain?"

"I do. My..." He paused and frowned, searching for the word he needed. Finally, he put his hand to the back of his neck and rubbed it, reaching as far down his back as he could to demonstrate. "Ah. I am sorry. Of course, you can't see me. Here."

He took my hand and placed it on his neck. I was so pleased that he really thought I was blind that I didn't snatch my hand away. Of course, being a gaijin, he had no idea how insulting it was to touch a stranger in such an intimate way.

"You have pain in your neck?" I asked. He had slackened his grip and I took my hand away as quickly as I could without drawing attention to it. "Pain that goes down your back?" I had spoken too quickly. He looked confused. Rather than repeating it, I turned away from him and ran my hand down my own back, from the neck to the small of my back.

"That's it!" he said. "Can you help me?"

I was confident I could. I guessed without touching him that the problem lay in the nerves of the neck. I noticed he stood with his shoulders hunched slightly. He probably didn't realize it himself, but he was tense. This was his body's way of telling him his posture was all wrong. I could help him, but did I want to? The thought of touching his strange body was distasteful. He was very tall, and looked quite muscular. But the gods alone knew what he was like beneath that robe. He would probably smell, as well.

I was about to refuse when he winced and rubbed his neck again. My conscience pricked; if he was an animal in pain, would I refuse to help him? Of course not. Very well. I would think of him as an animal, not a man at all.

"I will help you. Are you staying near here?"

"Thank you." He sounded relieved and I was pleased I had not turned him down. My pleasure turned to horror when he took my elbow in his hand and began to walk slowly forward. "Please, allow me to guide you. My lodgings are close." I gritted my teeth. He was an animal, I told myself. He knew no better. I stared straight ahead, relieved I could ignore the disgusted glances and murmured comments from everybody we passed. Not only was I walking with a foreign barbarian, he was actually touching me! "Here we are."

He pushed a shoji back and stood aside. I realized after a moment that he was expecting me to enter in front of him. What strange ways these barbarians had! No Japanese man would ever allow a woman to walk in front of him unless she was of far higher rank than him. But an anma?

Unthinkable. I shivered as I wondered what other shocks my patron might have in store for me.

"Can I offer you some sake? Or tea, perhaps?" At least he was polite. I would have loved some tea, but I declined. The sooner I was out of here the better.

"Could you lie down, please." I wondered if he had understood me as he stared around, apparently confused.

"On the floor, you mean?"

I almost laughed. The tatami was scrupulously clean. Why not? "Yes, on the floor. Lie in your stomach."

I approached him cautiously and sniffed carefully. He didn't smell too badly. I was deeply relieved. Everybody said the gaijin stank of butter and milk and undercooked red meat and that the smell came from their insides through their pores and no amount of washing could cure it. I relaxed slightly and felt the back of his neck.

His skin texture was different from a Japanese person. His hair was bristly and seemed to grow very far down into his neck. I fingered his skin curiously, finding it rather coarse. Perhaps I hadn't been so very far wrong when I thought of him as an animal. He grunted, and I wondered if I had hurt him.

"Your nerves are very tight," I explained. "I will soothe them for you, but it will hurt."

"Go right ahead. It will be worth it."

I worked on his neck until I was satisfied. I ran my fingers down his spine, pausing to prod occasionally. He shifted beneath me, and I apologized.

"Oh, you're not hurting me. Not at all." His voice sounded odd.

"Please take off your robe. I need to massage your back."

"With pleasure." What a strange thing to say! I averted my head politely as he shrugged the robe off. Of course, I was supposed to be blind, but it was the courteous thing to do.

His back was hairy. I hesitated to touch it, in case it felt as unpleasant as it looked. Like a pig's back, I thought. I shrugged. I was here to relieve pain. I had come so far, I would not flinch away now. I put my palms on each side of his spine, and leaned forward, pressing hard. Gradually, I worked my way down his back. The hair was far softer than I had expected, and his back was very muscular. I admitted to myself reluctantly that he obviously took far greater care of his body than Lord Akafumu. After a while, I almost forgot he was a gaijin as I concentrated on doing my work.

"You have an excellent technique." His voice was rather husky, and it took me a while to interpret his words. "This is far more interesting than just taking one of Doctor Serturner's pills."

I paused, wondering if I had heard him correctly.

"There is a pill in your country that works like an anma?" I asked incredulously.

He laughed and wriggled beneath my hands. "No. Not quite. But we do have pills that take away pain completely."

I was astonished. I had spoken truly when I told Akafumu that potent opium helped to relieve pain, but not for long. Some herbs could also help soothe pain, as could lettuce sap. But as far as I was aware, there was nothing that could take pain away completely. Even the most skilled anma could not do that.

"Is it magic?" I asked.

He shook his head. "No, no. Not at all. I don't know a great deal about medicine, but I believe this pill is a form of what you know as opium."

I carried on massaging his back, trying to hide my shock. A pill made of opium that could cure pain completely? But opium had been used in Japan for hundreds of years! Surely, if this were possible, someone would have discovered this miracle?

"And this pill works for all pain?" I probed.

"Oh, yes. It's called morphine, and it's very clever." I mouthed the strange word silently, trying to remember it. "But you have to be careful with it. I've only taken it a couple of times, when my pain was unbearable. A friend of mine started to take the pills to ease the pain when he broke his leg. They worked very well. He said that not only did they take the pain away, but they made him feel very relaxed, as though all his problems in life had gone."

This sounded like a very special gift from the gods. I couldn't believe it. Why would the gods give such a precious secret to the gaijin and not to us? This could not be so!

"Then these pills are far wiser than I am. I can only help reduce pain, not cure it entirely." I hid my cynicism behind polite words.

"Ah, but you do that very well, anma." I smiled, pleased. "And unlike morphine, you are not addictive."

I carried on massaging as a worm of excitement began to coil in my stomach. "Men come to depend on this pill?" I asked.

"Oh, yes. After a short time, my friend found he had to take more and more of the drug. Not just to ease his pain, but because without it he felt ill in a different way. He began to have headaches and to be deeply depressed. His food made him vomit and he became a changed man. The more morphine he took, the more he found he needed. The last time I saw him, I found it hard to recognize him. He had lost much weight, and it seemed as if he could not understand anything I said. He had lost his job, he told me, because he could not concentrate on anything. I told him he had to stop taking morphine, and he said he could not. He told me he would die without it. I think it would kill him if he carried on taking it."

I said nothing, simply rubbing his back as if he had said nothing of any interest.

"Ah, that's better. Thank you."

I took his polite words to mean he'd had enough of my hands on his body and I sat back on my heels. I was so distracted by thoughts of the morphine—I repeated it again to myself, to make sure I had it right—that the sight of my gaijin when he turned over made my vision swim.

If it had not been for the training of mind, as well as body, that I had undertaken to become onna-bugeisha, I would have gasped out loud and probably scrambled away from him.

Everybody had heard the tales about gaijin. Some said they were truly foreign devils. The parts that were visible—their heads, hands, and feet—were strange enough. The ones that had hairy faces were generally thought to be very high-ranking devils, those that were arrogant enough not to bother to disguise themselves greatly. Even the clean-shaven ones were ugly beyond belief, with their pallid skin and prominent noses. But rumors abounded about what the gaijin were like beneath their clothes. Some people insisted they had tails. It was widely known their bodies were covered in hair like a bear; now that, I could vouch for. Some said they had no toes, that their feet were cleft like a pig's. As they never wore sandals, one could not tell. My gaijin did have toes, but they were long, knobby things and —yes!—they were also covered in hair. I had been almost disappointed to find he did not have a tail.

Or at least, not until he turned and faced me.

I stared at his navel. I kept my face expressionless,

grateful that I was supposed to be blind. Even so, if my mind had not been so disciplined, I would have gasped out loud in shock.

His tree was huge. Was this the tail of legend? I rather thought it was. The thing reared up and up. I kept my eyes fixed on the gaijin's stomach.

"I am finished. If you are happy with my services, then I will go now."

"Oh. Are you sure I cannot persuade you to take some sake with me? You are a remarkably beautiful woman. I would be very glad of your company a while longer, anma."

The gaijin's voice was very throaty. I realized with rising astonishment that it was not just my massage that had aroused him. He really did find me attractive. On reflection, I was not surprised. Of course the gaijin found me attractive. He was ugly himself. No doubt it was like calling to like. Then I thought of my own dear Yo, who also obviously found me deeply lovely, and I was ashamed.

"I must go, sir." I rose to my feet. He stood with me, pulling his robe around him.

"That is a pity." He fumbled in his purse and took out two coins. Before I could hold out my hand to accept them, he reached out and opened my fingers and pressed the coins into my palm, closing my fingers around them with an oddly tender gesture. How odd these gaijin were! So polite in some ways, yet so grossly discourteous when it came to keeping their distance. "Thank you for your help. My back feels wonderful. Should I have need of your services again, anma, where can I find you?"

"I am often about the Floating World, sir." I tucked the coins into my obi. He had given me far too much, so much it was almost insulting. Had he no idea of the value of money? I shrugged to myself. As the saying has it, 'Wealthy people have many worries.' Perhaps I was doing him a favor by relieving him of some of his wealth!

"I see." He sounded disappointed. "And if I were to ask for you? What name should I use?"

"Kamakiri, sir."

He thought about it, and I could see he was searching for a translation. Finally, understanding came to his eyes. He smiled widely.

"Mantis. An ugly name for a beautiful woman, anma." He raised his eyebrows in obvious amusement. "Or perhaps it isn't. Like your namesake, are you so lovely that your mate will face certain death to make love to you? Well, Kamakiri, my name is Adam. I hope you will remember it."

I pretended not to understand him and bowed my way out. I was absurdly flattered by his words.

"Even an onna-bugeisha likes to be told she's lovely," I explained to Matsuo on the way home. He made no response. But to a dog, his owner is always perfect.

ELEVEN

Enjoy your honey.
It cost a bee the whole of
Its life to make it

*I*t was clear that Yo didn't understand my excitement. If anything, he was angry as I told him about my chance encounter with the gaijin.

"You should have walked away from him. Refused to touch him. The gods only know what sort of diseases they carry with them. They're even worse than burakumin."

"He was clean enough." I was angry with Yo in my turn. We were equals. He had no right to try and tell me what to do. And if it came to that, if a burakumin—an untouchable—had come to me for help, I would not have refused them. I had a sudden insight that shocked me. Before Reiki had taught me the art of healing, I had known I was responsible for my family, which to my mind included all those who worked for us. Now, it appeared my circle of commitment had widened to anybody I could heal. "He didn't even smell." Not too much, anyway. "But that doesn't matter.

You're not listening to me. The point is that if what he says is true about these morphine"—such a difficult word for my tongue!—"pills is true, then it's the answer."

Yo was sulking. His lips were set in a straight line. He shrugged.

"And how are you going to get them? You said yourself your gaijin only used your services as an anma because he didn't have any of his magic pills." I didn't like the way Yo said "my" gaijin, at all. Nor the sneer in his voice when he said "used." "And if you do get some, how are you going to persuade Akafumu to take them?"

"I don't think it would be a problem to get Akafumu to swallow them." I kept my temper. I would not allow myself to be goaded. "The wretched man's a coward when it comes to pain. And I can inflict such pain on him that no amount of opium will cure it. He'll be delighted to take anything to stop it. And as to where I'm going to get them from? I hoped you would be able to find some for me."

"You're looking forward to hurting Akafumu," Yo said flatly. I tensed; how dare he say that to me?

"I think you forget the injustice he has inflicted on me, Yo," I said stiffly. "I am the only one left to bear my family name. He should have acknowledged that. Instead, he wants to marry me off to an old man so that eventually he can get his hands on what is rightfully mine. I am being merciful in allowing him to live."

We glared at each other. Matsuo sat between us, turning his anxious gaze from one to the other.

"Be careful, that's all I'm saying. Don't let your need for vengeance make you careless." I understood he was worried about me, but at the same time, I was determined that I was not going to give into him. I was right; he was not.

"I will. But if you can't—or won't—get me these magic

pills, then I will have to get them myself. And the only way I can do that is to seek out the gaijin again."

"You must do as you think fit," he said coldly. "I'm going out."

I stared at his retreating back incredulously. He had just come in!

By the time Yo came back, I had veered from fury to worry. I had convinced myself that something terrible had happened to him and was relieved when he finally slid the shoji open and kicked his sandals off. I hid my pleasure and offered him tea very politely.

"Sake, please." I was immediately positive he didn't want sake; he was just being difficult in refusing the tea. And then I was angry with myself for offering to get him tea. Was I no more than a traditional wife—no, not even a wife—a concubine, who would leap to her man's needs without even being asked? That I was not.

"I'll take some with you," I snapped. Yo blinked with surprise. I rarely drank alcohol. I knew I did not handle drink very well, and I preferred to do without it altogether rather than have it betray me.

"Thank you." He accepted the brimming cup I handed to him. We both sipped in silence. I decided I would bite my tongue off rather than ask him where he had been.

"I was in error." I paused with my cup a hand's breadth away from my lips. He was apologizing to me? "I'm sorry, Keiko-chan. I was so angry at the thought of you being alone with that gaijin, and of you being made to touch his body. It made me feel ill."

I smiled and held my hand out, palm up, in a gesture that said he had no need to worry. All was forgiven. I sipped my sake to hide my true thoughts. I was delighted he had apologized. But I still found it deeply hurtful that he made it sound as if I had humiliated myself by taking the gaijin's hurt away. As if by touching him, I had infected myself with his strangeness. Reiki had always insisted that an anma should be prepared to treat any living thing, human or animal. I knew instinctively that she would have considered the gaijin as merely a fellow being that was hurting and in need of her services. Surely I should do no less?

Yo was looking at me with a worried expression, and I buried my doubts. Shinobi or not, he was still a man, and it must have taken considerable effort for him to apologize to a mere woman. Even one he insisted he truly considered to be his equal.

"If I can obtain some of the magic pills, do you not think my plan is a good one? Even better than getting Akafumu addicted to opium? After all, you said yourself it could take months, even more. I don't know if I can wait that long," I said frankly. "But Adam said it took only a very short time to become addicted to the magic pills. And if I don't supply them to Akafumu, he can't get them anywhere else. He'll be lost. And quickly."

I knew I had made an error in using the gaijin's name. Yo's face was stone, but I could see the bitter fury in his eyes. I winced at my own tactlessness as I suddenly understood the real cause of his anger.

Yo was jealous.

I patted Matsuo to hide my surprise. I wondered with some amusement how Yo would have reacted if I had told him how Adam's gigantic tree had found me so very alluring. I pushed the thought away before it could make me smile.

"I cannot get your magic pills," Yo snapped. "That's what I've been doing. I asked everybody I thought might know about them.

"A certain apothecary who has helped me in the past had heard of the gaijin's pills. He said he had been so interested, he had tried to make them himself, but nothing he tried worked any better than simple opium. He's convinced it's some sort of gaijin enchantment. He strongly advised me against trying to find them. As he pointed out, they may work for gaijin, but that didn't mean they would do us any good at all. In fact, they could be poisonous to us. Forget it, Keiko. If you kill Akafumu with gaijin poison, you would be dead as soon as he was."

"You may well be right," I said judiciously. Yo looked pleased. He stretched and yawned, very obviously.

"It's not worth the risk," he agreed. "We'll think of something else. Or it might be worthwhile simply getting him the sort of opium that even his chamberlain can't buy and persuading him to smoke that to relieve his pain. I've heard rumors that Akira, Hana's yakuza, has very special opium grown just for his own use. He's a very strong man, both mentally and physically, so it has little effect on him. For somebody who isn't used to it, it could be very different. It may well be that Akafumu becomes addicted to it very quickly."

Yo sat back, obviously pleased with his own idea. I nodded absently, still thinking about Adam and his magic pills.

"What?"

Yo had said something I had missed.

"I said, I'm tired. Absolutely worn out, tramping the streets all afternoon for you. I think I'll lie down for a while."

I was lost in my thoughts, and it took me a while to recognize the broad hint that Yo was dropping. He paused in the doorway, looking at me from lowered eyes and pretending to fuss Matsuo. I smiled to myself as I got to my feet and followed him into the second room. I *was* pleased to see him back. Even more pleased that he had worked so hard on my behalf. Surely it would be appropriate to reward him for his efforts!

Whilst the temple's house was tiny compared to my family home, it was a mansion compared to Reiki's miserable hut. She had a single cold and drafty room for all her needs. We had the luxury of a second room for a sleeping apartment, so I could leave our futons made up. Yo shut the door firmly on Matsuo's disappointed face and slid elegantly to the floor. His body was sinew and muscles worn as smooth as river pebbles by constant exercise.

He patted the futon beside him. I was amused and wanted to tease. I stood with my hands on my hips and leaned forward slightly. When Yo grabbed for me, I evaded him easily.

"You're going to have to do better than that, shinobi!" I mocked. "Are you so out of training that a mere woman can evade you so easily?"

He frowned, and I wasn't at all sure if he was pretending to be angry.

"If I am out of training, whose fault is that?" he demanded. "I can hardly keep myself in peak condition if I am spending all my time caring for you."

That did it. I threw myself at him. Yo rolled aside, but the futons took up most of the floor and he had nowhere to go. I caught his legs between my feet, and rolled over, trapping him beneath my body. I was deeply disappointed when he didn't even try to wriggle away.

"I can care for myself, shinobi," I mocked. "See how easily I caught you?"

But Yo was not as beaten as I had thought. In a heartbeat, his arms were around my waist and he was rolling me over so that our roles were reversed. He was straddling me so hard the breath was thrust out of my lungs.

"Really?" He wasn't even short of breath. I stayed as still as a trapped animal, pretending that he had winded me. As a finishing touch, I leaned my head against his ribs and sobbed for breath. "Give in? I'll let you go if you promise to behave."

"I promise!" I panted.

The second he relaxed his grip, I shot myself sideways. Yo grabbed for me, but clumsily. I realized at once that he was deeply aroused by our mock battle and that his own lust was distracting him. I was amused. If a shinobi, a man trained in all the arts of deception, could be so easily diverted, how much easier would it be to take advantage of an ordinary man? The idea that a woman could have crafts that could undo a man with almost no effort made me want to laugh out loud with pleasure.

"Not so fast, woman!" Yo had a few tricks left it seemed. He glanced at the door as if he heard something I had not. I was not fooled and refused to be distracted. Then his eyes widened in shock and I couldn't resist a glance over my shoulder. A mistake; Yo slid under my guard as sinuously as a fish and his hand grabbed my hair, forcing my head back. It hurt, and I retaliated by biting his wrist. Not too hard, but hard enough to make him grunt.

We were deadlocked. A slow grin stretched his lips, and I smiled with him.

"Enough." I bent my head. "We could carry on all day and end up no further forward."

"You give in?" Yo demanded.

"Certainly not. It was a fair fight, and neither of us won or lost," I said firmly.

He let go of my hair. I kissed the sore spot on his wrist. I found I was breathing far heavier than I had been during our activity. I leaned forward and kissed Yo hard on his lips. It was apparent that my lover was as deeply aroused as I was. He pushed my robe aside and grabbed my breast, rolling the nipple between his fingers. It was acutely, deliciously painful and I rubbed against him, forcing his hand to grasp me even more tightly.

I licked Yo's mouth, savoring the salt of his sweat lingering on his upper lip. At that moment, it seemed to me to be more delicious than any banquet I had ever tasted. Yo bit my tongue. I snapped at his lip.

He twisted and threw me on my back. I didn't even consider fighting back. The time for resistance was gone. I threw my legs so wide I felt my tendons protest at the sudden movement and grabbed Yo's shoulders, demanding that he enter me. He paused for a mischievous second, and I knew he was teasing. I was having none of it. I arched my back so that the hood of his tree flirted with the entrance to my sex. Yo could stand no more. With a gasp of pleasure, he slid inside me.

I moved with him, our rhythm as certain as if we had been lovers forever. For a fanciful moment, I wondered if we had known each other like this in a past life. If—should the gods smile on us—we would be together again in the next life. Then Yo bit my neck, hard, and I screamed with pleasure. I kept him tied in my grip as I slid forward to take him. I moved with slow, even strokes, feeling all sensation except for my own urgent need recede. I was greedy and craved a little more; with a jerk of my hips, I felt Yo's black moss rub against the splayed-wide lips of my sex. The friction was delicious, and a moment later I felt my yonaki blossom and my toes curled beneath my feet as I threw my head back and moaned with pleasure. I released my grip on Yo's tree and a moment later the waves of my yonaki were intensified as I felt his heat spill into me.

A long time later, Yo raised himself on his elbow and looked at me seriously.

"Give in?" he asked. I started to chuckle, and then Yo was laughing with me and I was pleased. We were one again.

TWELVE

A leaf takes a year
To fall to the ground if I
Am apart from you

"You should have more than enough cash. The house is ours for as long as we want it. If you need me urgently, then go to Jokan-Ji Temple and ask to speak to the kannushi. He will be able to get a message to me. Will you be all right?"

I nodded as patiently as I could. Yo was fussing around me like an old hen with her brood of chicks. He had received word that his services were needed, and he had to accept the commission.

"I'll be in Kyoto to begin, and then Kobe. I guess the journey will take perhaps seven days, more if the weather is bad. I don't know how long I'm going to be needed there. It could be only a few weeks, but depending on how things go, it could be a few months or even more."

"Really?" I asked questioningly. "Will you be in danger?

Should I pray for your safe return?" Yo shrugged and stared at his feet. I was intrigued. I put my head close to him and breathed softly on his cheek. "Tell me, or I shall not let you go at all."

"And you think you could stop me?"

"I could do my best to try." I smiled and Yo laughed finally.

"Stop making it worse, Keiko. You know I don't want to leave you. I wouldn't go if I thought there was any danger here for you. But I don't believe there is, and there should be no danger at all for me. I'm going to help a very wealthy merchant in Kobe. A man who claims to be a high-ranking civil servant from Kyoto has asked to marry his daughter. The merchant is pleased, of course, but he's a very shrewd man and he is suspicious. This man is unknown to him. He's very fond of his beautiful only daughter, and he wants to be sure that the marriage would be a good one. He wants to be absolutely certain her suitor isn't just a fortune hunter."

I was deeply impressed. A man who was so fond of his daughter that he would hire a shinobi to find out about her suitor? I thought sourly of the match my own father—and Lord Akafumu—had proposed for me and hoped the girl realized how lucky she was.

"Can't he ask about this man himself? If he really is a high-ranking civil servant, people will know about him, surely?" I asked.

"He claims to come from Kyoto. Kyoto society is not Kobe society." Yo pointed out. "And my patron's nothing but a merchant. No matter how wealthy he is, he's still a riverbed beggar in the eyes of the aristocracy. He can hardly simply go to Kyoto and barge into society and start asking questions."

"And you can?" I asked.

"I can. I will become a very minor noble from Edo. As a man of good family, I can mingle with society with no suspicions. But even then, it will take time. I must establish myself in Kyoto society. Make myself known to the right people. Only then can I begin to find out if the suitor is who he says he is."

"Sounds as if you'll be safe enough," I teased. "Hardly any need for you to unsheathe your sword, I would have thought."

Yo smiled reluctantly in response to my words. "I'm sure I'm not going to be in any danger this time. But what about you?"

I shrugged off his concerns. I would continue to visit Lord Akafumu in my role as an anma, I said. I would cause him pain, as much as I could. I shook my head at Yo's disapproving face. Afterward, I would persuade him to take a pipe of a particularly strong opium Yo had obtained for me.

"If the gods smile on us, you might find I have avenged myself to my satisfaction by the time you get back," I said innocently. I made a great effort not to think of Adam's magic pills; Yo knew far too well how my mind worked.

He stared at me for a long time and then shook his head.

"You are truly a brave woman, Keiko-chan." I was pleased, but his next words took my smile away. "But because of that, you make yourself vulnerable. Take care, I beg you."

"Go away," I said cheerfully. "Do your best for your rich patron. Come back laden with cash, and then we'll talk again."

I shooed him out of the door and closed it behind him. He would not expect me to watch him walk away, and I would not do it. It was only when I could no longer hear his footsteps in the quiet street that I realized he had told me to contact the *kannushi* of the temple if I needed to get in touch with him. Why hadn't he simply told me how I could contact him? Didn't he trust me? I was annoyed, and it took me a long time to realize that Yo was trying to protect both of us. If I genuinely did not know where to find him, then if there were problems I could not betray where he was.

I might be onna-bugeisha, but truly I had much to learn about the art of deception.

The house felt oddly empty without him. Matsuo came and put his head on my knee. I patted him absently and let my thoughts wander. Yo had gone. The moment I had been waiting for had arrived. I had no idea how much time I had to myself. There was so very much I had to do, and Yo would approve of none of it.

"Just as well he's not here, isn't it?" I said to Matsuo. He raised his paw to me as if he wanted me to take it, and I grasped it with a smile. Matsuo whined and I relaxed my grip. When I probed, I found he had a long thorn embedded in his pad. I pulled it out quickly, but the area looked sore and inflamed.

"Oh, poor Matsuo!" I comforted him. I bathed his paw carefully with water infused with herbs and told him firmly not to lick it. That was a nuisance. I had expected him to accompany me today, but it was now clear that he should stay in the house. I put one of my old tabi socks around his paw and tied it off.

"Don't lick!" I said again. I picked up Yo's staff, which he had left at the side of the shoji. Matsuo whimpered when I left him behind. I felt sorry for my poor dog, and also quite irritated on my own behalf. Kamakiri the anma had become so used to having him at her side, I felt naked without him. Well, it was no good. A broken mirror cannot be made to shine; I had my staff to pat my way with, and that would have to do.

I was relying on chance today. I hoped Adam would be in his house. If not, I would simply have to wander casually up and down the streets near his home until I found him. If not today, then tomorrow. Or the next day. I could be as patient as necessary. Once I found him, I would obtain his morphine pills. How, exactly, would depend on how events played out once I was in his house. Whatever happened, I had no intention of leaving without them.

The staff still felt slightly clumsy in my grip. It had been made to balance for Yo, and he was of a different build than me. I concentrated on the sounds it made, listening to the soft echoes and calculating how they bounced back from my surroundings. This, I thought, was how Reiki had found her way about so confidently. I wondered if she was happy with her son, and I hid a smile as I guessed her daughter-in-law was far less happy.

"Ah, anma. I have the most dreadful pain. Do you think you could help me?"

A young man's voice. Mocking and sly. I stopped instantly, angry that I had let my thoughts wander to the extent that he had been able to approach quite closely without me noticing. There was another man behind me; I could hear him trying not to laugh.

"I will do my best to help you. What is your pain?"

"Ooh. I really don't think I could describe it to you, anma. Here, feel."

I really had put too many drops in my eyes. My vision was so blurred the man's outline wavered. He snatched my hand and pushed it against his tree. He was already half-erect, no doubt with amusement at the thought of teasing a helpless blind woman.

"It feels perfectly healthy to me," I said crisply. "Let me pass, please. I have a patron waiting for me and I don't have time to waste with you." I was pleased with the fluency of my lie.

"Now there's a nice way to treat a man in pain." He was laughing openly now. His friend touched me on the shoulder. I had felt him move, but I pretended to jump as if I was startled.

"Please, young sirs," I whined. "Let me pass by."

"Treated some patrons already today, anma?" The man who had been behind me had moved to stand at the side of his friend. "Got some cash hidden in your obi, have you?"

"I have nothing," I said firmly. "No money at all. Let me pass. I've nothing to interest you."

"You think so? Well. It's a shame you've no money. But you're very young for an anma. And they do say that you blind women know your way around a man's body better than those who can see. I think we might get our money's worth out of you anyway."

I guessed he was nodding to his companion. There was a narrow alley to my left; I could feel the empty space. They had chosen a secluded spot; I could hear nobody nearby. Although I was angry to think I had to waste my time on these two, they surely needed to be taught a lesson, and I would be pleased to provide it.

The first man lunged at me. I hit him sharply on the knee with the padded end of my staff. Out of all the joints in the human body, the knee has the most nerves. A blow that would cause no more than annoyance elsewhere is intensely painful if the right part of the knee is struck—as my tormentor found out. A second later, he was crouched over, howling and rubbing his knee fiercely.

"Get the bitch, Teo. Hang on to her for me."

Teo was as noisy as he was inept. I heard the rustle of his kimono and the slap of his *zori* on the hard-packed earth of the street and was ready for him. The metal-tipped end of my staff hit him square in the ribs. He went down with a grunt and didn't rise again. I turned to face the first man, who had stopped rubbing his knee and was squaring up to me, his fists jabbing the air in front of him.

"Got lucky there, didn't you? Well, it's not going to happen twice. We would have been nice to you. But not now. Get up, Teo." He prodded the gasping Teo with his foot. While he was distracted, I ducked under his flailing fists and thrust my staff into the hollow beneath his chin. Unlike Teo, he went down silently, his eyes rolling back in his head.

"Ready for a bit more, Teo-san?" I asked sweetly. I held my staff across my breasts, both hands holding it firmly. "As your friend said, this poor, blind anma was just lucky the first time. How could I possibly hurt a big, strong young man like you?"

I didn't need to look to see him scrabble to his hands and knees and run down the street, bent double as he wheezed for breath. I gave the first man a brisk kick in his ribs, just in case he was pretending to be unconscious, but I needn't have bothered. He didn't even flinch. I rolled him into the alley with my foot and walked away jauntily, wishing they had put up more of a fight.

The blood was still singing in my veins as I joined the main street. Men jostled past me carelessly, and I found it quite difficult to resist the temptation to trip them—accidentally, of course—with my staff. If it hadn't been for the need to make myself as inconspicuous as possible, I would have left a few bruises to mark my passage.

"Anma?" I realized I was still wound up from my fight when I whirled around, my staff up and ready to strike. "Kamakiri, it's me, Adam. Has something frightened you? Are you all right?"

I almost laughed in his face. I was still alight with my victory; Yo would have recognized the emotion immediately. I reminded myself that this was a gaijin. His insights would surely be as different as his appearance.

I lowered the staff quickly. "Adam-san. I am so glad it's you. Two men tried to rob me. I was lucky I escaped from them."

"Where? Close to here? Would you recognize them again?" I heard him take a sharp intake of breath. "Forgive me. That was very tactless of me. Of course you wouldn't be able to recognize them. Never mind, you're safe now with me."

He paused, and I put my head on one side as I tried to identify the surge of emotions that were flowing from him. Genuine embarrassment for his supposed mistake. But beneath it, I caught real concern. For me? I was amazed. This gaijin barely knew me. Why should he care about me?

"Thank you, Adam-san." I bowed my head. "How is your back? Good, I hope?"

"Do come to one side." Adam took my arm and coaxed me out of the crowd. I did my best not to flinch and pull away. "I'm afraid it's not good at all. In fact, I'd hoped to find you. I've kept an eye open for you for days." I wondered absently if his words had become tangled in the translation. Why would he keep only one eye open for me? What was wrong with both eyes? His next words drove all desire to smile away. "I think I must have injured my spine when I took a fall not long after I met you. It's been so painful, I had to risk asking our doctor to let me have some morphine pills. As I told you, I hate taking them, but it was the only way I could get a little sleep."

"Well, I'm here now. Perhaps I could help you?" I smiled, and my smile widened as Adam looked flustered and then pleased. Even with my smeared vision, his pleasure was palpable. "Would you like me to massage your back for you?"

As I waited for him to answer, I wondered how it was possible for one of the gaijin doctors to be so skilled they could make a pill that vanquished pain and yet at the same time be so foolish they didn't understand that Adam's pain had nothing at all to do with his back. I had not long to wait. He spoke eagerly.

"If you have time, I would be very grateful. My own doctor is very skilled, of course, but he certainly doesn't have your magic touch."

My touch was magic? What nonsense! It had nothing to do with magic and everything to do with understanding how the body worked. I smiled graciously, acknowledging his words.

"Has something happened to your dog?" I was absurdly pleased. How unexpected that he should notice Matsuo's absence. "Does he truly guide you? How does he know where you want to go? I find that amazing."

There it was again, the strange gulf between wisdom and ignorance of the obvious. Isamu had told me that arquebuses—the gun that had killed both him and our father—were made from some process so advanced it was unknown to us Japanese, the secret of their manufacture known only to the gaijin. Yet every Japanese person simply accepted that the bond between a dog and its owner meant that the animal was easily capable of guiding their master—or mistress—away from any danger. Yet that common knowledge appeared miraculous to Adam.

It was all very strange.

"Matsuo's paw is sore. He picked up a thorn in it, so I thought it best to leave him inside," I explained. "I manage well enough with my staff."

"So you do." Perhaps Adam remembered his manners; he let go of my arm as abruptly as if it was red hot. "I think you're incredible. If I didn't know you were blind, I would never believe it."

I cleared my throat, wondering if my act was perhaps too good. Fortunately, we arrived at Adam's house at that moment. Once more he stood back to let me pass through. I heard a man in the street laugh, an ugly sound, and I was glad when the shoji slid closed behind us. I was sure that, in his own way, Adam was a good man. Gaijin were disliked enough anyway; I had no wish to bring any more disgust down on him.

"Please, do sit down. Can I get you some tea?" Such politeness to a blind anma! I was enchanted and spoke warmly.

"Thank you, but no."

"You're smiling, Kamakiri-san. I know my Japanese is not good. Have I said something amusing by mistake?"

He sounded so worried, I hurried to explain.

"Not at all. Your Japanese is excellent. I was smiling at *you* offering to get tea for *me*. In Japan, it is always the woman who serves the man. Have you visited a teahouse?"

"Oh, yes. A number of them. I've been entertained by many very beautiful and talented geisha. Why do you ask?"

I was surprised to find I was annoyed. Adam found the highly painted and highly paid geisha beautiful? I shrugged casually.

"Then you must have noticed that it is accounted a great virtue here for a woman to understand that she is less worthy than her patron. A Japanese man would never offer to serve a woman with tea. Or anything else for that matter. The man must always come first."

"I noticed that. In my country, it is considered polite for a gentleman to always ensure a lady's comfort before his own."

"Then the women in your country are truly fortunate, Adam-san," I said politely. "Would you like to make yourself comfortable on the tatami? Then I can ease your pain for you."

"Thank you." He sounded grateful, and I wondered again if the gaijin women understood how truly blessed they were. And yet...would I be happy if Yo subjugated himself to my wishes? If he asked me my advice before he did anything? If he agreed with me all the time rather than arguing with me? I knew I would not. Surely, it was far better for both of us to have a voice and to wrangle an answer out between us.

"I'm ready, Kamakiri."

Adam had taken off his robe and was lying face down on the tatami. I knelt beside him, looking carefully before I touched. That had been the first lesson I had learned from Reiki. *Don't assume you know what the problem is just from what your patron has told you. Always remember most men are not only fools, but babes when it comes to pain. They may be convinced the pain and numbness they feel in their hands at night is caused by too much tight gripping on a pen or a sword. It is your place to know that the pain comes from the nerves in their neck and is nothing to do with their fingers.* So now I inspected Adam's neck and back carefully, in case anything had happened to him since I had last seen him.

He had a large bruise halfway down his back, no doubt from where he had fallen. I was about to run my finger over it when I paused. He was a young, fit man. What had caused him to lose his balance?

"Adam-san, you told me you fell in the street. What caused you to fall? Did you trip over something? Did you slip?"

"No, nothing like that." His voice was muffled by the tatami. "It was very odd. I was just walking along and suddenly I felt as if my body no longer belonged to me. The next thing I knew, I had fallen and was lying in the street."

Ah! Reiki had been right yet again. I was certain the problem was caused by his neck.

"And what did your doctor say to you?" I was cautious. Surely, the gaijin doctor would know far more than a simple anma.

"He said it was just a dizzy spell." I didn't understand what Adam meant. He must have picked up on my uncertainty as he went on to explain. "Just a passing thing. He thought it might have been caused by a cold in my head, or possibly too much sake the night before. Although I did explain to him that I had drunk very little."

"I see." The doctor was half wise, half fool, then. "Did he examine you?"

"No. He said there was no need. Told me I was fit and not to worry about it."

I began to wonder if Adam's doctor had any wisdom at all. But of course, he was in Japan and not his own country. Surely, even the most skilled acupuncture master would find himself at a loss if he tried to cure a gaijin's ills; truly, the saying "ten men, ten colors" was very true.

"I'm sure he was right," I agreed soothingly. I probed carefully at the point where his spine became his neck. Adam grunted with pain. I took no notice and prodded harder. Adam tensed, and I changed the gesture into a gentle stroking motion until he relaxed.

The room was not warm, but by the time I was certain I had unknotted the nerves in his neck, I was sweating from the exertion. I sat back and flexed my fingers.

"That's better," I said. It was a statement, not a question. Adam stretched, his body quivering.

"The pain's gone completely. How can I ever thank you, Kamakiri?"

I was about to tell him simply to pay me my fee when he rolled over. Just as before, his tree of flesh stood out rigid from his body. Perhaps my victory over the thugs who had tried to rob me, together with the knowledge that I had more skill than his gaijin doctor, made me overconfident. Whatever it was, this time I did not avert my—supposedly unseeing—eyes from his rearing tree. Instead, I looked at it with interest, wondering with all the curiosity of a true anma how he managed to support the organ without fainting from lack of blood to the rest of his body. My heartbeat surged as I recognized that my chance had arrived. I spoke quickly.

"Is there anything else I can do for you, Adam?" I asked casually.

"I'm sure there is, Kamakiri." He paused, and I guessed he was trying to find a polite way of asking for what he obviously wanted. "I don't mean any offense, but I have heard that anma are very skilled in areas other than healing."

"Is that so? Are you sure you're not confusing me with a

geisha, Adam?" I was still stinging from his compliment to the geisha who had been paid—and no doubt very well indeed—to make this gaijin feel like a god.

"I could never do that. None of the geisha I've seen were as beautiful as you are, Kamakiri. None of them could ever be as caring as you. And even though they did not have the burden of blindness, none of them moved with the grace that you possess." He spoke in a gush of words; I felt great pleasure as I realized he meant it.

I smiled and shook my head modestly. "You are very kind, Adam-san." At least I could acknowledge his generous words. "But alas, I'm nothing but an anma, doing the best I can. Now, if there is nothing else you need, I shall go."

I had become impatient, both with Adam and myself. He could pay me, and I would be on my way.

"Well, there is something. But I hardly know how to ask…"

I waited, holding my breath. When Adam remained silent, I spoke myself.

"You are suffering somewhere else?" I asked.

"No. I mean yes." He sounded miserable. I sighed, barely able to hide my impatience. We would be all day at this rate.

"It is often the case that a very deep massage is stimulating," I said seriously. I ran my hand down his chest and pretended amazement when I found his tree of flesh. "Ah, I see. It may not be so in your country, Adam, but here in Japan, it is considered a very bad thing for a man whose tree is deeply aroused to go unsatisfied. It is believed that if a man is so aroused and does not find satisfaction, then his seed will go bad and cause his bodily organs to putrefy. Perhaps I may be able to help you avoid such a terrible fate?"

I didn't bother to wait for his answer, but instead began to massage his flesh gently. I was apprehensive about his lack of a hood. No doubt a gaijin woman would know what to do to stimulate him. I had no idea if what aroused Yo would interest him in the least.

Adam made a sound deep in his throat as if I was hurting him. I stopped at once, and he wrapped his own hand around mine, gripping it tightly. I was reassured and continued my gentle up and down movement. When he thrust out his belly toward me, I tightened my grip and began to move quickly, and then quicker still.

He burst his fruit unexpectedly, with a roar of pleasure that made me flinch with surprise. I slowed my rhythm, relieved that his eyes were closed so he couldn't see my astonishment. Finally, I took my hand away completely and Adam slumped back on to the tatami. He was breathing very deeply, and appeared to be on the verge of sleep.

It seemed to me then that gaijin men were not so very different from Japanese. Perhaps men the world over enjoyed kenjataimu—the short period of release from all tension that comes after orgasm. I hoped so.

I stood up silently and moved very quickly. I would have to assume I had only a few moments to find what I was looking for before Adam came to his senses. I guessed what I wanted would be kept somewhere secure. Adam must have a woman to clean for him and cook his meals. Naturally, she would be curious about anything that looked in the least odd and would probably want to look at, and even taste, anything unusual. Adam would want to conceal anything that might interest her. There was a chest against the wall. I lifted the top and glanced inside. Robes, folded carefully. Several obi. Some documents, covered in strange symbols. I was about to lower the lid when the light glinted on something in the corner. I snatched the small, glass bottle up and slid it in my obi. The contents rattled and I stiffened, afraid Adam might have heard. It might not be what I was looking for, but I had to take the chance.

By the time Adam sat up, I was kneeling on the tatami at his side, my eyes lowered and my expression suitably anxious.

THIRTEEN

> When my fingers form
> Words on paper, how do they
> Know what my mind wants?

Adam was deeply embarrassed. I felt his discomfort; it surprised me. Reiki had warned me that many of her customers believed that a "happy ending" must be included in the price of their massage. I had raised my eyebrows in surprise, and then felt absurdly guilty when she appeared to read my thoughts.

"It doesn't matter to them that more often than not I'm old enough to be their mother, or even their grandmother," she said crisply. "Anma have a reputation for being skilled in all the sensory arts. With some of them, you would have to cut their tree off at the root to dim their enthusiasm for a more intimate sort of massage."

"Do you oblige?" I asked.

She shrugged. "Depends on my mood. If I fancy the feel of them." That made my jaw drop! "I might give them a little extra. Otherwise, I make sure I get my money and then get well away before they can get their clothes on."

I was grateful for the warning, but I was surprised that Adam was ashamed of his perfectly natural reaction to my skilled hands. He fumbled in his purse and handed me a gold ichibuban coin. I pretended to weigh it in my palm before I protested.

"This is far too much, Adam-san." I held my hand out to him, inviting him to take the coin back. Instead, he wrapped my fingers over my palm, enclosing the coin.

"It is very little for the pleasure you have given, Kamakiri." He was actually blushing. How very odd these gaijin were! "May I make an appointment for you to come and see me again?"

"I'm sorry. I will be away from the Floating World for some time, and I don't know when I will be back." The lie came fluidly, and I was sorry. I was beginning to become quite fond of my polite gaijin; good enough reason in itself to keep away from him.

"I will look out for you."

I heard the disappointment in Adam's voice and bowed politely as I left.

Even though it was only mid-morning, the streets of the Floating World were seething with people. I marveled anew that this city within a city never seemed to sleep and was always restless, always searching for pleasure. I tapped my way forward, using my staff to feel my way. It was already comfortable in my hand.

My thoughts lingered with Adam. He had seemed genuinely unhappy that he could not make another appointment with me. Would he feel the same, I wondered, when he found his bottle was missing? Or would he perhaps blame the woman who cared for his house for stealing it? I guessed he would know it was me who had taken it, and I hoped he would think it was merely curiosity on my part.

My train of thought was broken abruptly. Someone was screaming. A high pitched, breathy wail. A young girl, by the sound of her voice. I paused, turning as I tried to locate the source. Men jostled past me as I stood. One of them cursed me for not moving. Another simply shoved me to one side. Two geisha tottered past on high geta. Neither of them spared me a glance. Not a single person appeared to even notice the screams.

The noise stopped abruptly. I was about to go on my way when the screams were replaced by sobs. I decided that the sound was coming from a house a little further down the street. I tap-tap-tapped my way down toward the noise. Another man barged into me so roughly that I guessed he had done it deliberately.

"Get out of my way, anma. Who do you think you are, taking up the whole street?"

"I am so sorry, master." I cringed, hunching my shoulders and bobbing my head. He grinned, clearly pleased with himself, and as I turned to move away, I jabbed my staff viciously against his shins. The man howled and hopped from foot to foot.

"You bitch!" he snarled. "You did that on purpose!"

"Master?" I stared over his shoulder. "Did what? I am so sorry. Did I catch you with my staff? Surely I could not have hurt you with a little tap!"

A crowd had gathered to watch the entertainment. One of the women called cheerfully at my assailant.

"Oh! Did the poor anma hurt the big, strong man?"

The crowd howled with laughter and the man I had hit was suddenly less brave.

"I realize you meant nothing by it, anma." He straightened up with visible effort. I had chosen to hit him precisely at the point in front of his shin that would cause the most pain. I bit my lip anxiously, tapping toward him with my staff as if I was searching for his legs. He hopped away from me quickly.

"If I have caused you pain, master, then I must heal it for you," I whined. I reached out as if to pat him and my wandering fingers jabbed him in the eye. The crowd erupted into more laughter.

"No, I'm fine. Forget it."

The man turned away and melted into the circle of people. They dispersed quickly, realizing the fun was over.

I had almost forgotten my quest, but I was reminded instantly when I heard the sobs again. They were much quieter now, and I had to listen carefully to distinguish them above the row of the street. A noodle seller shouting his wares close to me obscured the sound I was listening for and I frowned in annoyance. He glared at me and moved away in search of more likely customers.

There. I had it. Not this house, nor the next. I walked forward deliberately and then paused to listen. Men's voices, loud, and I guessed the worse for drink. But that was all I could hear. Still, I was sure that this was the right place.

I was torn with indecision. I needed to get away from here as quickly as possible. There was a chance that Adam would look into his chest for something and find I had taken his bottle. If he did that, he would surely come searching for me. But the voice I had heard from this house had been very young and deeply distressed. I was torn. The voice was silent. I decided quickly that it was probably only a child being smacked for some small thing by its mother and none of my business.

"Please, let me go." The child's voice. Her plea called to my heart and I turned immediately, knocking politely on the wooden lattice of the shoji with my staff. After a pause, a man's voice called out angrily.

"Who is it?"

"Sir, is this the house of Tanaka-san? He is expecting me."

"No. Go away."

"Oh, sir. I am so sorry to disturb you." I spoke humbly. "I was sure that this was where I was told to come. Tanaka-san sent for me especially to give him a massage. Do you know where he lives?"

I heard the mumble of voices behind the door and then a loud, lewd laugh. The shoji slid back far enough to show a young man's face.

"You're an anma, are you?" he asked.

"Yes, sir. Please, do you know where I can find Tanaka-san? He will be furious if I don't find him."

"Come in, anma." The shoji opened wide. I stared blindly at the man. He was grinning widely. "Tanaka-san isn't here, but perhaps one of my friends can direct you."

"Thank you," I said politely. The room stank of sake. Beneath that was a different odor, the raw smell of animals in rut. I paused, staring around apparently aimlessly, flickering my eyelids and allowing my gaze to wander without direction.

The girl was sitting in the corner. She was naked. Her thin arms were looped around her knees as if she was hugging herself. There was a red mark across one of her cheeks, I guessed where somebody had used their knuckles to strike her. Her eyes were wide and bright, as if she was holding back tears. I felt a surge of tenderness for this unknown child who had refused to cry.

"Anma, are you?" Four men crowded the small room. The eldest pushed his face close to mine as he spoke. I steeled myself not to flinch from his sake and pipe breath.

"Yes, sir," I said politely.

"Young for an anma, aren't you?" He was grinning at me. At the same time, he raised his fist and shook it in front of my face. When I didn't respond, he unwound his fingers far enough to make an obscene rubbing gesture. The other men laughed.

"I may be young, sir," I smiled, lowering my head. "But I am very good at my art. Nobody in the Floating World can give a better massage than me."

"Is that so?" The first man had joined his companion. They looked at each other and exchanged grins. "Well, I daresay we might enjoy a bit of pampering to get us in the mood before we get down to things with her." He nodded at the girl huddled in the corner. She stared straight back at him, her mouth tight.

"I thought I heard a child screaming," I said. "Does the poor thing have pain? Is it something I can help with?"

The girl sighed loudly and I moved toward the sound. Instantly the oldest man put his hand out, stopping me.

"Forget about her, anma. It's we who need your services."

"I'm so sorry, sir," I said. "I must find my way to Tanaka-san. He's expecting me and will be very angry if I'm late."

I turned. As I expected, the nearest man put his hand on my shoulder to stop me. I paused, feigning surprise.

"Oh, come on," the man coaxed. "I don't know how much Tanaka is going to pay you, but there are four of us. We can make it well worth your while to stay."

The two men who hadn't spoken looked at each other and then hunched over, shaking with amusement, their hands smothering laughter. I smiled sweetly, forcing my fury to be tame. For the moment. All the men were grinning widely, nodding at each other and laughing at the foolish, blind anma who had walked in just in time to enhance their fun. I had no doubt that they all thought themselves deeply iki; all men of the world that no woman could resist.

"Wonder what she looks like underneath that dirty, old robe, Choki," one of the men called loudly. I stiffened. *Choki.* What felt like a lifetime ago, one of my brother's friends had tried to rape me. He had been staying at our house as a guest of my brother. He had also been called Choki. I felt the shadow of karma fall upon me and I bared my teeth in what the men could take as a nervous smile if they were stupid enough.

"Nothing special, sir, I assure you." I cowered, miming fear.

"All women are special in their own way." Choki grinned. "Come on, let's have a look before we buy."

He grabbed for the knot on my obi. I let him concentrate firmly on it before putting my hand over his fingers quite gently. I didn't want to frighten him off. Not yet, at least.

"Would the gentlemen like a massage?" I asked.

Choki glanced at his companions and raised his eyebrows. "Part of me would," he said. He took his hand off my obi and grabbed for my hand, placing it firmly against his robe. His tree was erect, and I gasped in mock awe. Compared to Adam's stallion of a tree, it was nothing. I bit back the temptation to ask if this was the best he could do.

"Oh, sir," I gasped. "Surely you couldn't expect a poor anma to take a river monster like that?"

The atmosphere grew suddenly ugly. I heard the other men draw in their breath sharply. I risked a sideways glance at the child, mentally telling her to keep out of the way. She stared at me as if she knew I could see her, and for a moment, I was worried that the men might have noticed. I relaxed as I realized they were all so deep in lust that it would take an earthquake to distract them.

"Oh, but I do." Choki leered. "I'll go first, and then you can see to my friends here. And when we've finished with you, you can use your other skills to restore us to full potency so we can finish what we were about to start with *her*."

FOURTEEN

> Green grass makes no noise
> Even in the wind. Sere stalks
> Whisper on a breeze

I learned a valuable lesson at that moment. I knew the men were drunk. Because of that, I had assumed that they would be slow and clumsy and easy to deal with. I was wrong.

Choki kept me distracted. He was leering at me, so close I could feel his breath on my face. He pushed his hand into my robe, clutching for my breast. I took a step back so I could take a good swing at him with my staff—the padded end could deal a blow hard enough to leave any man reeling—and found that one of the other men had moved right behind me while I was fully occupied with Choki. I was angry with myself, but recovered my wits quickly.

The man behind me tried to wrap his arms around me. I sidestepped him easily, but the room was small and I had little space to maneuver. My staff dealt Choki a brisk blow to his ribs and he bent double, in so much pain he couldn't even speak. One of the other men laughed loudly.

"By all the gods, this one is spirited! Get her from your side, Hideki!"

I would not be deceived twice. I saw one of the other men dart forward, but I ignored him and concentrated on the man behind me. I kicked back hard, striking him on his knee. The blow must have hurt, as I saw his face contort with what I thought was pain. But to my surprise, it had little effect.

"Leave her to me!" he called, and Hideki stood still immediately. I raised my staff in warning, but the man I had hit took no notice. He lunged forward and I hit him on the side of the neck. I thought I must have misjudged the blow when it appeared to have no effect. He threw his head back and laughed.

"Delicious! If that's what an anma can do for a man, I must try another one. Come on, anma. Want to hit me again?"

I was astonished as he clutched at his robe and tugged it aside, baring his chest to me.

"No good showing her, Tadayo," Hideki called. "She can't see you. You'll have to tell her what you want!"

Even Choki had shaken off his pain and straightened up. He and the other two men watched me and Tadayo avidly. I was thrown off balance and confusion made me careless. I took the nearest target that was offered to me—Tadayo. Not bothering with my staff, I grabbed his kintama and twisted them. He should have been on the ground in a moment, wailing in agony and freeing me to concentrate on the others.

He was not. He gasped and bent over, snatching my

hand away from his *kintama*, but he was straight again in a flash.

"By all the gods, she has some fight in her!" he said. His eyes were shining and he licked a dribble of saliva from the side of his lips. "I do so like that in a woman. But can she take as good as she gives?"

All the men stood back a pace, forming a circle around me. I pretended to worry, clutching at my throat and panting. Tadayo snaked his hand out and grabbed my hair. He tugged at it so hard my scalp screamed. I kicked out and hit the large muscle in his thigh with no effect at all. I was about to try again when his fist connected with my jaw and I crumpled to the ground, my senses reeling. Quite casually, Tadayo kicked me in the belly. He was bare-footed, but the blow was still hard enough to knock the breath out of me. I choked back nausea and rolled onto my side, curling up as if he had hurt me very badly.

"Leave her alone!" The girl who had lured me here in the first place had left her corner and launched herself at Tadayo. She barely came to his waist, but even so, she was flailing at him with bunched fists and was trying to kick his legs. He seemed amused by her assault, holding her at arm's length.

The circle of men exploded with laughter as Tadayo tossed the child to one side. She immediately jumped straight back at him and he tucked her beneath his arm. I watched from beneath my now loose hair as he bent down and bit her naked buttocks hard enough to draw blood.

Enough. I had my breath back. I had come here to rescue this child, and now she was suffering on my behalf. The civilized part of my mind was embarrassed at the ludicrous turn-around. I quickly pushed the thought away. For the time being, I would exist on instinct.

And that instinct told me that now was the moment to act, while the men were distracted from me.

I focused on Tadayo. If he was happy to both accept and give pain, he was going to be more of a problem than the rest. I got to my feet as fluidly as a snake. Tadayo was laughing as he turned toward me. He had blood on his lips. His tongue poked out with the intention of licking it away, but I didn't give him the chance. I was standing to the side of him at the perfect angle to strike his temple. I do not have large hands, nor do I have more strength than the average woman. Thanks to my sensei's training, I knew that what I had would be more than sufficient.

I made a fist and launched a short, hard blow at the side of Tadayo's temple, level with his eyes. His head rocked sharply. I thought for a moment that my blow had been misjudged, but then he fell to the floor as if he were boneless. As he fell, his arm dropped outward and the child he was holding bounced off the tatami. The rest of the men stared from her to Tadayo.

It was so very easy to take advantage of their shock. The one called Choki went down with a punch just above his abdomen. One of the others lunged at me and I kicked him in his kintama. Unlike Tadayo, who had obviously enjoyed the experience, his face turned an ugly greenish color and he fell to the floor retching. The last man didn't bother to wait about. He backed away and was sliding open the screen door before I could lay a finger on him.

"Come on. You need to get dressed. Where's your robe?" I said briskly to the girl. "Stop that!"

She was kicking Tadayo as hard as she could with her bare feet. I grabbed her arm and pulled her away.

"He hurt me!" she panted.

"And now I've hurt him," I snapped. "Get dressed quickly."

She darted to the side of the room and picked up what looked like a bundle of rags. A heartbeat later, the rags were on her back and her hand was inserting itself into my fingers.

"I'm ready," she said simply. "I haven't got any sandals." She tugged me toward the open shoji and I followed her, feeling my surging fury transform into amusement. At the door, she stuck her head out and looked up and down the street carefully, and then ducked back in. "I think it would be safest if I pretended to guide you. Nobody will notice a blind anma being led about."

She was right, of course. The man that had escaped had probably gone to find some help. He could be back very quickly. I picked up my staff and put my other hand on the child's shoulder, urging her forward. Just as we were about to pass through the door, she wriggled out of my grip.

"Just a moment," she said urgently. Choki lay in a heap where I had left him. I watched in disbelief as the child scrabbled in his obi and came back to me clutching a purse in her hand. "That's it. We can go now."

I was so astonished, I allowed her to guide me into the street without another word.

She led me at a brisk pace. I gathered that she was very familiar with the Floating World; she walked confidently and appeared to know where she was going. We turned right and then left, walking forward until my guide steered me into a busy teahouse.

"Please, anma," her voice was suddenly high-pitched and polite. "May we stop and take tea? And perhaps daifuku cakes? I'm very hungry."

I was going to refuse but realized that I had nowhere to go, except home to an empty house. Empty apart from Matsuo, of course. And I was intrigued by this scrap of a girl who appeared to have as many facets as a fly's eye; she clearly was not the helpless child I had taken her for. She not only knew how to take care of herself, but was also, I was sure, perceptive enough to recognize that I could see as well as she could. I sat down on the bench the child led me to.

A disdainful waiter was at our side quickly. "Got enough to pay for it, anma?" he sneered. Before I could answer, the child spoke for me.

"Of course she has. My elder sister is one of the best anma in the whole of the Floating World. And probably the best rewarded."

The procession of expressions that passed across the waiter's face was so clear it took a great deal of willpower for me not to laugh out loud. He glared at my companion, switched his fierce expression to me and—when neither of us flinched—obviously became confused. Finally, he bowed his head and walked away, smiling unctuously.

"What's your name, *sister?*" I said quietly.

"Niko." She beamed at me. "And your name, elder sister?"

I was tempted to laugh out loud at the paradox of the situation. A few moments ago, we were fighting for—if not our lives, then certainly our virtue—and now we were exchanging names as if we had just met at some polite party. Niko inclined her head, waiting for my answer patiently.

"I am called Kamakiri." Even as I spoke, I wondered at the way I had phrased my answer. Niko raised her eyebrows but didn't comment.

Our order arrived then, and Niko was silent as she

stuffed the cakes in her mouth. She was hungry, I realized, not greedy. I broke one of the cakes in half for myself and pushed the rest toward her. Only when the platter was empty of every last crumb did she speak again.

"Oh, that was good. I'll pay for it," she said. I almost laughed at her and then remembered the purse she had taken from Choki. I was about to refuse, to tell her that the money was stolen and not hers to spend, but then I saw her dignified expression and instead I smiled and thanked her. What if the money wasn't really hers? The poor child had suffered enough at Choki's—and his friends'—hands to earn it. And I knew that she would have been deeply offended if I refused her.

"Thank you," I said gravely.

She sat back with a contented sigh and I stared into space, careful to preserve my anma personality. Not that it mattered greatly. Although the teahouse was crowded, nobody had chosen to sit near us. Niko was in rags and I was blind and obviously equally poor; nobody would want to sit near us in case our bad luck passed to them.

"Thank you for rescuing me," Niko said. "I thought I'd had it that time."

"That time?" I repeated in disbelief. "What do you mean, *that time*? Do you make a habit of being taken by strange men?"

"Of course not." Niko looked so injured I almost apologized. When she continued, I was very glad I had kept silent. I listened in disbelief, understanding what Yo had meant when he said I had much to learn outside of the code of the samurai. "I've never actually been taken by a man yet. Mind you, I've been pretty close to it a few times, but never quite as bad as this morning."

I licked my lips, searching for words. "You've been with men before?"

"No." Niko looked irritated. "You're not listening to me, Kamakiri. I've never actually been taken, I told you that. I've always managed to get away. Generally, if I scream really loud, they get worried enough to throw me out. If that doesn't work, I give them a good kick in the kintama. I'd been worried when I saw there were four of them, but when you grabbed Tanaka there and it didn't have any effect on him, I knew I really was in trouble. You were wonderful. If you hadn't have come in when you did, I would have had it for sure this time. I owe you my life, elder sister."

Niko looked at me with shining eyes. I gathered my scattered wits.

"You don't owe me anything," I said firmly. "I heard you screaming and sobbing and felt I had to help. It wasn't personal. But I still don't understand. How did you come to be there in the first place? Did they grab you off the street?"

"Of course not." Niko smiled as if my question was absurd. "My father gave me to them. Or rather, he sold me to them."

I was silent, absorbing her words in disbelief. My own father had been prepared to give me in marriage to a much older man. I had rebelled against the idea, but at least it was honorable. Could any father really choose to sell his young daughter to men to do with as they wished? And not once, but—if Niko was telling me the truth—over and over again?

"Why?" I asked finally.

"Because he needed the money, of course," she said simply. "Father used to be a carpenter, and a very good one. But he made the mistake of arguing with his master and he lost his job. No one else wanted to give him work after that, and his savings were soon used up, so we went hungry.

When Father couldn't pay the rent, our landlord was going to throw us out, so I went begging for a while." She sighed deeply. "I wasn't very good at it. After a while, Father said he would have to sell me to a brothel. I didn't like that idea at all. I asked him to give me a bit longer to see if I could make some cash begging, and he said I could. He's very good to me," she said with pride.

"But you didn't end up in a brothel?" I managed to ask.

"No. I would have done, but one day when I was begging, a man gave me a coin and told me if I went with him, there would be much more. I knew what he was after, but I pretended to be innocent. He took me to a really nice *ryokan*, and once we were in his room in the inn, he told me to take my clothes off."

"Did you?" I asked faintly.

"Of course not." Niko looked at me scornfully. "I told him I was too shy to do that. He seemed really pleased, and he tried coaxing me for a bit. When I burst into tears, he said I wasn't to worry, and he would take his clothes off first, to show me it was all right. You should have seen his tree of flesh! Bent as a twig, it was. After I saw that, I had half a mind to stay anyway, I was that sure he couldn't do me any harm."

Niko sounded so amused, I began to smile with her. The waiter approached at that moment, clearly intent on clearing us out. I stared straight through him and held a silver coin out in the palm of my hand.

"Will this keep our table until we're ready to go?" I asked. He took the coin so quickly the movement was a blur and walked away without a word.

"What did you give him that for?" Niko asked. "I could have started scratching at my head, and he would have been so worried I had lice he wouldn't dare lay a finger on us."

"It was easier that way. Money can buy almost anything very easily," I said wisely.

Niko nodded in agreement. "You're right about that," she said. I felt a pang of regret that this child should be so worldly-wise.

"So, tell me what happened," I urged.

"Not a lot." Niko raised her eyebrows comically. "Once he had all his clothes off, I told him I had never undressed in front of a man before and was shy. The stupid man offered to close his eyes until I had taken everything off. As soon as he did, I shuffled about as if I was taking my robe off. I had seen his purse inside his obi, so I grabbed it and ran off. Not a lot he could do, him being stark naked and all. I was out of the ryokan before he even knew his purse had gone. Of course, I gave the purse to Father, and he was delighted. We paid our rent and had food for weeks. When that ran out, Father suggested I do the same thing again. But this time, he came with me. He took me right into the Floating World, and we just sort of stood about on a corner. I thought it wasn't going to work, but eventually a man came up to us and chatted to Father for a while. I saw him give Father some money, and then he put his hand on my shoulder and tugged me away with him. That one was so pleased with me that he just took me down the nearest quiet alley and tried to have his way with me there. I let him get his tree out and then grabbed his kintama until he let me go."

Niko paused for breath, smiling as if she had told me something she was proud of.

"And after that? Did your father sell you often?"

"Whenever we ran out of money," she said simply. "I never had any real problems. More often than not, the men took me to a ryokan or a lodging house. If I screamed really loudly, they generally let me go in case anybody came to see what they were up to. If that didn't work, I would sob at them and pretend to be really upset. If nothing else worked, I would shiver and let them think I was really terrified of them. Then when they got close enough, I would give them a good kick in the kintama and run away as fast as I could. I never took anything from them over and above what I thought they owed me," she added virtuously. "Not until this morning. And anyway, I felt as if I'd earned what I took." She was looking at me adoringly.

"You probably did," I said briskly. "Well, you're safe now. Get back to your father. And if I were you, I would tell him that this was the last time. You see how dangerous it was? Those men would have taken you if I hadn't turned up. They would have hurt you very badly."

"But you did turn up, didn't you?" Niko breathed. "Anyway, I can't go back to Father. Not now. I don't want to do that anymore, and if I tell him that, he'll be very angry with me. He'll probably beat me. You wouldn't want that to happen to me, would you?"

"No, of course not. But if you don't go back to your father, where are you going to go?"

"With you, of course." Niko's face lit up in a wide smile.

FIFTEEN

How does a pine tree
Count the children it bears from
Each one of its cones?

A sudden throb of pain behind my temple made me put my fingers to my forehead. Had I not been so exasperated, the irony of it would have made me laugh. Surely an anma should be able to heal herself?

"No, Niko," I said firmly. "You are not coming with me. I'm only a poor anma. I barely make enough money to feed myself and keep a roof over my own head. Go back to your father. Explain to him what happened to you this morning. I'm sure he'll understand that you can't go on like that."

"He'll sell me to a brothel if I do." Niko's eyes were wide and bright, as if she was trying to hold back tears. "I'm still whole. He'd get a good price for me."

"He wouldn't do that!" I was appalled. How could any parent contemplate such a terrible thing? Then I remembered the danger Niko's father had been happy to accept on his daughter's behalf and was no longer so sure. "He couldn't. You're far too young. No brothel would accept you."

Niko stared at me disbelievingly. Suddenly, I felt it was I who was the innocent, not her.

"I'm twelve," she said incredulously. "Geisha have their mizuage when they're thirteen and nobody thinks twice about it. There are brothels out there in the Floating World that specialize in children a lot younger than me. Father wouldn't have any trouble selling me."

"I thought you were younger," I mumbled. "In any event, you can't come with me."

"Fine. If you don't want me, I suppose I'll have to go back home." Niko heaved a huge sigh and passed her hand over her eyes, as if she was wiping away tears. I felt hugely guilty, but reassured myself it was for the best.

"Good girl. Tell your father he isn't to sell you to a brothel. Tell him he'll have me to deal with if he tries."

An idle threat, of course. Niko had no idea where I lived, nor did I really suppose her father would be at all afraid of an anma. But for all that, it seemed to work. And I was relieved I had been wrong about Niko seeing through me earlier; she obviously thought I was what I appeared to be.

"I'll tell him." She beamed at me, and I understood that —in spite of her amazing courage—Niko was still a child. Now, she was full of tea and cake and was happy. I hoped very much that her father would realize the error of his ways and start to treat her as his daughter rather than something to be sold to the highest bidder.

I patted Niko's hand and stood, tapping my way out with my staff. I didn't look back. I felt immensely guilty at leaving her, and I knew if I saw she was crying, I would relent and take her home with me. But how could I? I was onna-bugeisha, and my way was clear. There was no room for a young child in my future; any danger she had already endured in her young life was nothing compared to what I was going to face. Besides, what would Yo say when he returned home if he found I had managed to adopt a young child? No, by far the best thing was for Niko to go home. Where she belonged.

It was, of course, the code of bushido that made me feel I had let her down. I protested to myself that I could not take in every waif or stray I encountered, and my conscience finally agreed with me. In any event, if this morning was anything to go by, Niko would survive very well without me.

By the time I arrived home, I had convinced myself I had done the right thing. The only thing.

I found it difficult to sleep that night. My futon was very empty without Yo. Matsuo obviously sensed my loneliness. He came and stood beside my futon, wagging his tail and looking at me hopefully. I gave in and patted the kakebuton, and he lay beside me with a happy, doggy sigh. I was grateful for his warmth; the night was cold and I hadn't bothered to light the charcoal-burner when I came in. I shrugged in annoyance as I remembered I hadn't cleaned out the ashes of the binchotan charcoal before I went out; another task to do in the morning before I set out to give Lord Akafumu his promised massage. I sighed, nostalgic for the easy life I had once led. A life I knew was gone forever. Matsuo whimpered and I rubbed his ears.

"I know," I said seriously. "You used to live on rabbit and chicken and now you get scraps. But it's worth it to be free."

He laid his head on my arm and I let him stay there. Just before I went to sleep, I remembered the old man I had been promised to and wondered if he was still puzzling over what had happened to his bride. The thought made me smile.

I was still in a good mood when I got up. I dressed and inspected Matsuo's paw. It had healed nicely. I would take him with me this morning. I poked the cold charcoal-burner with my foot. I could do without tea this morning; cold water would do. I had become used to the feel of Yo's staff. I picked it up and ran my hand down the smooth wood. Yo's hand had touched it here, and just so had he carried it with him. It was comforting in more ways than one, and I smiled as I opened the door and stepped out.

"You're late, anma." Lord Akafumu was sulky. I was actually slightly early for my appointment, and I had been surprised when the lecherous chamberlain had ushered me into the daimyo's private apartment at once.

"I am so sorry, lord," I murmured sincerely. "Are you in pain?"

"Pain? I have terrible pain. You had better be able to relieve it for me or it will be the worse for you."

I looked deeply concerned. Inside, I exulted. If he truly thought he was suffering great pain, it would surely make it far easier to persuade him to take one of Adam's magic pills. I prayed it would be so; I could detect no sign that the opium I had prescribed was having any effect on him.

"If the lord could kindly get undressed?" I said out loud.

Akafumu obeyed at once, peeling off his clothes and leaving them where they fell. I would have done the same once. But that was before I had learned that clothes neither hung themselves up nor washed themselves.

"Well? What are you waiting for?" Akafumu snapped. "I'm in the most dreadful pain. The opium you told me to take has done no good at all."

I looked concerned, even as I wondered cynically if the chamberlain was cheating his master. Charging him for the most superior opium and providing nothing special at all.

Akafumu was lying on his back, his tree of flesh folded rather neatly on top of his kintama. He looked perfectly well to me. Well-fed and sleek. An idea came to me and I put my ear against his stomach. I was rewarded immediately by a jumble of gurgles and wheezes. To make my examination look realistic, I felt his stomach in various places. I had no need to bother. I knew exactly what was wrong with the daimyo. He had been over-eating, and his stomach was sulky. A good dose of daikenchuto herb would act as a laxative and reduce the bloating, and he would be fine in a couple of hours.

I sat back on my heels and shook my head reluctantly.

"My lord," I said. "I think the situation is worse. I can see you have great pain. Is it coming from your back?"

"I believe it is." Akafumu nodded, prodding his belly carefully and wincing when he hit a sore spot. "You said last time that it would get worse. But so soon! Can you do anything?"

His voice was shaking with fear. I tried the effect of a reassuring smile.

"It is a grave condition, lord," I sympathized. "And I can see it is excruciating for you. A massage could ease the symptoms." A bit of prodding and poking in the right place would have him running to the lavatory. He would be cured instantly. Such a shame that wasn't going to happen! "But it would only be temporary. As I told you, it's the fault of the nerves at the base of your spine. They are fusing together far more quickly than I thought."

"Then do something, woman!" he howled. He was shivering with fear. "If you can't help me, I'll get somebody who can."

"Lord," I soothed. "Since Reiki left us, I am the most skilled anma in Edo. No other anma could do as much to ease your pain as I can. I promise you that. You might find it helpful to call in an acupuncture master." It wasn't as risky as it sounded. I knew perfectly well that if Akafumu continued eating and drinking to excess, acupuncture would do no good at all. In any event, it was obvious that I had hit a sore spot by mentioning acupuncture. Akafumu's face turned white, and I knew instantly that he was terrified of needles.

"No. No acupuncture. My father ordered it for me once when I had a fever when I was a child. The master stuck me so full of needles I was in greater pain when he finished than when he started. And it did no good at all."

"I see. Well, in that case, there is only one alternative, lord." I paused, rubbing my palms together in a nervous gesture as I waited for his reaction.

"What? If you can't help me, and I'm sure an acupuncture master would make things worse, what is there left? I've already made donations to a number of temples to ask the gods to intercede for me. That did no good at all. I could call in a witch, I suppose, but if the gods can't help me, I doubt a spirit could."

"You've done everything that is known, lord," I soothed. I waited to see if he would take my bait. He did, snapping like a koi carp at an evening mayfly.

"What do you mean? Out with it, anma. What do you know that you're not telling me about? Come on, before I have it beaten out of you."

I bowed my head and trembled. "My lord. I have something that will cure you. I know it will. I have gone to great lengths to obtain the remedy for you. It was very dangerous for me, but if it helps my lord to be restored to health, then it was worth it."

"What are you babbling about, anma?" He was obviously intrigued. "What is it? Some potion or other? If it's dangerous, I don't know if I want to try it. Are you sure it's safe?"

"Lord," I lowered my voice to a whisper. "Lord, it is safe enough. I'm sure of that. And I also know it will work. But I must tell you the truth. Only the bravest of men would dare to take the pills I have."

I stopped, as if I was thinking carefully about my next words. Akafumu was having none of it. He sat up and prodded me hard in the ribs with his toe. I winced theatrically and hunched into myself, as if I was still reluctant to speak further.

"Tell me. Now. If you don't, I'll have your head taken off. What use are you to me if you have a cure and refuse to share it with me? What is it? Some sort of vile-tasting potion? Does it have to be taken at certain phases of the moon? Does it take away pain but have negative effects elsewhere? What? Stop mumbling, woman, and tell me."

He had obviously forgotten the pain in his belly in his interest in what I had to offer. I cringed, wringing my hands together.

"Lord, it is a pill. Nothing more," I whimpered. "It should be taken three times a day, each day. If the pain is very bad, it can be taken more often. It relieves all pain, and I understand it is also very relaxing, which is just what your body craves above all else. It may well be the only cure for your malady."

"You think so? Why all the secrecy about it? What's it called, this magic pill?"

"Morphine, lord," I said.

"Never heard of it. What's so special about it?" Akafumu demanded suspiciously. "If it's that good, why doesn't everybody know about it? Is it very expensive? Is that it? Trust me, anma, I can afford it."

I'm sure you can. I thought wryly. Aloud, I said, "Lord, the morphine cannot be purchased for any amount of money. The reason it's not widely known is that it is made only by the gaijin."

I waited. Akafumu's expression turned from curiosity to anger and then became cunning.

"I see." He stroked his chin in an effort to look wise. "And how did a humble anma come to get her hands on these gaijin pills? Especially if they are so very exclusive?"

He was as easy to read as it is to see through clear water. He had begun to suspect I had been sent to assassinate him rather than heal him. I had expected this, and I knew I had to tread very carefully at this moment.

"I stole them for you, lord." I turned a trusting face toward him. "A gaijin came to me in great pain. I helped him to recover, and he was very grateful. He spoke quite good Japanese, and he told me how in his country there were no anma. Instead, the gaijin took the morphine when they had pain."

"So, why did he have need of your services?" Akafumu interrupted.

"He explained that his gaijin apothecary was away from Edo, so he could not obtain any of the magic pills. When I went to see him again, he told me he had no need of my services any longer as his apothecary had returned and he had obtained his morphine. I was astonished by the change in him, lord. When I had first seen him, he had been bent almost double with the pain in his spine. He found walking difficult and could not sleep at night for his pain. He was not a young man, but now he walked as if he had shed twenty years in a matter of days. He had no pain at all since taking the morphine, he said. But in spite of the fact that he was well, he had enjoyed my massage a great deal and asked me to treat him again. He had been very generous the first time, so I was happy to treat him again. He fell asleep when I had finished, giving me the chance to steal the magic pills."

"How did you know where to look? You're blind." Akafumu leaned so close he could have touched me, he was so interested.

"The gaijin was very foolish, as are all the gaijin. I told him as a healer I was very interested in the morphine and so he put one of the pills in my hand so I could feel it and smell it. When I said it didn't seem very special to me, he wanted to impress on me how clever the pills were, so he explained to me how many he had taken, and how wonderfully they worked. He put them away before I gave him his massage, but of course I heard where he had put them. I made sure to give him a very deep massage, and he fell asleep as soon as I had finished. I took them before he woke up and left straight away. I didn't even wait to get paid for the massage," I added pathetically.

"So." Akafumu sat back. "You have these pills with you?"

I reached into my obi and produced the pill bottle. I had taken a huge risk in bringing them here, but I had decided if they were found I would be honest. I would simply explain that I had brought them with me in hopes of helping to relieve Akafumu's pain. In any event, I had been fortunate. The chamberlain had obviously been lashed by Akafumu's anger already; he ushered me through to the presence-chamber without bothering to search me. There had been over a hundred pills in the bottle originally. I had taken them out and put twenty back in. I held it toward

Akafumu. He took the bottle carefully, holding it in his fingernails.

"This is the morphine, lord," I said.

"I'm sure it is. But have you thought, anma? You said yourself these were gaijin pills. They may work very well for those savages; after all, it is often the case that animals can eat things that would kill us. It may be the same with these pills. They may heal the foreign barbarians, and yet be deadly to us Japanese."

I put my hand over my mouth in a gesture of shock. "Oh, Lord Akafumu! I had never considered that! Please, forgive me. I am nothing but a stupid anma. I do not have your wisdom. Please, believe me when I say I was just trying to help you. If you give me the magic pills back, I will throw them in the river."

I kowtowed, hitting my head on the tatami. I wondered if I had overdone it, but it soon became clear I had not. Akafumu held on to the bottle, shaking it gently.

"You may rise, anma. All the pills appear to be the same. If they are as magical as your gaijin said, it would be a great shame to pass up the chance to try them. Here." He shook out a single pill and held it out on the pad of his finger. "You swallow that. If you're so certain they work, and they're harmless, you'll be fine. Open your mouth."

I did as he instructed and he put the pill on my tongue. I am not very good at swallowing pills. Usually, I would have needed a good gulp of water to get one down. This time, I swallowed hard, grimacing as the bitter pill stuck at the back of my throat. Akafumu instructed me to open my mouth wide, and he peered between my teeth thoroughly until he was sure it had gone.

"Sit there, anma. I want to see what effect it has on you."

I kneeled back down, lowering my head to my breast

and praying that the morphine would not kill me. I had expected this, and had decided that there was no way out of it. It had seemed to me that Adam was as normal as any Japanese man, apart from his height and other interesting features. Surely, if the morphine pills had not hurt him, then I would survive taking just one.

Quite suddenly, I felt a wave of anger so intense it made me shake. Here was the great Lord Akafumu, so worried about a bit of indigestion that he was willing to see me die before he would take a little, harmless pill. What a nasty, heartless coward the man was! I had to struggle hard to keep my face passive. I must have shown some emotion, as Akafumu leaned toward me eagerly.

"Well? Is it having any effect on you?"

There was, I noticed dreamily, something very like a rainbow around his head, where the sun reflected off his oiled hair. So very beautiful!

"I feel very well, lord," I assured him. And I did. I was so relaxed, I wanted to sway in tune with some music I could hear from far away in the palace. I put my hands on my knees and closed my eyes, wishing he would stop talking to me. I wanted to go to sleep. To sleep for hours and hours and wake up completely refreshed.

But Akafumu was having none of it. "Well? Do you feel any pain? Anything unusual?"

"I feel remarkably well, lord," I said dreamily.

I stared at him with lazy interest. I noticed that his eyes —as far as I was aware, formerly an average sort of dark brown—were suddenly glowing like topaz. How beautiful they would look strung on a bracelet. I could pluck them out quite easily. If only I could find the energy to reach up to him. Instead, I smiled. Akafumu seemed pleased about that. He sat back, tapping his finger on his knee. His fingernails were long and curved like a hawk's talons. They reminded me of my beautiful Soru. I wondered absently if my golden eagle was happy with his freedom. I hoped so.

The music was still drifting around me. It was so faint, I had begun to think it was in my head and not really being plucked from a samisen by human fingers. Then the musician struck a wrong note. The sound made me grit my teeth with annoyance. It caused a crack in my being for a moment. Then the music began again, flawless, and I relaxed. But the single fault had roused me long enough for me to realize that this was wrong. I struggled with my own inner being; the morphine beckoned to me, luring me back to a fine place of peace and gentleness. A place where nothing mattered at all except the joy of having no cares, of being perfectly happy. It would have been so very easy to give in, to relax and enjoy the perfection. But I would not. My sensei, Riku, had trained not just my body, but also my mind. Time after time, he had impressed on me that being a samurai was far more than the ability to fight, and win. That far more important was the ability to understand *why* I was fighting. To be able to temper violence with mercy; to understand that we humans were set on this earth by the gods, and because of that each of us had a little of the divine in us, if only we were aware of it.

I was onna-bugeisha. I was here to right the wrong that had been done to me by this man. This bully who was prepared—without so much as a thought—to see me die if it meant he could remove a minor irritation from his life. Once awareness was back with me, the iron fist of the drug began to relax. Still, it tugged, offering me the enticement of a little part of heaven here on earth. Akafumu was watching me intently. I stared over his shoulder at a beautiful scroll on the wall behind him and began to count silently. I got to ten before I lost my thread. I started again. By the time I had reached thirty, I was confident I was in full control of my mind again.

"I don't feel any ill effects at all, lord." My voice sounded odd, a little throaty and indistinct. I cleared my throat and tried again. "In fact, I feel very well. Very tranquil."

Nothing but the truth there! But Akafumu was still cautious.

"Stand up," He barked abruptly. I obeyed. "Touch your toes with your fingers." I did so, feeling as elegant as a dancer. "Kowtow. Properly, full length."

I stayed face down on the tatami, waiting for my next order. Mentally, I was elated. If the morphine could have such an effect on me, one who had been trained to use my mind to obey every command of my body, what would be the effect on a man like Akafumu, who expected the world to pamper him? I had kept back most of the morphine pills with the idea that I could feed Akafumu a few at a time and watch his progress. But surely there were enough that I could keep back a few for my own use? I smiled with pleasure at the thought, and then closed my eyes tightly as the reality of the thing smacked me like a blow.

Just one tablet of the morphine had released the divine in me. It had led me to pleasures that should rightly belong only to the gods. And the gods were said to be very jealous of anything that was their gift alone. I remembered Adam telling me how his friend had come to depend on the drug and had lost everything in his desire to dwell in its pleasures. I shuddered; Akafumu could have all the pills. I wanted nothing more to do with them.

"I'm certain that the morphine will cause you no ill effects, lord." I spoke into the tatami, grateful that I had no need to show my face as I lied. "Quite the contrary."

"It appears not. You may rise, Kamakiri." He had used my name instead of merely calling me anma. He was pleased, then. "Well, as you stole them in the first place, I don't need to pay you for them. And you haven't even given me a massage, so I don't owe you for that. Still..." He fingered the pill bottle, turning it in his fingers. "I shall be kind. Ask my chamberlain for your usual fee on the way out."

I rose and began backing toward the door, bowing humbly as I went. My hand was on the shoji when Akafumu's voice stopped me. I paused, my breath held in my throat as I wondered if he had, somehow, suspected me.

"Three of these a day, you say? More if I have pain?"

"That is so, lord," I replied quickly.

"There are not many pills here. Will there be enough to cure my pain?"

I pretended to think about his question carefully. "Perhaps not, lord. Would you like me to try and get you more? It will be very difficult for me, as I'm sure the gaijin will know it was me who stole them. If I go back to see him, he will surely be angry. And he might not even have any more of the magic pills."

I shuffled my feet and hunched my shoulders, hoping I appeared to be terrified.

"I don't care if he's angry or not." Akafumu sounded irritated. "You will go back and see your gaijin. If he doesn't have any more pills, you will persuade him to get some for you."

Even knowing how selfish Akafumu was, I was surprised. I spoke with genuine astonishment. "But, lord, how am I supposed to make him get more pills? He'll want to know what I did with the first lot and why I want more. It's impossible, lord."

I could have handed over the lot today. But caution told me to walk carefully. I would feed them to him slowly so that he didn't realize that the drug had taken him entirely in its power. Only then, when it was too late, would there be no more pills.

My only regret was that I would not be there to see him sink into degradation. I was so delighted with my plan that I was almost ashamed of myself. For a second, at least, then Akafumu's next words drove any sympathy away.

"Impossible? You dare say that to me?" Akafumu sounded incredulous. I hung my head and moaned with pretended fear. "You will get me those pills. If you don't get them for me, then I will have you executed. I'm sure that knowledge will sharpen your wits."

"Yes, lord," I said quickly. I was almost through the door when Akafumu spoke again.

"A moment, anma. Where do you live? I may have need to send for you."

"On Willow Road, lord," I said smoothly. "My dwelling is between two houses, perhaps halfway down. It is not much, but it keeps the rain and cold from my poor bones."

That was where Reiki's poor hovel had been. If Akafumu sent his men there, they would not find *me,* but they would find the sort of home they expected.

Akafumu was grinning. I guessed he thought he had been cunning, fooling the poor, blind anma into telling him where she lived.

"Excellent. I want you back here in five days, at this time. You will bring me more of the magic pills. If you do not come, then my men will find you. And if they have to search for you, I tell you now you can expect no mercy from me."

"I understand, lord. I will get you more of the magic pills."

I was so elated, I almost neglected to ask the chamberlain for my fee. Almost, but not quite. I turned the small coins he gave me over in my hands, comparing them with the gold ichibuban that Adam had given to me. Truly, Akafumu deserved everything the gods—with a little help from me—bestowed on him!

Matsuo was waiting for me. I untied him and trudged behind him, tapping carefully with Yo's staff. I was pleased I had it. The wood was very smooth from much use, and if it hadn't been so very hard, it would have reminded me a little of his skin. I sighed, wishing I could share my triumph with him. He would laugh, I knew, when I told him how very selfish and very stupid the great lord Akafumu was showing himself to be.

He would be back soon. But I hoped not too soon. I had a great deal left to do before he returned.

SIXTEEN

> Just as the moon has
> The sun for a lover, so
> Are you my reverse?

"Matsuo. What's the matter with you?"

My akita had stopped at the entrance to our home. He wasn't growling, but his hackles were raised and he was sniffing the air with his head up. I glanced around; there was nothing out of the ordinary that I could see. Still, if my dog was anxious, then I would be careful.

I slid the shoji back smoothly, without hesitation. If there was someone inside, I wanted them to think I was unaware of their presence.

"Come along, Matsuo," I said cheerfully. I tapped my way in with my staff, keeping up my pretense of blindness. All my senses were working with great clarity, and I understood at once there was something wrong. I could smell a clean, sharp odor. The charcoal-burner had been moved and looked different. I bent to pat Matsuo and heard a movement off to my left. I snapped upright immediately, my staff raised ready to strike.

"Niko!" I stopped my swing abruptly, my staff barely a hand's width from her head. "What in the names of all the gods are you doing here? And how did you find me?"

Obviously realizing Niko was no threat, Matsuo had abandoned his defensive stance. He was sitting on the old kakebuton that served as his bed and was scratching behind his ear. I poked him with my foot, but he took no notice. I was furious, both with Niko and myself. She had no right to be here. And my shock at seeing her had been so great that I had forgotten I was supposed to be blind. I caught myself up at once; this would be a lesson for me in the future. No matter how distracted or surprised I was, I must always remember that I was an anma. Niko appeared not to have noticed. She flung herself against me and wrapped her hands around my waist, muffling her face in my robe.

"Kamakiri, I've been waiting ages for you! I thought you were never going to come back. Look, I've cleaned everywhere for you. And the kettle's ready to boil for tea. I would have prepared a meal for you, but there's no food."

I glanced around. She certainly had cleaned. There wasn't a speck of dust anywhere. And everywhere was so *tidy*. The house was as clean and sweet as my apartment had been when I had had servants to care for my every need.

"Thank you." I tugged her away from me. "But what are you doing here? And how did you find me?" I took a sharp breath as I saw her clearly, then remembering I was blind stopped myself commenting on the cuts and bruises that puffed out her face.

"I followed you yesterday." She beamed. "The shoji was unlocked, so today I just came in."

Of course the shoji was unlocked. What was the point of locking something that could be torn apart with a sharp knife? Unlike my family home, where the great doors to the outside walls had been securely barred at night to deter intruders. Even better, the entrance hall to the house had a nightingale floor. The wooden blocks looked completely normal, but they had been laid by cunning workmen. Random blocks were fitted so that they moved at a footstep, and with each movement, they creaked and groaned so the noise echoed through the silent house. When I was a child, I had spent hours learning which blocks moved, and had amused myself greatly by learning to tread over the floor in absolute silence. Even Isamu caused the blocks to scream occasionally, generally when he was very late in returning at night and careless through too much sake. Once Yo and I had a house of our own, I decided I would speak to him about having a nightingale floor in the entrance. It was an extravagance, but if it ensured our safety, it was worth the expense.

"But what are you doing here?" I recalled myself to the moment.

"Aren't you pleased to see me?" Niko's lip trembled. I was grateful I was not supposed to be able to see it. "I've been worried about you. I suppose you were out, pretending to be an anma again?"

I sighed. I suppose I could have laughed at her. Told her she was talking nonsense. That I had no need to *pretend* to be an anma. But what was the point? Niko was as sharp as a needle. She knew I could see as well as she could.

"Never mind all that. What are you doing here? And what happened to your face?"

"It's nowhere near as bad as the rest of me." Niko seemed quite proud of her cuts and bruises. She stood back and unloosed her obi, spreading her kimono wide. I winced. She was so thin, I could count each rib. But apart from that, her belly and chest were black. I could make out the marks of knuckles, where individual blows had landed. I felt her pain.

"Your father?" I guessed.

She nodded. "I told you he would be angry with me." Niko shrugged. "When I went home and said an anma had rescued me from the men he had sold me to when she heard me screaming, he was furious. I think he'd been drinking, and that always makes him bad-tempered. He said he wouldn't be able to take me out again in case any of the men saw him, and it was all my fault for not keeping my mouth shut. I tried to tell him that they really would have taken me this time, but he didn't care. He was so annoyed with me for answering him back, he beat me."

She fastened her robe again and hunched her narrow shoulders at the memory.

"You ran away," I said. I found it very difficult to hide my anger at her father's treatment of her.

Niko shrugged her shoulders. "He shut me in the bedroom. And then he went back to his sake. When he started snoring, I crept out and came here." She looked at me anxiously and added, "I haven't come empty-handed. I've still got the purse I took off Choki. I was going to give it to Father, but I decided he didn't deserve it when he beat me."

Niko delved in the sleeve of her kimono and held the purse out to me.

"Keep it. You'll need it," I said firmly. "You don't want to go back to your father, I suppose? He might be in a better mood when he sobers up."

"I'm not going back," Niko said defiantly. "He said he

was really going to sell me to a brothel this time. And he meant it. If you don't let me stay here with you, I'll use Choki's money to buy myself some nice clothes. I might as well set myself up as a yujo and go on the streets. It's no worse than being sold to a brothel, but at least that way I get to keep whatever I earn."

I stared at her rebellious expression and realized she meant it. For all her apparently worldly wisdom, I thought that Niko could have no idea what she was considering. A child of her age, offering herself on the streets? At the very best, a yakuza would soon get to hear about her, and she would find herself offered the sort of "protection" that she could not refuse. At worst, she would be snatched and end up in the very brothel her father had considered for her. What was I thinking of? Of course, that wasn't the worst that could happen to her. The very worst—and the most likely—outcome was that she would be murdered by one of her patrons. A man who either enjoyed inflicting extreme violence or one who thought so little of her that he preferred to kill her rather than pay her fee.

Niko obviously interpreted my prolonged silence as irritation. She kneeled quickly at my feet and spoke humbly.

"Please, Kamakiri, let me stay with you. At least until the bruises fade. I'm not going to attract many customers in this state, am I? I don't eat much. And I'm very good at cleaning and washing. I've looked after Father since I was ever so little. Please?"

What could I say? For a fleeting moment, I wondered how I was going to explain my new sister to Yo when he returned. I shrugged the thought away as irrelevant. With a little good fortune, Niko would be gone before he came back. The kannushi at Jokan-Ji Temple might know somebody who wanted a servant. If Niko really could clean and cook, and came with a recommendation from the kannushi, she would soon find a place.

And if Yo's business was finished quickly? Would he really be so very sorry to have somebody about the place who knew how to cook and keep the house clean? After all, I knew I was sadly lacking in domestic skills. Like every other samurai daughter, I had been taught the traditional tea ceremony. My *ikebana* flower arrangements were exquisite, and I could sing and dance beautifully. But I could not cook—even the production of a simple bowl of rice was beyond my talents—and the idea of cleaning made me feel helpless. I felt deeply disloyal to Yo as I had a sudden pang of longing to be pampered at least a little.

"Please, can I stay?" Niko's pleading broke in on my thoughts. I shrugged. Even if she was no better at household tasks than I was, I had to let her stay. Turning her out to fend for herself in the Floating World was unthinkable. The code of bushido was perfectly clear; the needy had to be cared for, without question. Niko was, whether I liked it or not, my responsibility.

"You can stay. At least for a while." I watched her face light up with pleasure and I was touched.

"Thank you!" She took my hand, pulling me around the house and showing me what she had already done. I was impressed. Every surface gleamed. The tatami smelled fragrant and had obviously been well brushed. There was fresh water in the jar in the kitchen, ready for use. "Shall I make us some tea?"

I nodded. I found Niko's pride in a job well done charming.

Niko's tea was very good. She handed me my brimming cup without ceremony, but I was pleased to sip the scalding hot liquid. I knew I was being grossly impolite, but I had to speak.

"Niko, you stink," I said bluntly. She sniffed her armpit and shrugged.

"Do I? I suppose I must. I haven't had a bath in ages."

The contrast between Niko's sweaty odor and the sweet cleanliness of the house was too much for me to bear.

"Come on." I stood up. "There's a good public bath close by. We'll go and get clean and then have something to eat."

"Yes, Kamakiri," Niko said meekly. "Are we going to take your dog with us or would you like me to guide you?"

I glanced at her suspiciously, but her face was innocent.

SEVENTEEN

All women know that
When clad only in their skin,
All men are the same

*T*he bath was wonderful. Hot and steaming and smelling faintly of the minerals in the water. We were fortunate; apart from us, it was empty.

Niko—obviously taking her new duties seriously—pushed the maid aside and soaped and rinsed me repeatedly herself. When it came to her turn, she allowed the maid to do her duty, lifting her arms and turning with obvious pleasure. Finally clean, she climbed in beside me and spoke loudly, for the benefit of the hovering maid.

"Anma, are you quite comfortable? When you're ready, I'll help you out. The tiles are slippery, and it would be easy for you to miss your footing."

I thanked her gravely. As soon as the maid left, I asked her the question that had been on my mind since I had found her in my home.

"How did you know I'm not blind?"

"I didn't. Or at least, I wasn't quite sure. Not until you didn't deny it earlier," she said cheerfully. I frowned; I must remember never to let my guard drop for a second in the future. "You do it really well," she went on. "Anybody would think you really were an anma. The only thing that made me wonder in the first place was when you came into the house where the men were holding me. You looked at me, and just for the tiniest moment, I could see you were furious with them. I knew you were going to look after me then."

"I'm not going to look after you," I said crisply. "You can stay until my man gets back, then we'll find a proper job for you."

"Is he a ninja?" I stared at this impossible child in disbelief. "Your man, I mean. Are you a ninja as well? I've never heard of a woman ninja, but the way you use your staff is just as good as a man ever could be. Will you teach me to fight?"

It took me a moment to sort out the flood of words. When I had, I spoke slowly, and very carefully.

"My man is shinobi," I said finally. "That's the correct name for a ninja. But you must never, ever tell anybody that. He would be furious if he thought I had told you. Secrecy is essential for a shinobi. If it became known that he was shinobi, his life would be ruined."

I shook my head to myself, wondering what enchantment this child carried that she could see and understand things that were hidden to all others.

"Of course I wouldn't say anything that you told me not to," Niko said indignantly. She lowered her voice and looked around furtively, even though we were alone. "Are you a ninja—I mean, shinobi—as well?"

"No. I am a warrior woman of the samurai. I am onna-bugeisha."

Niko repeated my words silently. I could see they meant nothing at all to her and I sighed, wondering how I could ever explain the code of bushido and my quest as a samurai warrior to her.

I had no need; after a moment, she said simply, "I don't know what an onna-bugeisha is. But I know who you are. You're the samurai lady whose family was slaughtered in the last uprising. You were supposed to marry some old man or other, but you refused him. The gossip said you had committed suicide rather than accept him. Everybody thought it was a very romantic thing to do, but I'm glad you're still alive. Why are you pretending to be an anma? Is it something to do with getting revenge? The rumors were about you, weren't they?"

"I suppose the rumors must be about me." I was so shocked I didn't even try to pretend I didn't know what she was talking about. "But how did people find out what happened?"

"Everybody in the Floating World loves gossip." Niko shrugged as if she was stating the obvious. "Especially when it involves the aristocracy."

"I'm not an aristocrat any longer, Niko," I said quietly. "Do you know the story of *The Forty-Seven Ronin*?"

She nodded. Of course she knew the story. Every Japanese child knew it.

"Is that like you and your ninja?" By the gods, but she was quick on the uptake! "Is that what you're both doing, taking revenge on all those who killed your family?"

"Not quite." I spoke indulgently, and then realized that in her innocence, Niko had spoken almost the truth. "It's not as simple as that. I'm the last of my family. If I had been born a man, I would have inherited the family name and the title and our estates. But I'm a mere woman, so I've been denied everything. You were right about me being promised to an old man. My father had planned the marriage before he was killed, and our daimyo, Lord Akafumu, insisted that I had to go ahead and marry Tadatomo."

"But if he's an old man, he'll die soon and you'll be left with plenty of money, and you'll be free as well. You can do what you like then," Niko said cheerfully.

"My old man has been married twice and has had no children," I said bitterly. "And if I have no sons by him either, what then?"

Niko considered my question seriously. I could see she was turning the thought over in her mind. Suddenly she gasped in almost comic surprise.

"You still couldn't inherit your family estate. But I know who would claim it. Your daimyo! It would all go to him and everybody would say he had done the honorable thing by not just taking it for himself when your menfolk died. It's just like a kabuki play, but in real life!"

"If it wasn't my life, I would probably agree with you," I said drily. "But it *is* my life. And unlike the kabuki, there isn't going to be a happy ending, nor am I going to commit suicide," I added drily. "No matter what the rumors say."

"No, of course not. Are you going to murder your daimyo to get your revenge on him? Can I help?" she asked eagerly.

I shook my head, smiling at her blood-thirsty enthusiasm. Niko watched me doubtfully and then began to grin.

"Have I said something wrong?" she asked. "Father always said I spoke before I thought, and I suppose I do. You will let me stay, won't you? I can help you, even if it's only by cleaning and cooking. That would clear the way for you to concentrate on your plans. Please?"

I stared at this girl who had been thrust into my life by forces above either of us and who obviously had no intention of leaving it again. Suddenly, my amusement vanished. She had called herself my younger sister. If I had dared to speak to Emiko in such a way, my elder sister would have told Father I had insulted her and he would have had me whipped. I was overcome with a growing pleasure at the understanding that the gods had granted me the chance to begin my life all over again. Not just with a lover who was prepared to accept me for what I was, but also with a younger sister who was everything my own sister had never been.

Niko was staring at me. I realized she was still waiting for a reply to her serious question.

"You can surely help me, Niko." Her face glowed with delight. "And not just by housekeeping, either."

"I can cook as well. And take your dog for a walk. And I'm very good at washing clothes."

I held my hand up to silence her. "And when do you expect to sleep?" I teased. Niko smiled, clearly delighted.

She reminded me of a stray dog that had hung about a house for weeks, barking at strangers and existing on scraps, always hopeful that one day the door would be opened and it would be allowed in. Just like the patient dog, Niko had found the home she had longed for. I had accepted responsibility for my stray, and that was all there was to the matter.

"I love you, Kamakiri," she blurted suddenly. "You're my elder sister and I'll do anything you ask me to do, I promise. You can trust me."

Yo had told me he loved me. Until that moment, he was

the only person in the whole of my life who had said that to me. And now here was this street urchin, a child I doubted Father would even have accepted as the lowest of his servants, telling me that she, too, loved me. I felt a great warmth for them both.

Suddenly, I had a family again. A family that was different from anything I had ever known. Different from anything I could even have dreamed existed. I blinked away tears, pretending that the steam had found its way into my eyes. Niko put her hand shyly into mine, and I stared at her fingers, shimmering like a white starfish through the water.

I suddenly understood how very fortunate I was.

EIGHTEEN

A dragonfly lives
On my maple. I think your
Spirit lives in him

I should have known that acquiring a younger sister as spirited as Niko would not be so very simple. She stared at me, frowning sulkily.

"I'm not going to put those rags on again. I've still got that horrible Choki's purse. If you won't let me have a new kimono and obi, I'll go and buy them for myself."

We glared at each other. I glanced at the dirty, patched clothes she was wearing, and relented.

"I'm supposed to be an anma," I explained patiently. "My clothes are no better than yours. It would look all wrong if the girl who was leading me was wearing a new, expensive kimono. People would suspect something at once."

"I hadn't thought about that," Niko said grudgingly. "Can I have some new clothes when you're not an anma, anymore?"

"Of course. In fact, it will be essential for you to have beautiful clothes. But not yet. First, we are going to see my daimyo, Lord Akafumu."

I was amazed to see Niko's usually happy face cloud with fear.

"Lord Akafumu? I can't go to his court. I'll stay here, Kamakiri. You take Matsuo, like you normally do."

"No," I said firmly. "I want you to come with me. I need you there. If anything goes wrong, you can slide away unnoticed. Nobody's going to notice an anma's apprentice."

Niko was insurance. If something went amiss with my plans, and Akafumu became suspicious, I needed Niko to get away. To come back here and contact the kannushi, who in his turn could get word to Yo to come back and rescue me —again. But Niko was shaking her head, her expression worried, and I was irritated.

"Why not? It was only yesterday you were telling me you would do anything for me. All I need you to do is pretend to lead me and keep quiet. If that's possible for you," I added tartly.

"I can't go there." Niko hung her head, but I could see her cheeks were burning with color. "Not so long ago, one of the men that Father sold me to belonged to Lord Akafumu's court. I don't think he was a noble himself, but you could see he was very wealthy."

"How did you know he came from Akafumu's court?" I asked.

"He said he did," Niko said simply. "I think he was trying to impress Father, but I didn't like him at all. He pinched and poked at me as though I was a piece of meat that needed to be made tender. As soon as he got me to his room in the *ryokan*, I screamed the place down and ran like the wind when the innkeeper came to see what was going on. If the gentleman saw me again, he would remember me, I'm sure he would. He didn't look to be the type of man who would be happy about being made a fool of."

"There are a lot of men at Akafumu's court," I said gently. "And even if we did see that particular one, you have to remember that you're no longer a girl who was sold off by her father. No one would associate the blind anma's apprentice with the girl you used to be."

Niko thought about it for a while. "You're sure? You promise I'm not going to get into trouble?"

"I promise," I said. I truly wasn't worried. I remembered Yo's wise words when he had told me that people only saw what they expected to see. The Niko who had been sold into prostitution by her own father was a world away from the anma's apprentice.

I took Matsuo as well. The huge akita was an excellent deterrent to any man who was foolish enough to think about robbing a poor, blind anma. And apart from that, he seemed to have taken a great liking to Niko and had started following her about. I was almost jealous of my dog's new devotion, until I realized Matsuo felt it was his duty to protect her as well as me.

"Not so fast, Niko." She had started off slowly, but had quickly begun to walk at her usual, brisk pace.

"Sorry. I forgot I was leading you."

I squeezed her shoulder gently. I had also taken my staff, and it felt odd not to tap my way with it. I could have left it behind, but it was comfortable in my hand, and also a comfort to me to know it was there should there be any trouble.

I reminded Niko of her duties toward the end of the long walk to Akafumu's court.

"I know what to do." She raised her eyes to the heavens

indignantly. "I don't speak unless someone asks me a question, and then only if you tell me to answer them. I stand looking at the floor. Wherever you go, I follow. When we're admitted to the daimyo's presence, I stop behind you. If there's trouble, and you get taken away, I run like the wind and go to Jokan-Ji Temple and ask to see the kannushi and tell him to get a message to Yo-san."

"That'll do." I smiled. "Here we are."

We waited at the great gate until a guard found the time to attend to us. Even though it was the same guard I had seen on the last two occasions I had been to the court, he still made me give my name and state my business before he let us through.

I tapped Niko's shoulder to tell her to stop as we came to the ante-chamber. I felt a tingle of anticipation as the chamberlain bustled up almost at once.

"You're here, at last. Lord Akafumu has been asking for you since this morning," he snapped.

"I am sorry, lord." I hung my head meekly. "It is a long walk from Edo."

"I'll announce you." The chamberlain paused, staring at Niko. "Who's this?"

"My new apprentice. I have no daughter of my own to pass my skills on to, and it would be sad for my knowledge to die with me, so I decided to take her on. She's an orphan and her name is Mina, if it pleases you, lord."

"Doesn't matter to me what she's called." The chamberlain glared down at Niko from his great height. "You might have cleaned her up a bit. She's as filthy as you, anma. Go on in, the pair of you."

Niko shuffled in in front of me, my hand on her shoulder. I could feel the tension in her slight body and gave her a little touch of reassurance.

"Anma. There you are." Akafumu sounded even more pettish than usual. Even with my eyes lowered, I could see that he was fidgeting, shuffling about on his seating platform restlessly. He was sweating freely, in spite of the cool breeze that came through the open screens. "Have you brought me some more of the morphine pills? For your sake, I hope you have."

"Of course I have, lord. I have them here." I patted my obi. "I had to visit the gaijin again to get them. He was very angry with me for stealing them in the first place. I had to tell him lies, lord. I told him they were for my poor, old mother, who was dying of an internal growth in her breast and that nothing I did could relieve her pain."

"I don't care what lies you had to tell." Akafumu almost screamed the words at me. "Give them to me now."

I pulled out a square of silk containing the rest of the pills and gave it to Niko. She shuffled forward, bent almost double, and placed it in Akafumu's outstretched hand. She retreated to me without turning around.

"I am sorry to have caused you distress, lord," I whimpered. "I came on the day you appointed. I thought you would have enough pills to ease your pain until I returned."

"You're a fool, anma." Akafumu was tugging at the knots that held the silk tied. They came loose unexpectedly, spilling the contents on his lap. He grabbed for them, his hooked fingernails trying and failing to grab a single pill. Finally snaring one, he put it in his mouth and swallowed. I saw his throat convulse with the effort of trying to get it down without liquid. "I finished the first lot of pills yesterday morning. I haven't felt at all well today without another one. When can you get me some more? I don't want to run out."

"Lord, you should have enough to last for more than

thirty days, even if you take the full dose of three each day," I murmured.

"I may have taken more than three a day," he said sulkily. "I found they helped me to sleep, as well as ease my pain. You will obtain more and bring them to me as soon as you can."

His voice was shaking. I could smell him. Beneath the odor of well-washed skin was a sour, nasty reek of something rotting. I suspected strongly that it came from within Akafumu's body and was seeping through his pores.

"I will bring you more as soon as I can, lord," I said. I fully expected him to demand when. He did not, and I felt a surge of satisfaction as I understood that already his mental sharpness had begun to deteriorate.

"Good. These are the same pills as last time?"

"Of course, lord," I said smoothly. "I am delighted that they have helped you so greatly. They have caused you no problems at all, I hope?"

I was so sure he would answer no that I was shocked when he spoke.

"They most certainly have," he snapped. "My pain is better. Much better. And even with the weight of court affairs on my shoulders, I find I sleep very well after I have taken a pill. But they have blocked my natural functions quite terribly."

For a moment, I had no idea at all what he was talking about. Had the morphine made his tree incapable of rising? Was he having problems breathing? I raised my hands in bewilderment, and Akafumu leaned forward and hissed at me angrily.

"I'm constipated, woman. I've sat on the closet and strained until I feel as if my stomach has come loose, but nothing happens. You can give me a massage to ease it. At least you can be useful for that."

"But of course, lord. Most certainly." I hoped I sounded sufficiently eager. I pushed Niko to one side gently and tapped my way forward with my staff. Akafumu glanced at her as if seeing her for the first time.

"Who is that? What is she, your daughter?" He didn't sound angry, just vaguely interested.

"Mina is my apprentice, lord. I have no daughter. I hope to pass my trade on to her."

"Is she blind?" The morphine was already beginning to take effect. Akafumu's voice was slurred and his fidgeting had stopped.

"No, lord. She is sighted. She guides me."

"Ah." He looked sulky. "Well, if she can see, I don't want the brat staring at my body. It's not for just anybody's eyes to feast upon. Get out of here. Stay outside until the anma's finished with me."

Niko went to her knees and kowtowed. She did it very gracefully, but Akafumu was unimpressed. He glared at her as she rose and backed out, bowing from the waist all the way.

"That's better. I'm not having her staring at me, anma. She's not touching me either. You can find her some peasant to practice on." He stretched and yawned widely. "I suppose you want me to lie on my back, do you?"

"If it pleases you, lord." I waited, expecting him to shrug his robes off.

"I can't be bothered undressing," he said lazily. "You may earn your fee, anma. Take my obi and robe off for me."

I bent hastily, pretending to fumble down his body until my fingers found his obi. The knot was large and intricate, and it took me so long to undo it, I thought he might have already succumbed to the opium and fallen asleep. He had not.

"Be careful with that." He tapped my shoulder sharply. "If you damage it, I'll take the value from your fee. If you damage it greatly, I'll take it out of your miserable hide."

I bowed my head silently and breathed evenly until I was sure I had my temper under control. When I was calm —or at least as calm as I could manage—I pulled the obi away and parted Akafumu's robe. He was wearing a silk loincloth beneath. The thin, slippery material was tented out by his thrusting tree of flesh.

I hesitated fractionally and then smoothly parted the loincloth. It was only when my fingers found his tree that I allowed myself an exclamation of surprise.

"Well? What are you waiting for? My stomach needs your attention. And I daresay when you've finished putting that right, which I'm sure isn't going to take long for an anma of your talent, you can attend to other matters."

"Of course, lord," I said quickly. I considered my options as I pressed on his belly, and decided I had none. If Akafumu was still awake when I had finished massaging his stomach, I supposed I would have to deal with his tree. At least it was clean, and not of any great size. I decided I would linger as long as I could on Akafumu's belly and pray he was asleep before I finished.

"That feels better. I'm sure I can feel something stirring."

I paused in surprise. I had barely started kneading Akafumu's stomach. Then his tree jerked at me, and I guessed he was making fun of the poor, blind anma.

In case I hadn't taken the hint, he took my hand and moved it to his tree, wrapping my fingers firmly around his flesh. I moved my hand up and down tentatively.

"I have heard that many of you anma are greatly skilled in all the bodily arts." Akafumu sounded dreamy, but his state of relaxation obviously hadn't reached his tree. "Reiki was very good at all aspects of her work. Was she a good teacher, I wonder?"

I clutched at his words like a drowning man grabbing for a reed. "She taught me the arts of relieving pain, lord," I said quickly. "But nothing else. I am sorry."

"Sorry? What for?" Akafumu's voice was soft, his words slurred. But when I stopped rubbing his tree, he slapped me at the side of my head hard enough to hurt. "You will be sorry if you don't get on with it. Reiki loved taking me in her mouth. It was a shame she had all her teeth. My favorite concubine was delighted when I had all her teeth taken out so she could give me greater pleasure. I was thinking of offering Reiki the same favor. Pity she had to die."

I carried on stroking his tree. I remembered Reiki warning me to be careful with Akafumu, and now I understood why. How many times had he insisted that she pleasure him? How dare he? The answer came to me immediately. Of course he dared. He was a daimyo. He had the power of life and death in his hands. I gritted my teeth in helpless fury and then shuddered at the thought of having them pulled out just to satisfy this man's lust.

"I will do my best, lord." I hoped he might take the tremor of anger in my voice for fear.

"You had better." He tapped me on the head sharply. "If you don't please me enough, I shall get that girl of yours to try. Only before I give her the privilege, I will have her teeth pulled. If her gums are tender, it should make the experience exquisite in the extreme."

It was obvious that Akafumu found the idea intensely erotic. His tree surged beneath my fingers, pulsing as if it was a living thing. There was no way I could avoid this. I leaned forward without saying another word and took his tree between my lips. I heard him sigh with pleasure; I wanted to get this over with as quickly as I could. I gulped him into my mouth so far that his hood brushed the back of my throat.

I told myself that this was nothing but a bit of flesh. It meant nothing to me at all. Akafumu pushed, and I gagged. He laughed and I bit him. It was instinct; I couldn't help it. He paused, as if trying to decide whether he liked that or not. I gathered he did, as he arched his hips and tried to push further. I was very grateful his tree was no bigger.

I closed my lips firmly around his flesh and sucked. I heard him exhale heavily and tensed, expecting at any moment that he would spill his seed in my mouth. After a heartbeat, I realized that although his tree was still erect, he had become still and silent. I pulled away a fraction, and when there was no response, a fraction more. I waited for a slap or instructions. When there was only silence, I drew my mouth away completely.

He was asleep. His arms had fallen to each side of him, and his mouth was open, showing nasty, yellow teeth. I glanced from his face to his tree and saw that the great daimyo might have succumbed to the embrace of morphine, but his tree was still very much alive. I thought of Reiki as I turned and walked away.

"For you, Reiki," I said very softly. "I hope he's still like that when his servants come in to attend to him. And I hope they wake him up so he can understand the state I left him in."

NINETEEN

The sun shines on my
Mountain. Why is it raining
Where you make your home?

"*D*id you see the man who said he was from the court?"

Niko was very quiet, and I thought she might be worried.

"No. Or at least, I don't think I did." She paused, frowning. "It was really odd, but they all looked the same. They all wore their hair in the same way and all dressed the same. They even sounded alike. Is that how they look at us peasants? I mean, do they think we're all the same?"

"Yes," I said simply. "I think so."

That started her off.

"You were rich. You were a samurai. But you don't think all peasants are like animals and not worth bothering about. Why? Why are you different?"

"I try to live by the samurai code of bushido," I explained carefully. "And if that is observed properly, it means not just loyalty to your peers and obedience to those of higher rank, but also compassion toward those in need, no matter who they are."

"But Akafumu's a daimyo," Niko protested. "He should live by the code of bushido as well, but look what he did to you. He has no compassion at all. All he thinks about is himself."

I thought of his idle comment about pulling Niko's teeth and shuddered. She was far more accurate than she knew.

"I know. A lot of samurai are the same." I was absurdly frustrated that I couldn't explain it to Niko and finally fell back on something I guessed she would understand. "Perhaps it's because I'm a woman. I'm not just samurai, I'm onna-bugeisha. That's means I consider far more than just obeying the words of the code. I have to live by the spirit of it as well and do what I think is right."

As I said it, I realized I was speaking no more than the truth. I was astonished by the revelation. Niko put her head on one side, thinking about it, then nodded.

We walked on in perfect understanding.

"Do you have to go back to Lord Akafumu's court?" she asked finally. "I didn't like it there. Even the servants looked at me as I was dirt and walked around me, making sure they didn't touch me. And I liked *him* even less."

"I don't think we'll need to go back," I said. "We'll listen for any rumors that circulate about him and then decide. But I believe it won't be long before we hear that the great Lord Akafumu is suffering from some strange malady that the doctors can neither diagnose nor cure."

"Good," Niko said with great satisfaction. "Is it those pills you gave to him? Were they poison?" Oh, but she was sharp!

"Not poison, no. They're meant to prevent pain. But if a

man takes too many of them, he will find he can't live without them. When Akafumu has finished the pills I gave him today, he'll crave more. And when he can't get them, his body will demand them until he can think of nothing else. He'll send his men looking for Kamakiri the anma, but she'll have disappeared, and there's nowhere else he can get the pills.

"I think a very strong man could overcome the spell the pills impose, but even for them, it would be very terrible. And Akafumu is weak. He can't stand pain, and my guess is that he'll turn to opium for consolation. When he finds his pipe isn't as good as the pills, he'll take more and more in an effort to get the same results. He'll get to the stage very soon where he can't make a decision, can't do anything at all. He has no future. He'll be enslaved to his drug."

"But he'll still be alive," Niko protested. "After what he's done to you, shouldn't you have killed him?"

"Better this way, you blood-thirsty child." I smiled. "His life will never be the same again. He has many sons. Sons who would be delighted to inherit his wealth and position without waiting for his death. When they see their father is no longer the man he was, they'll fight amongst themselves to take his place. The family will tear itself to pieces. The shogun will be forced to step in. He may side with one of the sons and put Akafumu aside for him. If he does that, the other sons will be jealous. There will never be any certainty for the new daimyo. But the shogun may not do that. He is a man who loves wealth and power. He may decide to give Akafumu's estate and title to one of his favorites. Or instead, he might decide to simply take Akafumu's land and title for himself. If he does either, no man would dare argue with him.

"Whatever happens, Akafumu will spend the rest of his

days as a ruined man who must sit in the corner of what was his own courtyard and watch his ancient and noble family being destroyed around him. Now tell me it would have been better to kill him!"

"Probably not," Niko said cheerfully. "So, what do we do now? Do we just sit and wait for your ninja to come back home?"

"Most certainly not. There's something I have to do before I can move on." Something Niko had said earlier had made me realize I had left a loose thread. A thread that had to be tied off before I could progress. And now was the time to address it. "You can stay here in the house for a while. I have to go and see the *kannushi* at Jokan-Ji Temple."

"And what brings you to see me so soon?" The kannushi's voice sounded slightly disappointed. "Our friend will barely have arrived in Kyoto. I doubt he will have had time to attend to any business yet. Has something happened? Do you need to get an urgent message to him?"

"No. I understand it's too early to expect to hear from him," I said quickly. "And I haven't come to you to ask you to contact him for me."

The kannushi looked exactly like all the other monks. I had been expecting him to be different; he was shinobi by training and presumably inclination. I had anticipated someone who still bore the marks of a warrior. This man was small and slight, his face unremarkable except for its tranquility. I wondered if I had made a mistake and then saw the shrewd look in his eyes and I relaxed. Yo trusted this man; if he did, then so should I.

"I see. Then why have you come to me, daughter? Is something amiss with the house?"

"No, not at all. I'm deeply grateful that you allow me to stay there." I spoke quickly. "I've come to ask you a favor, kannushi."

"Ask," he said simply.

His expression did not change as I explained what I needed. When I finished speaking, he was silent for a long time. My hopes sank when he finally spoke.

"I am a Buddhist priest, child. You should know that the fourth precept of Buddhism—the *Theravada*—instructs that an adherent of the Lord Buddha must abstain from falsehood. Because of that, I cannot do as you ask."

I bowed deeply. "I apologize, kannushi. I hadn't thought of my request in that way. Thank you for your time. I will leave you."

Before I could rise from my knees, the kannushi's voice stopped me.

"Sit, child. I'm sure our mutual friend told you that in a former life I was shinobi." I nodded. "I have put all that behind me now. But it does mean that I am perhaps a little more worldly than my fellow priests." He was smiling, as though something unsaid was amusing him. "As I told you, I cannot commit to a falsehood. But perhaps there may be a way that I can help you."

I watched him and waited in silence, busy with my own thoughts.

Niko's innocent words had reminded me that I had left something undone. When she had told me that the rumor in the Floating World was that I—the Lady Keiko—had committed suicide, I was delighted. If I no longer existed, then I was free to do as I liked.

On reflection, I understood that there was one serious

problem with my reasoning. The Floating World might believe that I no longer walked the earth, but I doubted that the gossip would have reached Tadatomo's ears. He would think I was still alive, and no doubt he was still expecting to marry me once my grief had abated. But how long would he wait? Eventually, he would try to find me. When it seemed I had disappeared without a trace, the natural thing for him to do would be to turn to the shogun to help him find me. I shuddered at the thought. Nobody would dare to lie to the shogun. Ironically, it was entirely possible that he might hire some of Yo's shinobi colleagues to track me down. If—or rather, when—the shogun discovered me, all my plans would be dead. I would be forced to marry Tadatomo. Or actually commit suicide. And I had no intention of doing either.

The kannushi's voice broke my reverie.

"I cannot lie for you, daughter," he said thoughtfully. "I understand that your cause is a just one. But you are sitting in front of me. How, then, could I send a message to Lord Tadatomo to tell him that I have buried your body in my temple?"

I was deeply ashamed. Of course this good man couldn't go against his religion for me. I would have to find another way. I bowed my head.

"I am deeply sorry, kannushi. I should have thought of that before I insulted you by asking for the impossible," I said humbly. Even with my head bent to the tatami, I thought I saw a flicker of interest in his face and I paused, my hopes rising.

"Your penitence does you great credit, daughter," he said gravely. "I think you must know that this temple is unique in that we care for the bodies of those poor unfortunates who die serving the Floating World." I nodded my understanding. "We take care of them all. Sometimes, the sad creatures come to the temple and die here, of hunger or cold or both. I often think that it is not their hurts that finish them, but the knowledge that they are fated to reach the end of their earthly existence here. They know we will treat their body with a respect that was never shown to them elsewhere in the world, and so they come here and die with the dignity that was denied to them in life."

I heard the bitterness in his words. This was truly a good man. I felt ashamed of my own trivial desires.

"I have money," I said quickly. "Could I give a donation to help your work?"

"You can. We have patrons who are sure that their donations will bring good fortune on them, or persuade the Lord Buddha to grant them what they desire. They're wrong, of course. Buddha does not care about money. Still, I take it of course. Otherwise we couldn't go on." I flinched, and he smiled kindly. "I understand that your motives are different, daughter. And because of that, I also think that there is perhaps a way Jokan-Ji Temple can help you."

He paused and I spoke into the silence.

"If it can be done without going against the Fourth Precept..." I shrugged, deeply uncomfortable. My family had been Buddhists for generations, but in name only. We resorted to the religion when it suited us; we observed the main festivals, but more as an excuse for amusement than anything. A Buddhist priest would never be turned away empty-handed, but what was a bowl full of food to us? I found myself wondering if it was possible that the Lord Buddha was using this as an opportunity to reprimand me for my neglect. I was sure the kannushi had read my thoughts when he spoke.

"The Lord Buddha forgives much, daughter. How could

it be otherwise when he has seen fit to allow me to serve his temple? A man who has spent the whole of his life lying and cheating—yes, and killing—with no motive except for my own gain."

I thought of Yo and grimaced. "But you were shinobi," I protested. "That was the way of your life."

"And now my life is here," he said simply. "The way to enlightenment is different for all of us, daughter. I understand that you seek revenge. In the past, I would have done just as you are doing. That is the nature of mankind. Each man—and woman—must do what they think is right at the time. As a priest, I cannot condone your actions. As a man —and a man who was once shinobi—I understand and sympathize with you."

I felt both comforted and relieved by his words.

"Can you help me, then? As the shinobi you once were?"

"I cannot." I closed my eyes in disappointment. "But it may be that circumstances allow you to be helped with no assistance at all from me. And if that is so, then who can say it isn't karma?"

I chose my words very carefully. "Can you tell me how this is to happen?"

"A poor unfortunate was brought to us only this morning." I was deeply disappointed. The kannushi was an old man. Clearly his thoughts were wandering. "She was left in front of the main door to the temple, as so many are. It was impossible to see how she met her death. She seemed to be well-nourished and there were no marks of violence on her body. But she was most certainly dead. Oddly, she looked very much like you."

I was nodding automatically when I realized what he had said. A small flame of hope made me catch my breath.

"She was dressed in rags, of course. No ornaments, not

even a pair of sandals on her feet. When somebody is left with us like this, we always wait for a few days, just in case somebody comes forward to tell us who she was. It happens very rarely, but who knows?"

"Indeed." I spoke into the silence. "I believe my adopted younger sister, Niko, knows many people in the Floating World. Perhaps she might be able to recognize the unfortunate woman? And no doubt her soul is still close by. Do you think it would give her satisfaction to have something nice at the very end?"

I put my hand up to my hair and tugged out the clasp from the back. It was a pretty thing, gold set with pearls. I held it out to the kannushi reluctantly. It had belonged to my mother and had initially been given to my elder sister, Emiko. But Emiko had never liked it and had passed it on to me without a second thought. And now I was passing it on, but this time, I hoped for a good purpose.

"That is most generous of you, Kamakiri." It was the first time the *kannushi* had used my name, and I hoped it signified approval. "I'm sure you're right. In life, no doubt the girl was very fond of ornaments. I will have it placed in her hair. And it would be very good if your younger sister could visit the poor creature. Even better if she could put a name to the unfortunate."

We smiled at each other in perfect understanding. I would speak to Niko as soon as I got home. She would, I felt sure, be delighted to be involved in my scheme. She would identify the body that looked so much like me as the missing Lady Keiko with appropriate grief.

"And if it turns out that the gossip of the Flower and Willow World is confirmed, and that the Lady Keiko is indeed no longer with us?" I asked. "In that case, surely it would only be right that Lord Tadatomo be told that his bride is dead?"

"One step at a time, daughter," the kannushi reprimanded me. "If karma says these things should be so, then no man should stand in the way." I nodded seriously and hid a smile as I saw the gleam in his eyes. *Kannushi* he might be now, but I was confident that in his dreams, he was still shinobi. "Your Niko will view her. If she is certain that she is the Lady Keiko, then word will most certainly be sent to Lord Tadatomo. May I ask if he knows his betrothed very well?"

I understood his meaning and spoke seriously. "No. In fact, I believe that he met Lady Keiko only once, when she was much younger."

"Excellent," he said promptly. I was about to take my leave when a thought came to me and I paused.

"Kannushi, may I see the poor woman who may be Lady Keiko?"

The kannushi seemed surprised. I thought for a moment that he was about to say no, then he shrugged.

"Of course. It seems there's nobody to mourn her. Her spirit will be pleased to receive you."

I stared at the woman's body. I felt great pity, and also great apprehension. In life, she might have been my sister. I shivered; in fact, she was so like me that it was almost like looking at my reflection. In death, her face was very tranquil. The kannushi handed me a bowl of clean water and a cloth, and I understood that I was to moisten her mouth, to give her the water of the last moment. It should have been done by her relatives just before she died;

I felt honored that the duty should fall to me. The kannushi handed me my clasp, and I pushed it carefully into her hair.

"Please, may I pay for a decent white kimono to clothe her in?" The poor woman was dressed in a tattered kimono, and her skin looked dull and uncared for. "And if she could be washed, I would appreciate it."

"Of course. All will be done as it should be. If Niko identifies her as Lady Keiko, then we will get word to Lord Tadatomo immediately. It may be that he will wish to claim her body and have her cremated and her ashes buried on his estate." I shuddered at the thought. That felt wrong to me. I was sure this poor unknown would want her earthly remains to lie next to those she had known in life.

"I hope not," I said impulsively.

"I doubt it myself," the kannushi said impassively. "We must tell Lord Tadatomo truthfully that we don't know how she died. If she stays here, we will intern her in the yujo graveyard."

I knew that he shared my wishes. I waited until we had left my dead "sister" before I asked my final favor.

"I don't believe I will need to use the temple's house very much in the future. But unless you have a pressing need for it, I would be very grateful if I could keep it."

"Our absent friend has been most generous in paying the rent on the house. It's yours for as long as you need it."

"Thank you," I said simply.

The kannushi escorted me to the door of the temple. As I walked away, he spoke very softly.

"Take care, Kamakiri. I don't want to find somebody else who looks like you on the steps of my temple."

TWENTY

Time doesn't care if
We are rich or poor. Our life
Is not in our hands

I was ready. I was sure everything had been done that was needed, but I hesitated in my doorway as if there was an invisible barrier in front of me. I was torn. Partly, I was elated. I was about to start my new life with nothing to hinder me. How many women in this world could truly claim that they were as free as I was? There was no past to tug at me, nobody to order me to do this or that. Lady Keiko was dead; her bridegroom had accepted the word of the young priest who had delivered the message. He would mourn her passing. Or so he said. Odd, then, that he was perfectly happy for her to be interred in the yujo cemetery. Just as Lady Keiko was no more, it appeared that the anma Kamakiri had vanished from the Floating World.

I would listen carefully for any gossip about Lord Akafumu. In any event, I was satisfied that he was already on the path to irredeemable addiction. He was in the past, and I would put him out of my thoughts. Truly, my future was my own at last. I was free to recreate myself in whatever image I desired. Exhilarating as the knowledge was, it was also terrifying. I had nobody to blame except myself if my plans went wrong. Niko slipped her hand in my mine; I found her touch oddly comforting.

"Ready, Kamakiri?" she asked softly. I nodded.

My adopted name was the one thing I was carrying with me into my still newer world. *Mantis.* It seemed appropriate for what I was about to do, and a good omen. And apart from that, it felt right in my mouth. Lady Keiko was dead. Kamakiri the anma was gone, but she had been good for me. I would honor her passing with her name. And why not? Who was ever going to associate a wretched, blind anma with a woman who dripped jewels and walked as if she owned the Floating World?

"That poor girl!" Niko had been loud in her sorrow when she returned from Jokan-Ji Temple. "When I first saw her, for a moment, I was sure it was you. I had no problem at all convincing the priest about that, I promise!" With the resilience of childhood, her mood changed in a flash. "So, now that you're dead and Lord Akafumu's out of the way, what are we going to do? Are we really going to be ronin and roam about the country righting wrongs?"

Her enthusiasm was endearing.

"I'm sorry to disillusion you, Niko. But no, we're going to stay right here in the Floating World. We have a lot to do, and if possible, I want to do it before Yo comes back."

"Why? Isn't he going to be happy about it?" The child was so shrewd, I wondered if she had read my thoughts.

"Probably not," I said honestly. "But that doesn't matter. As of today, Kamakiri the anma is no more."

"Yes, elder sister." Niko waited hopefully for me to tell

her about my plans. When I explained, her face broke into a huge grin.

"Leave all to me, elder sister," she said cheerfully. "I will take care of everything."

All the arrangements had been made so smoothly, I was amazed. Niko's knowledge of the Floating World helped, of course, but I was suspicious that she had managed everything so well on her own. So suspicious that I suspected the kannushi must have had a hand in it. When I challenged her with it, Niko turned innocent eyes on me.

"How could Aishi help us, Kamakiri? He rarely leaves the temple. He would know little of the practical workings of the Floating World."

My suspicions intensified. How did Niko know the kannushi was called Aisha? He had never mentioned his name to me. Then common sense came to my aid. Just as Yo had insisted that I knew nothing about his mission, not even where I could find him if I needed him, I understood that Niko and the kannushi were protecting me now.

I smiled and let it go.

In any event, whoever had actually made the arrangements for my new life had done it superbly.

Niko left our old home in the temple house in the morning. A short time later, Kamakiri the anma entered an elegant little house in a reasonably quiet part of the Floating World. She was never seen again, and in her place Kamakiri, the sumptuous oiran, a courtesan of the highest caliber, emerged. I was deeply thankful that Yo was not here to see the transformation. He would not approve, and I had no time to waste in arguing with him.

I had thought long and very hard about what I wanted to do. What I was *going* to do. My first, overwhelming priority had been to seek vengeance for the destruction of my family's honor. Now that I was sure I had achieved that in destroying Akafumu, I could move on.

Akafumu had not been alone in humiliating Lady Keiko. There had been others, and now the time was coming for them to receive justice for their actions. I anticipated their downfall eagerly.

In spite of my pleasure at the knowledge of what was to come, I still didn't feel at all comfortable in my new persona. I put my hand up to pat my vast wig uneasily and Niko frowned at me.

"Don't disturb it," she scolded. "It's perfect as it is."

"You don't think it has too many ornaments?" I questioned. "It seems to be bristling with them. I feel like a porcupine fish."

"You look wonderful," Niko insisted.

"Not too much makeup?" I felt as if I was plastered in white paint so thick it would crack if I smiled. Niko had painted my lips bright red. I had to resist the urge to lick them constantly. When she had shown me my face in the mirror, I didn't recognize myself.

"You are an oiran, Kamakiri," she explained patiently. "You must look like one. Without the expensive clothes and makeup and wig, you could be mistaken for a common woman of pleasure, a yujo. It has to be obvious that you are something much better class than that. Especially if you're going to break with tradition and parade yourself around the streets." She sounded so disapproving, it amused me.

"I have to become known," I pointed out. "And I have no intention of getting a place in a teahouse. I need to be completely different from every other oiran in the Floating World. Very special. And it's essential that I'm able to do what I want, not what my master tells me. Besides, I could hardly walk into a teahouse and demand to become their oiran, could I?"

"By the gods, no!" Niko was clearly horrified by the thought. "The other girls would never stand for an unknown usurping the place of the most sought after girl in the house."

"You see? I have no alternative. We go, Niko. By the end of this evening, I want the Floating World to be buzzing with yet more rumors. This time, about a new oiran, one who is the most unique oiran ever to be seen in the place. Will you follow me, please? And remember, no matter who speaks to you, no matter what they ask you, stay silent. I want to be a mystery until it suits me to reveal myself."

I stood very straight. No humble hunching of the shoulders and downward glance for me! My kimono was so gorgeous, it dazzled the eye. Lady Keiko would have died of shame if she had been seen wearing such gaudy robes. Kamakiri the oiran paraded proudly, her head held high. I walked slowly, but with confident strides, more like a young man about town than a woman. Unlike every other woman on the street, I looked at men I passed fully in the face and did not drop my gaze. My sumptuous kimono was tied very tightly to emphasize my slenderness and height. After a few minutes, I began to enjoy myself and relaxed easily into my role.

Men and women alike stared at me. I heard the murmurs that followed our progress.

"Who is she?"

"Where did she come from?"

"What's she called?"

"Why hasn't she been seen before?"

"Why isn't she in a teahouse?"

"How does she dare walk the streets with only her maid for protection?"

"Whoever she is, she's very glamorous."

Within moments, Niko was approached by a man. He walked alongside us for the length of a street, pestering her with questions.

"Who is your mistress? Is she for hire? What's she called?"

Wouldn't you like to know, I thought smugly. Becoming bored with the man's attention, I gestured to Niko to turn aside into a tearoom. I was delighted when a crowd immediately gathered outside, watching me sip my tea. When I rose to go—leaving Niko to pay the reckoning, as though money was beneath my notice—the crowd parted before me. One or two of the men even bowed to me.

Many of them followed us home. That pleased me greatly. It was essential that my house should be known. Niko told me that there were still some men lingering outside when we were ready for bed. She also said that the teahouse owner had refused payment.

"He said it was honor enough that an oiran of such magnificence as you should grace his humble establishment!" she said gleefully. "The gossip will be all over the Floating World by tomorrow."

"Good," I said absently. "Would you take Matsuo out, please? He must be in need of a pee, poor dog."

Niko was still full of the excitement of our excursion. I could feel the unrest vibrating from her. She jumped to her feet at once and clapped her hands at Matsuo. He glanced at me for confirmation, and when I nodded, he walked after Niko, his tail wagging happily.

I blew the lamp out when Niko had gone. The closed air in the room felt as if it was drugged from the scented oil. I watched a spiral of smoke rise from the wick and waited until it had dispersed before I moved to the shoji. The screens were made of silk, opaque for anybody looking in, but far more sheer from the inside looking out. That had amused me when I had first seen our new house. Had its former occupant had the screens made specially, I wondered, so she could see without being seen? It suited my purposes perfectly, and I was pleased. There was a young moon in the clear sky, and I could see effortlessly when my eyes adjusted. I stayed very still, barely breathing. I knew that somebody was out there. The same somebody who had followed us all night, always keeping just out of my line of sight. A number of men had clustered around us continually, but they had wanted to be noticed by the new oiran, and their presence had been obvious. The unknown somebody had stayed in the shadows.

For a moment, I wondered if it might be Yo, returned early and amusing himself by watching what I was up to before he announced himself. I dismissed the idea almost at once. At our first meeting, I had only been aware of Yo's presence because he had wanted me to know he was there. If he had not, even I—with my sharply honed senses—would never have suspected him. No. This man was clumsy. He had kept himself concealed, but with no great skill. He was not shinobi.

I waited. I cast no shadow in the darkened room and was completely still. My breathing was so shallow, I could barely hear it myself. Finally, my patience was rewarded. Unlike me, he had not been able to wait. I opened my eyes wide, trying to make him out. A tall man who walked with his shoulders hunched. Dark grey robes that merged into the darkness far better than black would have done. I could tell from the set of his head that he was staring at the house.

Did I know him? I doubted that even a cat would have been able to make out his features; I certainly could not. I searched my memory for the way he walked, the way he stood, and an infuriating itch of recollection told me that he was known to me. I willed him to walk forward, but at the same moment, I heard Niko's voice calling to Matsuo, and the man turned and walked away briskly.

I had a moment to think that was odd before Niko came back in. If he had been shinobi, he would have melted back into the shadows without so much as disturbing the air around him. If he were samurai, he would have stood his ground and made Niko walk around him. If he was one of the men who had been fascinated by me earlier, I was sure he would have taken his chance to try and bribe Niko to get some information about me.

Who was he? I didn't know, and it irritated me.

Perhaps that was why I slept badly.

Matsuo curled up beside me, yelping and twitching as he pursued something in his dreams. I poked him in the ribs and he subsided with a deep sigh. Thoroughly awake now, I got up and stared out of the shoji for a long time, but I saw nothing but the shadows, coiling like sleeping monsters.

Matsuo grunted enquiringly, and when I didn't go back to my futon, he stretched and walked out. I heard him lapping at his water. I could hear Niko's even breathing. The child slept like the dead. For a selfish moment, I wondered about waking her, just for the pleasure of having somebody to talk to. But I did not. Instead, I simply sat until I heard the bells chime the toll for the hour of the rat, and then I lay on my futon and wondered all over again.

TWENTY-ONE

What use is silver
And gold when I have all that
I want except you?

"Another one!" Niko was jubilant. The bell outside our house jangled and she came back with a folded sheet of paper in her hands. She handed it to me unopened, a frown clouding her face. "Do you think that you could find the time to teach me to read, Kamakiri?" She sounded humble, and I looked at her in surprise.

"Why? Not many women can read," I pointed out. "My own elder sister, Emiko, can barely read and it never bothered her at all."

"But you can read," Niko said. "Can you write as well?"

"I can," I acknowledged. I can read very well, and I am very proud of my beautiful calligraphy. Isamu had caught me looking at one of the books in Father's collection when I was very young. He had teased me that there was no point in looking at something I couldn't understand, and in a fit of pique, I had demanded that he teach me to read. It must have amused him, as the next day I found he had hired a young man to teach me to both read and write. I had found the lessons tedious and complicated, and it was only the knowledge that Isamu would gloat if I gave in that made me determined to go on. After a while, I was glad I had persevered, and soon I realized that my stylish kanji were better by far than anything even Isamu could produce.

"Will you teach me, then?" Niko asked hopefully. She dug her toe in the tatami and looked down, and I understood that my bold, spirited younger sister was, for once, embarrassed. "I need to be able to read at least. When I go shopping, the merchants always have to tell me what the prices are because I can't read what it says on the goods. They could overcharge me for everything and I wouldn't know any different. And if we go outside the Floating World, I would be lost because I can't even read the street signs. Besides..." She paused and I knew the real reason for her request was coming. "I would like to be as skilled as you are, elder sister."

I was touched. "I can't teach you to read and write, Niko," I said. Her lips quivered and I went on quickly. "Teaching is a very difficult thing to do. I wouldn't know where to start. But I'm sure if I ask Aisha, he will find one of his monks who could teach you. Would you like that?"

She beamed at me, all distress forgotten. "When?" she demanded.

"I'll ask him next time I see him, I promise. In the meantime, could you make me some tea?"

I read the note she had handed to me while she busied herself with the kettle. It was short, and I read it quickly and put it down, disappointed. Like all the other missives that had been delivered this morning, it was from a would-be patron. And like most of the rest, it had obviously been written by a professional calligrapher. I was even beginning to recognize individual calligrapher's styles. This was the third from the same hand. Cynically, I thought that the tradesmen of the Floating World should be on their knees before their household shrines, giving thanks for the arrival of the new *oiran*.

Like all the rest, this letter protested how my beauty had dazzled the applicant. My lips twisted in a mocking smile. What fools these men were; could they really be deceived so easily by a layer of paint and some gaudy clothes? How strange that in what I still thought of as my "real" life I had been regarded as completely unattractive; the plain, insignificant younger sister who was kept hidden away. I watched Niko fidgeting as she waited impatiently for the water to boil and my thoughts strayed. Yo found me beautiful. The knowledge pleased me greatly, but he was my lover. Of course he found me pleasing. And now, it seemed, other men also found me lovely to look at. I wondered why now? My sister, Emiko, had never worn makeup, and her clothes were drab compared Kamakiri the oiran's flamboyant kimono and hugely knotted obi. Yet nobody had ever questioned that Emiko was beautiful. When I had been Lady Keiko, just as when I had been Kamakiri the anma, nobody had spared me a glance. Except for Adam, of course. But no doubt his gaijin eyes saw beauty differently from everybody else.

Now, I was Kamakiri the oiran, and men who had never even spoken to me lusted after me. I was bewildered; all three were the same woman. All three were me. Was it possible that the answer lay within me? I turned the thought around in my head. When I had lived my first life, on my father's estate, Emiko had always told me I was ugly, and I had believed her. Was it because I saw myself as being of no consequence that the rest of my world perceived me in the same way? Just as when I had acted the part of Kamakiri the anma, I had presented myself to the world as a humble blind woman of no consequence and that was how I was accepted.

And now? Now, I walked proudly, as if I expected men to look at me with hunger in their eyes. And strangely, that is what they did. Now, I was Kamakiri the *oiran*, a special woman who knew she could demand what—or who—she wanted and get it without question. Was the answer to the riddle as simple as that? That others saw me as I chose to be seen?

I put the conundrum aside for the moment. I would think about it later, when I had less urgent calls on my thoughts.

I glanced at the latest letter again and sighed. I threw it down casually. Niko glanced at me but did not speak, clearly deciding it was best not to disturb me. I barely noticed; I was lost in my thoughts.

I had taken my revenge on Lord Akafumu for the wrongs he had inflicted on me and my noble house. And at the same time, I had avenged Reiki for his treatment of her. Akafumu was no longer of interest to me.

But now three other men had taken Akafumu's place. Just as he had insulted me when he laughed at my attempts to give me what was mine by right, so those three men had treated me with contempt. They had stripped me of my honor without even giving it a thought. I licked my lips, eager for the sight of the names I longed for. Even though my prison in the Hidden House had been dim, and the men who came to see me had been shielded by Hana's artful shadows, I knew their names. How could I ever forget them?

There had been many men in that dreadful time. Some had come to look at me more than once. But there were only three that interested me now. The final trio, who had decided to bid for me. The three men that Hana knew could afford her price. These she had allowed to touch me as much as they wanted. To squeeze my breasts and slide their fingers into my sex. To sample my delights before they decided that I was worth buying. Hana had called them all "lord." Even now, I could recollect the gloating note in her voice as she mocked them with her excessive courtesy. And all of them had simply accepted it as their due. What fools they were!

I saw their faces in my mind and matched a name to each.

The youngest was a man probably barely in his twenties. Hana had called him Lord Sato. By the way he slouched and stared around as if he was wondering why he had honored the Hidden House with his presence, I guessed that he was the spoiled son of at least a minor noble family. He had tried to disguise his interest in me. But I had seen it clearly enough in his eyes. He had not only fingered my black moss, but had also fondled my buttocks and scratched his nails cruelly right inside my anus. My lips peeled back from my teeth in a primal snarl as I remembered how he had made me feel soiled by his very touch.

Number two was Lord Hara. Out of all of the men, he had puzzled me. He had said little, merely listening to Hana extol my virtues. He, too, had walked around me, inspecting me with eyes and fingers. His hands had been icy, the palms oddly rough. I couldn't pin a class on him. Not noble. Nor did he strike me as being a merchant. He had money, a great deal of money, or he would not have been there, bidding for me. There was something cold about him, something ruthless. Before he left me, he licked my neck, watching me all the time for a response. When I stayed still as stone, he smiled and told Hana I would do very well. I tried not to think about what he had in mind.

The third and last was Ikeda. Not a daimyo, nor a samurai. If he had been, I would have placed him instantly. But possibly he might have been the son of some noble's favorite concubine. He had the air about him of somebody who expected to be obeyed instantly. He had loitered in the shadows just inside the screen door and had simply stared at me, with Hana hovering at his side. Out of all of them, he had been the one who asked Hana the most about me. Because he hadn't wanted to probe me, at first, I had thought him kinder than the others, and I had even felt a little pity for his dreadful appearance. Until Hana told me spitefully after he had gone that he was riddled with baidoku, or "plum poison." The disease takes its name from the appearance of the cankers that appear on a man's tree of flesh in the early stages of the incurable illness; they are thought to resemble plum blossom clusters. Such an innocent name for a truly dreadful disease.

"He's undergone treatment with mercury several times, but it had no lasting effect. Now, he's convinced that the only true cure for his disease is intercourse with a virgin. He's fool enough to take my word that you are still whole and that's why he's here." Even Hana seemed a little uncomfortable about the terrible death she was condemning me to if Ikeda won. She shrugged and added, "He's not the wealthiest of all of them. He may well not win you."

Out of the three, Ikeda was the one I would recognize instantly. Once he was seen, it would have been impossible to forget him. Although he lurked in the shadows as he watched me, I had seen that his face was the stuff of nightmares. His terrible disease had progressed to the extent that his nose was almost rotted away. He constantly sniffed, wiping his face with a piece of silk. At first, I had thought the marks on his face and neck were smallpox pits. When Hana told me about the baidoku, I guessed that they were yet another aspect of his vile condition. His voice was odd as well. He spoke thickly, as though his words were fighting their way through a mouthful of food. I guessed he smoked heavily; even from a distance, the odor of his pipe hung about his clothes and hair. As he watched me, he fumbled at his obi and drew a pipe from an ornate ivory kiseruzutsu pipe holder. Hana lit it for him from a candle, and when I saw his face more clearly in the wavering light, I shuddered.

It was with minimal regret that I decided I would have to exclude Ikeda from my plans at the moment. He had wanted a virgin. Kamakiri the oiran would have no allure for him. The most sought after oiran combined the talents of a geisha with the attractions of a yujo, but at the end of the day, they were still top-flight women of pleasure. Ikeda would hardly be lured by me. I would return to him later, when I was satisfied that the other two men had received their just reprisal.

I felt instinctively that the remaining two would be interested in Kamakiri the oiran. Something told me that that they had wanted Hana's offering at least in part because I was both rare and sought after. Both men had been interested in beating the competition, in obtaining the unobtainable. Kamakiri the oiran was a similar proposition. A brilliant new oiran who had set the Floating World on fire with gossip. An oiran who was said to be waiting for the single patron who she would choose because she felt he was the very best.

Hana had told me that all the other men who had been

to see me had dropped out of the competition when my price went beyond their purses, leaving these three to bid up my final price between them. Yo had helped me escape before the victor could triumph, and I had been intensely grateful for that. But now, the time had come when I would seek out those three remaining men who had wanted to buy me and turn me into their slave. Find them and destroy them, just as I had already destroyed Akafumu.

Niko passed me my tea, and I turned my thoughts away from my prey. "We will go out for our walk again tonight, Niko." I smiled at her. "Just as last night, you will not answer any questions."

"How long do we do this for? What's the point?" Niko asked. I wished I could tell her, but caution held me silent. I wanted to keep Niko away from any possible danger. I knew that the three men I was seeking were not only rich, but well connected and important men, as were all Hana's patrons. I was playing with fire, and I had to tread very carefully if I was to triumph and walk away safely.

We would take our evening walk, night after night, until I caught the attention of those I was seeking. If I failed, then I would be forced to find my quarry in some other way. I hoped that would not be necessary; it was too much like setting a trap and walking into it myself.

"We will do it for as long as it takes," I said simply. Niko puffed out her cheeks and then shrugged her shoulders, smiling. The movement said more clearly than words could that I was her elder sister, and as far as she was concerned, anything I said or did was correct. I was touched.

There was already a crowd waiting for us when we left the house. Niko's impatience was contagious. I held my head high and walked with apparent indifference to the throng that flowed behind us, but inwardly I was exasperated. Surely, at least one of the trio I wanted must have heard the gossip about the amazing new oiran? Heard and been intrigued enough to take a look. We were almost at the teahouse where we had stopped yesterday when I heard somebody whispering to Niko. My heart missed a beat as I caught a name. *Hara-san.* I glanced around lazily, as if I was simply bored, and saw a man who looked like a well-dressed servant close to Niko. I cursed my own stupidity. Of course my victims would not show themselves. *They* would expect *me* to allow myself to be summoned to their presence.

The servant pressed a piece of paper into Niko's hand and then turned abruptly and thrust his way through the crowd that hemmed us in. He was gone in a moment. I took the note from her and read it casually, my expression betraying nothing of my inner joy. Hara hoped that I would honor him by visiting his home. I crumpled the paper between my fingers and tossed it aside as if it bored me. I had him! I was so pleased that my plan was beginning to move forward that we were inside the teahouse before I remembered the shadow that had followed us home yesterday and waited outside the house. I concentrated my mind on feeling if he was nearby. I was puzzled when I sensed nobody.

When we finished with our tea and cakes, two of my followers competed loudly and at length to pay our reckoning. I allowed the victor—who was grossly overcharged by the teahouse owner—the smallest of smiles. I almost laughed aloud at the obvious delight in his face. What fools these men were.

I allowed myself the hope that Hara would be just as easily deceived.

TWENTY-TWO

> I watch you smile in
> Your sleep, and I wonder, is
> It me you dream of?

"**Y**ou will be safe on your own? What if somebody comes with a message? Who's going to answer the bell?"

Niko fussed like a hen with wandering chicks. I shook my head at her. Now that the time for her first lesson at the temple had come, she was intensely nervous.

"Go," I said firmly. "I shall manage without you for a day. Take Matsuo with you. There's far more danger for a young girl walking alone than there is for me in my own house. Listen to the monk and do as he tells you."

She went, finally, slouching and with many a backward glance. Matsuo walked obediently at her heels. I felt very alone without either of them, but I knew it was necessary.

As soon as Niko was out of sight, I drew water from the well and heated it. I washed as carefully as I could from a bowl and then put my makeup on. Not as thickly as I had worn it for our walks, but still enough to disguise my real face. I untied my hair and brushed it until it hung thick and lustrous. It was as far from Kamakiri the anma's scraped back hair as it could possibly be. Finally, I changed my plain house robe for a beautiful kimono and then simply sat and waited.

He would come. I could feel it.

I had awoken in the darkest hours of the night, bewildered as I wondered why I could feel my heart pounding against my ribs. I lifted my head and listened. There was nothing except for the murmur of the Floating World in the distance. The city that never slept, Isamu had called it. Rightly so. I closed my eyes and concentrated on letting all thoughts slip away from me. When my mind was empty, I listened with my essential being, but there was still nothing. I was confused. Something had startled me into wakefulness. A dream, perhaps? I could remember nothing. But I trusted my instincts. I waited quietly, staring into the darkness.

Complete relaxation had me trembling on the verge of sleep again when the answer I was seeking slid into my mind. I knew who had waited outside yesterday. No shinobi, this. Not even one of the admiring throng who had crowded closely around us during the evening walk. I smiled as a face formed itself out of the shadows.

Adam. The gaijin who had been kind to Kamakiri the anma. The man whose trust I had repaid by stealing his morphine pills. Did he know that Kamakiri the oiran was also Kamakiri the anma? I had no way of knowing for sure, but I felt instinctively that he had not made the connection. But clearly he had seen Kamakiri the oiran and had been so entranced that he had hovered outside my house for hours, silent and—or so he thought—unseen. I smiled as the thought came to me that it was also highly unlikely that he would recognize me for another reason entirely. I had no doubt that to him all Japanese women looked much the same.

He would be back. If he had found his plain anma attractive, how was he supposed to resist the lure of the sumptuous oiran who bore the same name?

I felt his presence when he drew close to the house. I felt good fortune was smiling on me. If he had chosen to arrive at my door when Niko was there, I knew she would have disapproved of him deeply. And she would, no doubt, have made her dislike known very vocally. I felt his hesitation as he hovered outside, unsure whether to call out or ring the bell. I was tempted to call and tell him to come in, but I held my words patiently. I was an oiran now. I had neither the special skills of an onna-bugeisha nor the acute senses of a blind anma. I had to remember that. It would be easy to make a mistake.

The bell jangled finally. I waited until I guessed he was about to ring again, and then called out for him to enter.

"Good day, sir." I stood and bowed, pretending to cover amazement that it was a gaijin who had entered my house.

"Good day."

He hesitated, clearly at a loss for how to continue. I watched him and hid a smile. I could see his discomfort; it was quite touching. And also obvious was the fact that he didn't recognize me.

"I'm sorry," he said finally. "I think I must have made a mistake. I saw you walking and I thought I knew you. But I was wrong. I apologize for intruding on you."

He bowed deeply and turned as if he was about to leave but still hesitated. One word from me would be enough. But did I want him to stay? Thoughts flew through my mind so rapidly that they felt like lightning striking inside my head. The way Yo's slightest touch could arouse me to ecstasy; the memory of Adam's tree rearing at me like a river monster; the many hours in the night when I had awoken alone and lonely.

"Please, do not go." I spoke without conscious thought, but I was not at all surprised at myself. I understood that this moment had been inevitable since I first realized he had followed me home. "I do not believe we have met before, but as you can see, I am all alone. I would welcome a little company. Would you care to take some tea? Or perhaps sake?"

"Tea would be wonderful. Thank you."

I gestured for him to sit, and he folded his height quite gracefully. He watched as I prepared the tea things. I guessed he had seen the tea ceremony performed before, in high-class teahouses where the performers had been well-trained geisha, but I was determined that never would he have seen it done so elegantly as today. I made sure that each movement was as fluid as a butterfly stretching its wings before flight. When I finally handed him the cup of green tea, I was satisfied.

"That was quite beautiful. As is your home. I'm beginning to think that all Japanese homes are decorated in exquisite taste."

Adam sounded surprised. I lowered my head and murmured my pleasure at his words. At the same time, I was slightly annoyed. Did he think me a mere yujo? A woman of pleasure who knew—and needed to know—nothing more than how to give pleasure with her body? Oiran were more akin to geisha than yujo. Just like geisha, an oiran must be able to pleasure all of a man's senses.

She must be able to sing and dance, play the samisen with exquisite skill, and make her patron feel as if he was a god come down to earth. And, of course, she must make the mere act of serving tea into a piece of superb theater. Everything flowed through my thoughts in the time it took me to smile politely, and then I recollected what he had actually said. How many Japanese homes had he visited? It was unheard of for a gaijin to be invited to a Japanese house; had I misunderstood? I would find out, but not for a moment. First, the formalities had to be gone through.

"I am delighted to make you happy, sir. I must apologize," I added smoothly. "But I do not know the honorable gentleman's name."

"Adam." He bowed his head politely. "And you are Kamakiri-san."

I allowed my face to express astonishment that he knew my name.

"I am called Kamakiri, yes. But how did you know me?" I bit my lip, pretending confusion. "Forgive me, Adam-san. Have we met before? I cannot believe that we have, for surely I would have remembered you."

A Japanese man would have accepted the flattery at face value and been pleased. I had forgotten that a gaijin would take my words differently. Adam's face clouded.

"I thought I knew you when I saw you from a distance. But now I realize I was mistaken. Apart from anything else, if you had met this clumsy gaijin before, you would have remembered me."

"Adam-san, I beg your pardon." I spoke hurriedly, appalled at my own mistake. "I merely meant that I am newly arrived in the Floating World. I have met many people in the short time I have been here, but I have an excellent memory for faces. Had we been introduced, I am sure I would recollect you."

"I see." He stared me straight in the face. It was rude, but when this awkward gaijin did it, somehow it was touching. I watched his expression trail off from hope into confusion. How easy it was to read these foreigners! They had no idea how to keep a stone face. I hid my own surprise behind a smile as I realized I found his almost childlike openness very attractive.

"Perhaps I remind you of somebody you know?" I hinted. Adam seized on my words immediately.

"Yes, yes, you do. I know it's ridiculous, but you remind me very much of an anma who helped me when I had pain." I raised my eyebrows in a show of astonishment, and even Adam seemed to realize he had insulted me. "She was young, and very beautiful, just as you are. Oddly enough, she was also called Kamakiri."

He looked at me and smiled shyly. I thought carefully before I spoke. He had found a blind woman, dirty and dressed in rags, *beautiful*? I was astonished that any man—especially an ignorant gaijin—could look beneath the surface of a woman's appearance and see that there was loveliness beneath. I was amazed, and very touched.

"I am flattered that I remind you of somebody you cared for, Adam-san."

Had I gone too far in assuming that he had cared for his anma? Adam's face flushed, and I guessed I had not. Suddenly, I was absurdly jealous of Kamakiri the anma. It was ridiculous, of course, but the notion was there and would not go away. How dare this man prefer a destitute blind woman dressed in rags to the sumptuous oiran I was presenting to him. I almost laughed at my own silliness, but the hurt was too deep.

"My anma was very special," he said quietly. "I didn't know her for very long. She disappeared suddenly. I would have liked to have known her better."

"And do I look like her, Adam-san?" I probed. Adam blinked as if his thoughts had been far away. I was oddly disappointed when he shook his head. I would have been pleased for him to find at least an echo of his anma in me.

"I thought you did when I saw you in the street. But now that I'm closer to you, I see the resemblance was more in the way you walk, how you hold yourself. Apart from the fact that you're both tall, you don't look alike. My Kamakiri may only have been a humble anma, but she took pride in herself and her skills. She wore no makeup and her clothes were very different from yours. She was very kind to me," he added sadly.

"I see." I lowered my head, and coincidentally, my gaze fell to his lap. I remembered the rearing tree of flesh that he had presented to me—or rather, to his anma—and an itch of arousal scratched inside my belly. I remembered all too clearly wondering at the time what it would feel like to ride such a river monster. Had Yo been here, I would have dismissed the thought immediately. But Yo was not here, and Adam was.

"I must go. Thank you for your time and the tea, Kamakiri. How much do I owe you?" I winced. If nothing else, I had to teach this gaijin some manners before he insulted the wrong person and found himself skewered on the end of a sword. He was fumbling in the purse that hung from his obi. I abandoned all subtlety and put my fingers around his hand.

"Adam." I squeezed his hand firmly and he looked at me in surprise. "It's unfortunate that your anma didn't explain to you the way things are done here. You seem to be confusing me with a yujo. A woman of pleasure." I had the satisfaction of watching his face flush crimson. I spoke before he could make matters worse. "I am an oiran. Unlike a yujo, I am very, very particular about my patrons. I accept only those few I know will give me pleasure, as well as take pleasure from me. It is like the courtship dance of cranes, understand? Anybody fortunate enough to be allowed into my company must be in rhythm with me. I have as many talents as a geisha. Never offer to pay an oiran for her services. Such things are arranged discreetly."

I was almost breathless with indignation when I finished. Adam's face was deeply embarrassed. He laced his fingers in his lap and stared at the tatami.

"I'm sorry. I didn't know. I must apologize for my ignorance. We gaijin must make many mistakes without even knowing we're causing offense."

"The error is mine," I said formally. I sensed he was so embarrassed he was on the verge of making his farewells. Not yet! I went on smoothly, smiling as I spoke. "It was beyond rude of me to speak to you so bluntly. No doubt you were better served when you visited other houses. I cannot apologize enough for my error."

I spoke quickly, every muscle tense as I urged him to take the bait. Honest man that he was, his expression was embarrassed.

"Well, to be frank, I've only visited with one other Japanese person, and that was in the course of business. I expect you know him? Hara-san? I guess he's an important man hereabouts."

It could, of course, be mere coincidence. But I knew instinctively that it was not. It was karma coming to my aid and guiding me onward. And knowing *that,* I also knew that it was pre-ordained that my plans would work. The knowledge made me deeply happy.

"I have met Hara-san a number of times," I said truthfully. "But I've never had the good fortune to be invited to his home." *Not yet, anyway.*

"I'm sure you will," Adam said innocently. I smiled; I shared his certainty. "Both his house and most of the contents are remarkably beautiful. There are a few pieces I didn't quite understand, but that is no doubt the fault of this ignorant foreigner. He has works of art scattered about casually that I'm sure must be worth a fortune. And he showed me his collection of jewels. I have never seen anything like them. Jade, precious stones, pearls. Any woman would think herself fortunate to own just one of them."

I thought contemptuously that I had been right about Hara. He had no class at all. A true noble would hide his wealth; my childhood home had been bare except for necessary furniture. Beautifully made, very expensive furniture, of course, but the beauty was in the wood and the craftsmanship. Not one single piece screamed vulgarity. Even prints were reserved for our own apartments, where strangers would never be invited in. And Hara chose to show off his wealth to a mere gaijin? I smiled sweetly.

"It sounds wonderful. Do you do a great deal of business with Hara-san?"

"Yes. He was one of the first contacts I made when I came to Edo. I was very fortunate to meet with him. He seems to have interests everywhere." He obviously saw my fascinated expression and added, "I've heard that he's quite new to Edo himself. Somebody told me he came from one of the other islands." He leaned forward confidentially, so close he could have touched my face. "In fact, I have heard that he made his money as a yakuza."

I sighed with pleasure. Not only was I going to take my revenge, I was going to rid society of a parasite who had no business mingling with decent people. Perhaps Adam thought he had made yet another mistake. He jumped back as if he had suddenly recollected his manners and moved awkwardly.

As I watched him, I remembered once more the tenderness Kamakiri the anma had felt for this honest, clumsy gaijin.

"Adam," I said quickly. "I have offended you. I am deeply sorry. You are my guest, and it seems my manners have deserted me. If you are not in a hurry, perhaps you would allow me to atone for my errors?"

"Any fault lies with me, Kamakiri," he said politely.

As he spoke, Adam raised his face to me. He looked cautious, but at the same time, eager. I sighed and threw subtlety to the wind. I had to. At this rate, we would still be apologizing to each other when Niko came home.

"Adam, I find I am tired." His face fell and I closed my eyes in exasperation. "I think I will lie down. But the knots in my obi are very intricate and my maid is not here to help me undress. Perhaps you could learn a new skill today? That of disrobing a Japanese woman?"

To my profound relief, he climbed to his feet rapidly and bowed deeply.

"If you will instruct me in the art, then I would be most eager to learn."

I smiled. Perhaps there was hope for my gaijin yet!

He waited courteously for me to walk before him. He had done that when he had taken me to his house. It pleased me, but it was yet another lesson he had to learn.

"You are most polite, Adam. And I appreciate that. But you should understand that here, the man always comes first. His woman follows behind and runs forward to open the door for her man."

"I have noticed that." Adam put his hand in the small of my back. I should, of course, also have told him that touching a relative stranger was forbidden. But his touch was warm through my kimono, and I felt my skin glowing where he pressed against me. One lesson at a time, I decided. "In my country, men are polite to women. Would you be pleased if I treated you as if you were my inferior?"

"No," I said simply.

"Then I will save that knowledge for when I am not with you."

I smiled, delighting in the inference that this would be the first time of many.

The knot in my obi was complex, and I waited impatiently as Adam fumbled at it. Finally, he lost patience himself and tugged until it came loose.

My kimono fell open, and he stared at my body as a hungry man might look at a feast.

"My God, but you are truly beautiful, Kamakiri," he said hoarsely. I was delighted, but shook my head in denial.

"I am too tall. And Japanese men prefer their women to have more curves than I do," I said modestly. "And of course, to treat them with the proper respect a man deserves."

"Then they're fools," he said softly. "Although I guess some of them must have better taste or you wouldn't be attracting crowds like you are. I'm honored," he added huskily.

Ah, but that was better!

But now that I had Adam where I wanted him, I found

myself at a loss. I doubted he would understand the subtle games a Japanese man would want to play, and I knew no others. I had no need to worry, though. Polite though he had been, now that I had made myself clear, Adam needed no urging. He crossed the few steps to my futon and took my face in both his hands. He held me still for a moment, staring down at me. I felt a flicker of worry; so close, would he see his anma in my face? I soon found I had no need to be concerned. He sighed deeply and then lowered his head toward me, placing his lips against mine. Yo had kissed me often. But he was exceptional. Japanese men did not kiss a woman. Or at least, not on the lips. The thought of Yo threw me off balance. Guilt ripped through my body like a lightning strike. What was I doing? Was my bodily need really so great that I could betray my lover?

I was about to draw back when Adam's tongue pried my lips apart and his tongue flicked into my mouth with a sensuous subtlety that left me shocked. Guilt retreated on a flood of desire and I kissed him back with a deep sigh of pleasure. *I am sorry, Yo. But you have been gone for a long time, and my body cannot wait for you forever!*

Even as the thought flickered through my mind, I knew it was no justification. Then Adam transferred his lips to my neck and I shrugged mentally. Yo and I were equals. I knew he would expect me to simply accept it if he had taken a lover in Kyoto. And did I really expect that he would be faithful to me in body as well as mind? I did not. I felt an overwhelming surge of freedom thrill through me as I understood that the old proverb was correct. *In the pursuit of pleasure, there is no difference between a woman and a man.*

And then Adam's hand was sliding inside my open kimono and I heard him sigh deeply as his hand found my breast and all thoughts went far away from me.

Adam muttered something I could not understand. No matter. I understood his meaning perfectly when he raised his face and looked at me. His mouth was ajar, his eyes wide, the pupils enormous.

"Yes, Adam," I said urgently. "Now."

Courtesy was obviously a thing of the past. He pushed me on to my back and kneeled across my waist. He needed no further urging. I was pinned like an insect taken by my namesake, the mantis. I shrieked out loud with the pleasure of it. For a moment, I thought Adam might worry that he was causing me pain, then I understood truly that Reiki had been correct when she had said that all men were the same when they were naked. Adam was no longer polite. He was like a wild thing, seeking for nothing but his own fulfillment. He shoved at me until I thought it wasn't possible to contain any more of him in me, and then I found that not only was it possible, it was delicious.

I felt my yonaki swelling deep inside. The sensation was so powerful, I sensed that Adam felt it in his own body. He burst his fruit into my yonaki, and the waves of pleasure repeated and repeated as I bucked against him. Just as he had felt my yonaki, I felt the heat of his seed cascading deep into my sex.

We lay together for a long time. Adam dragged the kakebuton over us and pulled me toward him so that my head was on his chest. It was deliciously comfortable and I was annoyed when he finally moved.

"I must go." He sat up and smiled down at me. I fixed a smile on my lips, remembering that I was Kamakiri the oiran, not a green girl annoyed that her lover was not lingering. "But I hope that I may come back."

"Of course, Adam." That was better! He was already on

his feet, tying his robe around him. "You are always welcome in this house."

"Thank you, Kamakiri. I wonder, may I ask a favor of you?" I put my head on one side, inviting his question. "I would very much like to know what has happened to your namesake, Kamakiri the anma. I've been worried about her. Should you happen to hear anything about her, could you tell me when we meet again?"

It was so stunned it took me a moment to gather my wits. I managed to find a smile and I spoke smoothly.

"If I hear anything, I'll be sure to tell you. But anma often disappear for long periods. It may well be that she has gone out of Edo altogether." I paused, trying to find the right words. "Were you very fond of her, Adam?"

"Yes," he said simply. "She had a goodness about her that isn't found often." It was on the tip of my tongue to say tartly, *even though she robbed you?* But I remembered myself and kept quiet. In any event, Adam answered my unspoken thoughts. "She stole some pills from me. I hope she wanted them to relieve the pain of some of her patrons, but I'm worried she might have tried them on herself first to make sure they were safe. They were very strong, and if she took more than one, they could be dangerous." He sighed and wiped his hands over his face. I nodded gravely.

"I see. You want her caught and punished. And your pills returned."

"Not at all." Adam frowned. "She had no need to steal them. If she had asked, I would have given them to her and explained how careful she had to be with them. I certainly don't want to see her punished. I just want to know I haven't inadvertently caused her harm."

He shrugged and made a curious gesture, putting his

fingers in front of his lips and then flicking his hand toward me.

"I hope to see you again soon, Kamakiri." He smiled and turned, pausing to call over his shoulder, "Please, stay there in comfort. I'll make sure your shoji is closed behind me."

As the shoji slid shut, it occurred to me to wonder what my innocent gaijin would say if he knew his precious anma and Kamakiri the oiran were one and the same. I guessed that he would be bewildered and deeply hurt.

Just as well that he was never going to find out.

TWENTY-THREE

Prince or whore, it makes
No difference. Neither can
Pull the stars to earth

"*I* thought you were pleased when Hara sent you the note. Aren't you going to respond to him?"

Niko was clearly puzzled. I smiled and shook my head.

"Not yet. Wait until he asks again. Then...perhaps. The longer I make him wait, the more interested he will be. How did your lessons go today?"

"Fine. I didn't know learning to read and write would be so difficult."

"Persevere," I advised. "Just like Hara, if something is worth having, it's worth waiting for."

We both laughed. Our amusement was interrupted by our outside bell clanging. Niko darted off to answer the summons and came back with a scrap of paper and a tiny package carefully wrapped in silk.

"Open it." I gave the package to her as I read the note. I smiled with pleasure as I read the brief message. Hara, begging for the honor of my company that same evening. I glanced up as I heard Niko's startled gasp. She was holding her hand out toward me. She rocked her hand back and forward slightly, and the jewel nestling in her palm reflected the light in a rainbow of beauty.

"What is it?" she asked eagerly. "I've never seen a gem this color before. Is it worth a lot, do you think?"

I took the stone from her and held it between my finger and thumb, examining it carefully. It was about the size and shape of my little fingernail. If it had been white, I would have thought it was a diamond. But it wasn't white. It was a pure, deep pink. I read my note again. In addition to begging for my company, Hara had written, "*It is my great pleasure to send this insignificant gift for you. I hope it will give you a little pleasure to receive it. It is almost as flawless in its beauty as you are yourself.*"

The hint was in the modesty of the wording; I guessed that the gem was precious indeed.

"I think it is a diamond," I said thoughtfully. "And I think it must be a very good one, as I notice that Hara's messenger didn't wait for an answer. He obviously thinks that his gift is enough to bring me to him. Shall we go for a walk, Niko? There's a merchant in Willow Street who sells excellent jewelry. I think we can trust him to tell us the truth about this stone."

I was greeted with deference. A bowl of water was produced instantly for Matsuo, who lapped politely. Even Niko was given a polite nod. The merchant bowed deeply before me, washing his hands before him in an oily gesture.

"Kamakiri-san, you honor my humble shop. What may I show you?"

"Nothing, Himura-san." I tempered my abrupt answer with a smile. This man was reputed to be the best goldsmith in the Floating World. I had received many presents from would-be patrons, and most had made a point of telling me that their trinkets came from this man. A couple of men had even taken me to his shop and told me grandly to choose anything I liked. My purchases had always been modest, which only added to my growing legend. "I have come to ask your opinion. What do you think of this?"

I took my pink gem out of my obi and handed it to the goldsmith. He was so astonished that he gasped out loud. I exchanged a look with Niko; I had been right. To have drawn amazement from this seasoned merchant, the gem must be very precious indeed. I was almost irritated by the knowledge. For no rational reason at all, Hara's jewel made me nervous. It had felt strange when I held it in my hand, and I was sure I could feel it all the time it was cocooned safely in my obi.

"May I ask where you obtained this, Kamakiri-san?" he asked.

I shrugged, as though it was unimportant to me. "A patron gave it to me as a present."

"Ah." The goldsmith's face was suddenly crafty. "I see. Oddly enough, I sold this stone to somebody myself only a short time ago. The customer is well known for his collection of precious and unusual jewels. I was under the impression that he wanted it to keep for himself to add to his collection."

He stared at me in something that looked like awe. I felt a shiver of excitement as I wondered how much Hara had paid for it, and, hence, how much he valued me. Politeness forbade me to ask how much it was worth.

I said casually, "It's very pale for a ruby. I take it that it has little value?"

I watched the goldsmith's expression change from shock to greed. He licked his lips and stared at me. I had made a point of wearing some of the more expensive items my admirers had purchased from him. To make my point clear, I raised my hand to adjust an ornament in my wig. A very heavy ornament, in very bad taste, made of gold and set with large turquoises and—I knew—bought from him. He sighed and handed the gem back to me reluctantly.

"It's a pink diamond," he said. "They're very rare, and this one is both flawless and unusually large."

I heard Niko stir with interest, and I thought even Matsuo raised his head from his water bowl.

"Really?" I tossed the gem casually in my hand, as though it was no more than a scrap of paper. Himura's eyes followed it greedily. "Well, in that case, I may have it set into a comb for my hair. I'll think about it."

"I hope, Kamakiri-san, you will entrust me with the setting if you decide to have it mounted?" Himura leaned forward anxiously, watching as I replaced the gem securely in my obi. "Or possibly you might worry about wearing such a precious thing? The streets of the Floating World are full of dangers, and such a jewel would be a great temptation. If you wish, I would be delighted to buy it from you."

I shrugged and remained silent, patting Matsuo. Himura spoke softly, but the price he named froze me in place. If he was willing to pay that much to get his gem back, how much had he charged Hara for it?

"It's a pretty thing," I said coolly. "I think I'll keep it for the moment. I would hardly like to upset my patron by selling his gift at the first opportunity."

The goldsmith obviously read more into my words than I had meant. He smiled so widely I saw a gold tooth gleaming at the side of his mouth.

"I understand perfectly, Kamakiri-san. If the time comes when you do wish to sell it, I assure you, I will give you the very best price. And equally, if you have a fancy for anything in my humble shop, I will be delighted to offer you an excellent price."

Niko was so shocked by the amount he had offered to me, she was silent all the way home.

"I think we will pay a visit to the kannushi at Jokan-Ji Temple, Niko." The stone seemed to me to be pressing into my flesh. Something other than its value made me nervous. "I would be glad for him to take charge of Hara's diamond for me. Keep it safe in the temple."

"Kamakiri." The kannushi, Aisha, bowed to me politely. There was a gleam of humor in his eyes that made me smile. "How nice to see you again. Have you come to inquire about the progress of Niko's lessons?"

"I hope she is attending to her teacher and doing well at her learning?"

"Of course." Aisha's smile widened. He exchanged a glance with Niko, who grinned at him cheerfully. She was already a favorite, I guessed. "And apart from that, what can I do for you? Alas, I must tell you that I have had no word from our friend, but that is hardly unexpected. No message points to good news."

I bowed my head in response, although I was a little disappointed. I had hoped for *something* from Yo, even if it was just a few words of reassurance to tell me he was safe.

"I hope he's back with us soon," I said cheerfully. "But I wanted to see you about this."

I held my pink diamond out in my palm. Aisha looked at it, but made no move to touch it. I watched him carefully and decided he liked the glittering stone even less than I did.

"I know this diamond," he said abruptly. "I've seen it before, many years ago, when I followed the trade of shinobi. It's very valuable—and very unlucky. It has blood on it. Where did you get it?"

I took a deep breath. I had been right, then, to dislike the stone.

"Hara sent it to me as a present," I explained. "He purchased it himself not long ago. Tell me about it, please."

The kannushi stared at my outstretched palm for a long time. I waited patiently until he nodded as if making his mind up.

"Close your fingers on it. Better still, tuck it away in your obi. I don't want it to hear us." If his voice hadn't been so severe, I would have laughed at his superstition. Instead, I put the gem back in my obi. I was sure I could feel it glowing hot through my kimono, as if it felt Aisha's distaste and resented it.

"When did you see it last?" I asked softly.

"A long time ago. And far away from here, in the Kingdom of Chosun. When I last saw it, it belonged to a very beautiful woman. A woman who had the greatest nobles in the land at her feet."

"Did you see her yourself?" Niko interrupted impatiently.

Aisha nodded. "I did. Often. She wore that thing—" He nodded toward my obi. "—set in gold in a necklace that clasped her neck closely. Necklaces were unusual in Chosun, but then again, so was the woman who wore it. She told me herself that it never left her neck, day or night."

I held my breath as he paused, his eyes looking at us but, I thought, seeing another time and place entirely.

"Who was she?" I prompted. I guessed from the way he spoke of the unknown woman that when Aisha had been a young shinobi, they had been lovers. I hoped he understood from my simple question that I was asking not for personal details about his relationship with her, but about his lover. Who she was and how she had come to own such an expensive gem.

His expression said his mind had returned to us. Reluctantly.

"Her name was Yebin. In Chosun, it is a very old name that means to be pretty. It was an insult to her. She was perfection in every way. She was a gisaeng, a courtesan. It was said that she could turn men to stone by her very glance, and they were glad to die knowing that their last sight in this life had been her face. She could sing and dance exquisitely. Even to hear her speak was to be enchanted." He paused, his expression longing even after the passage of so many years. Niko was about to speak, and I nudged her to silence. Aisha needed to tell his tale in his own way, in his own time. "She enchanted me in the end," he said finally. "Just as she enchanted every other man who saw her. You have to understand, in those days I was young and handsome. Also, I had something of a reputation as a daredevil, a man who cared for nothing and nobody. Yebin couldn't stand for that. She had princes of the blood at her feet. The idea that a mere shinobi, and not even a Chosun at that, could refuse to fall for her charms was anathema to her. I did some work for one of her patrons, which was how I met her. I fell in love with her at once, of course, but I pretended indifference. She hated that and went out of her way to attract me. I gave in, in the end. If you had seen her, you would understand." He spoke as if we had laughed or made fun of him. I nodded seriously.

"Some women are like that," I said quietly. "They always have to have what's out of their reach. And you say she had my diamond?"

My diamond? I was astonished even as I said it. I had just acquired the jewel and already I was beginning to feel possessive about it. I didn't like that idea at all.

"There can't be two like it," Aisha said. "It was specially re-cut for her in that pattern. Even then, it had a bad reputation. In its original form, it was said to have been given to a noblewoman who in turn gave it to her lover. The man was stupid enough to flaunt the magnificent jewel, and they were both executed by her angry husband. He sold the diamond on, and it disappeared for many years. It was found again in the ashes of a terrible fire, clutched in the hand of a priest. It was rumored that this priest was so besotted by a certain courtesan that he robbed his temple to buy the jewel for her. And when she still refused him, he kept the diamond and then set fire to himself and burned his temple as well.

"How it came to be in the possession of Yebin's lover, I have no idea. He was a very great noble, of true bone rank. In Chosun, that signifies a member of the highest ranks. Only a man of true bone rank could ever become king. This noble wanted her to become his concubine, but she refused. Perhaps all the flattery had gone to her head, but she insisted that she would go to her noble as his wife or not at all. I was her lover by then. I pleaded with her to forget it. A noble of his rank could never marry a gisaeng. It was laughable. I tried to tell her that if she persisted, he would put her aside altogether, but she wouldn't listen to me. She told me I was jealous. I suppose I was, to be honest."

"What happened to her?" I asked.

"She died. Or perhaps it would be more truthful to say that her vanity was so great that her death was inevitable." I heard Niko take a deep, satisfied breath at this revelation. I was vaguely irritated; she had surely seen too many kabuki performances for her own good! "Yebin was pregnant. She was convinced that her baby had been fathered by her noble. I was equally convinced that the baby was mine, but she wouldn't listen to me. Suddenly, I was turned away when I went to visit her. When I was finally admitted, she told me brutally that she no longer had any interest in me. That she didn't want to see me again. I pleaded with her, even told her that I wanted to marry her. She stared at me as if I had gone mad, and finally, she summoned her servants and had me thrown out. I was bewildered. I couldn't believe that she meant it and continued to hang about her house in the hope of seeing her and persuading her to change her mind."

Aishi was a very old man. The story he was telling us had happened almost a lifetime ago, yet there were still tears in his eyes now. I put my hand on his sleeve to offer comfort and he patted my hand absently.

"She was very beautiful," he said apologetically. "Outwardly, if not within. Eventually, one of her maids took pity on me. This girl warned me to stay well away, that there was nothing but danger for me there. Yebin wanted her maid to support her story that the father of her baby was the noble, so she had confided in her what she was going to do. Her pregnancy was beginning to show. Yebin had decided that the next time her noble visited her, she would tell him he was to be a father. Her maid would swear on her life that it was so, that Yebin had had no other lovers. The noble had no children by his wife or any of his concubines, so she was sure he would be so delighted that he would put his barren wife aside and marry her. He didn't, of course. He was pleased, but the best he would offer her was to be one of his concubines. She flew into a fury with him and actually slapped him. She was lucky. He simply walked away from her."

"What happened?" I asked when he stopped speaking.

He shrugged. "Yebin had many gifts, but common sense was not amongst them. She summoned me back to her. At first, I was overjoyed. But not for long. She told me of the insult her noble had offered to her and demanded that I use my skills as shinobi to kill his wife in such a manner that her death would appear to be accidental. In return, she promised that she would take me as her lover after her noble married her, as soon as it was safe. She offered me the pink diamond in payment. When I refused in horror and told her she was playing with fire, she turned cold. If I would not help her, then there were plenty of others who would, she said. I begged her not to be so foolish. I told her she was risking death, not just for her but for her—our—unborn child.

"She laughed at me. Called me a coward and told me to go away. Said she did not want to see me again and advised me to leave the Kingdom of Chosun because when she became a princess of the bone, she would have me hunted down and executed. I suddenly knew beyond any doubt that I was the father of her child and that she meant to keep me quiet by whatever means she could.

"At that moment, love turned to stone. I walked away from her without a second glance. I made preparations to get out of Chosun as soon as I could, but before I could leave, I heard the rumors. Yebin had persuaded one of her other lovers to try and assassinate the noble's wife. The idiot had been clumsy and was caught. No doubt hoping that he and Yebin would be together in the next world, he had confessed all. They were executed together. I saw them die." He shuddered and closed his eyes at the memory. "The noble had decided on a public execution, no doubt to warn off anybody else who displeased him. When Yebin's head left her body, he walked over to her corpse and fished her necklace out of her blood. I haven't given a thought to that diamond since that day. And I wish I had never seen it again."

"Will you take it?" I asked. Aisha's expression was horrified. He put his hands out in front of him as if warding off evil. "I don't mean for yourself," I added quickly. "I know it's worth a fortune, but I don't want it. Will you take it and sell it? Use the proceeds to help the temple and those poor, unfortunate girls who come here as their last refuge? If anything could remove the stain from it, then surely that will."

He held out his hand reluctantly and I retrieved the diamond and dropped it into his palm. My fingers must have been warm, as it seemed to adhere to my skin and be reluctant to leave me. It caught the light and shed a rainbow of colors all around it. I was suddenly reluctant to part with it and almost snatched it back. Aisha folded his fingers around it and took it away from me.

"I think that there is something wrong with this jewel," he said thoughtfully. "Perhaps all the jealousy and desire it has attracted over the years has found a home inside it.

Perhaps it was evil on the day it was dug out of the ground. Either way, I will do as you ask. Perhaps for the first time in its existence, it will be used to do good. And I also think that the sooner it is away from you, daughter, the better. The souls of many women will thank you for this."

He held the diamond between his fingernails as if he was reluctant to even allow it in contact with his flesh. A young monk came running at his call, and he took the diamond with as much interest as if it was a piece of fish. He barely glanced at it when the kannushi told him to put it safely away.

"Ayya is a good man." Aisha smiled. "But he has no imagination at all. The diamond will not be able to hurt him."

Niko walked very closely to me on the way home.

"It was a lovely thing," she confided. "But I didn't *take* to it, if you know what I mean. I didn't like it before I heard Aisha's story, and I liked it even less afterward. I can't believe it was just a coincidence that we took it to probably the only man in the whole of the Floating World that knew its history.

"I'm sure it was the gods offering you a warning about it. I think it would have been very unlucky for you, elder sister. And it seems to me that—until today—it was always given for the wrong reasons, so it became unluckier each time it changed hands. The temple will look after it now, and that's an end to the nasty thing." She beamed at me, and I nodded. She was right, I was sure. "Now that it's gone, will you go to see Hara? I think it'll be safe now. The blood will be washed off his present. It can have no hold on you."

I stopped and stared wide-eyed in amazement at the innocent truth of her words. As we walked on, I thought of the kannushi's innocent unborn baby dying with its mother and I swallowed as if a lump of food had lodged in my throat. The pain that even seeing the pink diamond again must have caused him had surely been almost beyond bearing. Yet he had taken it from me gladly, knowing that he could do good with the money it brought. Just like Niko, I didn't believe it was a coincidence. Again, karma was showing me the way.

I wished suddenly that Yo was back with me, if only so I could tell him that his choice of friend was even better than he could have known.

TWENTY-FOUR

> What does the breeze know
> Of the pleasure it gives when
> It touches my face?

I peered at Hara's house through the curtains of my palanquin. Even from the outside, everything was just a little too well finished. The wood was bright with varnish, the beams picked out in red as if it were a temple rather than a house. I smiled as I wondered if ever a bird would dare to shit on the splendid roof! The door gave me pause. Instead of the normal sliding shoji, this was solid wood. It reminded me very much of the substantial doors in the wall around our family's estate. What, I wondered, did Hara have to fear that he needed a door like that?

The palanquin had been waiting for me when we returned from Jokan-Ji Temple. Even though I had already decided that I would go to Hara as he had asked—not to go would have thrown good intent back in karma's face—I kept the bearers waiting until I had washed carefully and applied my makeup. I took my time over-dressing as well.

"Am I to come with you?" Niko asked hopefully. Her face fell when I shook my head.

"No. Stay here." Matsuo leaned heavily against my legs and I pushed him away gently. "Don't let anybody in, and don't stay awake for me, Niko. I have no idea how long I'm going to be."

Niko sighed theatrically and bent to put her arms around Matsuo's neck. They both looked at me reproachfully, but I refused to change my mind. I had no idea if there was danger for me here. I hoped that even face-to-face, Hara would not connect me with Hana's captive firefly. As Yo had said, people saw only what they expected to see, and it was Kamakiri the *oiran* who had been invited here. But there was always a chance. If it came to it, I was willing to fight my way out, and Niko would distract me. She was safer here, with Matsuo to protect her.

"If you're not back by morning, I'll go to Aisha for help," she said firmly. I nodded in agreement.

"Kamakiri-san, welcome to my house!" Hara bowed to me with exactly the right degree of courtesy. I smiled graciously and allowed myself to be seated in the place of honor, in front of the tokonoma alcove. A beautifully executed scroll hung in the alcove behind a single pillar bearing an ikebana flower arrangement. The ikebana held nothing but a single spray of orchids with a bare branch to support them, but a strong odor of incense pervaded the atmosphere. It made me want to sneeze.

"Hara-san." I bowed my head graciously. "I am honored to be invited to your beautiful home."

I smiled at my host. He was grinning happily. I could feel his sense of triumph that I was here. Very well. If he could be obvious, then so could I. I stared around in genuine amazement. The room I was sitting in was large. So large that part of it was lost in the shadows. What I could see was opulent. Each wall had many woodblock prints on them. All the masters were there— Hokusai, Utagawa, Torii, and others I could not immediately identify. Hara followed my glance and beamed at me.

"Ah. I see you like my prints." He closed one eye in an unforgivable leer. "I have others in my private apartment. But those are, shall we say, not for casual guests to enjoy."

He paused, waiting for my reaction. He meant shunga, of course. Erotic prints that were meant for private enjoyment between lovers. I smiled politely, refusing to respond. I hated him anyway for trying to buy me from Hana, but now that I was in his presence there was something more. He made me...uncomfortable. Although he was reasonably polite, his gaze slid over me as if he was assessing me. Calculating if I was truly worth his time and, presumably, money. I was deeply grateful when he moved away from the subject of shunga without further comment.

"You are clearly a woman of great taste, as well as beauty, Kamakiri. I hope you liked the little present I sent for you earlier."

"Of course." I smiled readily in relief. "It is a remarkably lovely diamond."

His smile widened fractionally at my words. "Ah. You recognized it as a diamond, then. Most people would have thought it a pale ruby. You have exquisite taste, Kamakiri."

I noticed that he was speaking to me as if we were old friends. Did he think he had already bought me with his expensive gift? I accepted his compliment silently, hoping he would sense my annoyance. He did not. I could see his mind was on other matters. His eyes flickered around constantly. I guessed it was so instinctual, he had no idea he was doing it. I was puzzled. What was there to be afraid of in his own house?

"I had never seen a gem like it before," I said honestly.

"I knew you would appreciate it. Now, would you like to see around my house?" Hara stood, using the movement to glance suspiciously around. It was both an odd thing to say—I had never met anybody before who wanted to flaunt their possessions, particularly to a stranger—and an indication that in spite of his wealth, my new patron was not quite the gentleman he pretended to be. Still, I was curious and stood up quickly.

Hara took my elbow to guide me. I stiffened but allowed myself to be steered around. His body was too hot for my liking and he pressed far too close to me for comfort. Hara knew not only each thing he possessed, but also the value of each piece. I almost laughed aloud as his catalog of rare and precious things droned on. They were lovely, most certainly. But there was far too much furniture, and each piece was topped by ceramics and metal ornaments. One large chest had a crisply pruned bonsai tree in a very old and very lovely Satsuma-ware pot on top of it. I suddenly recalled Adam's puzzled words about some of the items seeming odd to him. Now, I understood. Perfect items were placed less than artfully next to the imperfect, the art form of wabi-sabi, the aesthetic that is centered on the acceptance of transience and imperfection. I noticed that Hara skipped over those lovely, flawed pieces almost as if they puzzled him as much as they had Adam, and I guessed that he had purchased them simply because they were costly without any understanding of why they were so beautiful.

I was almost overwhelmed by the crudeness of it all, and I was glad to sit down again. A maid brought in flasks of sake. I sipped mine. Hara gulped his down greedily, and I leaned toward him solicitously, filling his cup to the brim. He steadied his cup with all his fingers and I saw that his little finger on his right hand was missing the first two joints. The wound was badly healed, as if the finger had been ripped off. Adam had said casually that he had heard Hara used to be a yakuza, a gangster. Now, I was sure Adam had been correct. It was quite common for a yakuza to cut off part of their little finger to show loyalty to their master. Particularly when that loyalty was challenged. I smiled and chatted and flirted, and all the time my mind ran in different directions. I was recalled to reality when Hara put his cup down and leaned forward, grasping my wrist firmly.

"Well, you've led me in a pretty dance, Kamakiri. I might as well tell you, I'm used to getting what I want. And quickly. I'm only interested in the very best, as you can no doubt see." He waved his hand airily at our surroundings. "I know you've caused a great stir since you came to the Floating World. And I've been told that even for a top-class oiran, you're remarkably fussy. And now that I've met you, I can understand that."

He laced his hands across his belly and sat back, a fat smile on his lips. I inclined my head and spoke politely.

"I thank you for your compliments, Hara-san. But I am at a loss. What do you want from me that any oiran in the Floating World couldn't give?"

"You're very blunt, Kamakiri." He nodded repeatedly, and I wondered how much sake he had downed before I had arrived. "But I appreciate that. I will get straight to the point. I want only the very best. Not only the best, but the rarest and the most beautiful. The most uncommon. I want you, the oiran who has the Floating World buzzing. The oiran who finds it amusing to walk the streets and acknowledges nobody. Just as you do, I'll come straight to the point. I'm offering to take you as my concubine."

I pursed my lips thoughtfully, as if I found his ludicrous words reasonable.

"You do me great honor," I said courteously. "But as you said yourself, I am an oiran. And not just any oiran. I value my ability to do as I want. I doubt there is anything you could offer me that would be worth losing my freedom."

He cackled with laughter. I smiled with him, as if his brashness was a rare and precious thing.

"You think so?" He broke off to pour another cup of sake and drained it quickly. I poured him another cup immediately. "I am a rich man, Kamakiri. Oh, I know it's not polite to brag about one's wealth, but I don't care for all that nonsense. The fact is that I could buy most of the nobles who hang around the shogun's court and not notice I had parted with any cash." He leaned toward me and smirked. "In fact, quite a few of them are well and truly in my debt already. I understand that you value your freedom, but everything has its price. Name it, and it will be yours."

"And in return?" I asked delicately.

"You will leave the Floating World. You will live here. I will be the only man who possesses you."

"You would own me." I stared him straight in the face, watching his expression. "I am sorry, Hara-san. But there is nothing in this world that could buy my freedom."

I was delighted. Revenge was mine, and so very easily! And if he did but know it, this was not the first time I had gotten the better of him. He had been desperate to buy me from Hana, but I had slipped through his fingers. Now, I had eluded him once more. I guessed he would already have bragged to his acquaintances of his plans for me. For such a man as he was, the lack of face would be devastating. I almost laughed as his cheeks reddened to the color of river clay. A nerve jumped in his left eye, his lips set in a tight, thin line.

"Everybody has their price," he grated. "You will not always be a young and lovely *oiran*. What if—just supposing, you understand—you were to survive a nasty fire? Burns are impossible to hide, and your loveliness would be destroyed in a moment. And never forget, the Floating World is a violent place. There are thieves out there who would slash a woman's face for the sake of her purse and think nothing of it."

I stared at him, fighting the desire to laugh out loud. Surely, if he wanted to threaten me, at least he could do it with some subtlety!

"And what if I did suffer some accident, Hara-san?" I enquired with amusement. "Surely, if I were no longer attractive, you would be deprived also? You would hardly want a disfigured woman as your concubine."

"Ah, but I would. It would delight me to have you by my side, every hour of every day. And to know that you had crawled to me in the end, your pride humbled and your looks destroyed. That would give me very great pleasure, *oiran*."

I knew then that he was mad and that I would have to step very carefully. I lowered my head and smoothed the front of my kimono.

"I see. You have given me much to think about, Hara-san. Perhaps it would be best if I went home now and considered what you have said."

I rose and bowed. I thought I had gotten away with it. Hara remained seated, watching me but making no move. His very stillness made me uncomfortable. I walked toward the entrance and slid on my *zori* as I put my hand on the strange wooden door and tugged. I was barely surprised when the door remained stubbornly in place.

Hara's voice was so casual, he might have been gossiping about nothing. "Please, do come and sit with me for a while. My stupid servant must have misunderstood my wishes and barred the door from the outside. Listen, I'm sure it's beginning to rain quite heavily. The man must have gone to his own quarters to shelter from the storm. Do stay awhile. Once it stops raining, my servant will come back and unlock the door and you can go home. I will, of course, be very sorry to let you go. But if we cannot come to an agreement..."

He left the sentence unfinished. He was trembling, although from the effects of the sake he had drunk in such quantities or from anger, I had no idea. I was irritated by his blatant ploy, but not enough to be worried about it. I watched as he poured himself yet more sake, and as I stared at him, I realized with surprise that he was neither angry nor drunk, but holding back laughter.

Hara held a cup of sake out to me. I shook my head, watching him carefully. Hara was not a young man, but he was still tall and bulky. In his youth he must have been very strong and determined to have succeeded as a yakuza. I could, I thought, beat him in a fight if I had to. But I was deeply reluctant to go down that route. Skilled as oiran were in many ways, I doubted that intimate knowledge of the martial arts was typically included in their repertoire. If I beat Hara in a fight, my persona as Kamakiri the *oiran* would vanish, along with the rest of my plans.

"Come now. I'm sure there will be no need to even contemplate any such misfortune in your future. Do sit down, Kamakiri," he coaxed, patting the tatami at his side. I folded down, knowing that at the moment I had no alternative. I would wait. My moment would come. Still, I was tense, wondering at Hara's sudden change from threatening to almost playful. "Are you a gambling woman?"

"Not really," I said. "I play mahjong quite well, but apart from that..." I shrugged and let my words tail off.

"That is such a shame. I have made a great deal of money by gambling over the years. The trick is to know one's opponent. Few men keep their wits about them when they gamble. For some reason, I feel certain you would make a worthy opponent."

"Thank you. Do you always win?" I asked. I waited with genuine interest for his answer. Was there no end to this man's vanity?

"Oh, yes. Only once did I forget myself, and I was severely punished for it." He stared at the missing little finger.

"That must have been very painful," I said. I was interested and wanted to know the answer. "Did you lose it in an accident?"

"Not at all. I cut it off myself." He stared at me intently, and I gasped in feigned surprise.

"But why would you do that? It must have been agony."

Hara smirked and then shrugged as if to say it was nothing.

"It was many years ago, when I was a very young man. I have not always been rich and respectable. I was born into a very poor family in Osaka. I was determined to get on in life, but the only way to do it was to join a yakuza gang."

He paused and I nodded quickly, as if I approved of his actions.

"And you were obviously successful, Hara-san," I said seriously.

"Indeed, I was. But not without cost." He held up the mutilated finger and stared at it. When he went on, his voice was animated. He might have been talking about something that had happened days ago. "My yakuza chief was a man of very great ambition. He had conquered Osaka and decided that it was time Edo had a new yakuza leader. I was one of a select band of men he brought here with him.

"We had all heard stories of the wealth that was to be had here in Edo, and we were all willing to take the risks involved. We soon found things weren't going to be as easy as we had anticipated. I was very ambitious myself in those days. I quickly decided that I was likely to be on the losing side, and so I went to the leader of the biggest yakuza gang in Edo and offered to join him. In return for a place of power in his organization, I told him I would become a spy for him and pass on all my old master's plans."

"That was very daring of you. But how did you come to cut off your finger?" I asked innocently.

"As I said, that was the only time I lost a gamble. I was so pleased with myself, I forgot one very important thing. Nobody trusts a man who is willing to change sides for his own advantage. At first, the Edo yakuza, Akira, seemed pleased to accept me." I felt the hairs rise in warning on the back of my neck. Akira. Hana's protector. No, of course not. My mind was whirling as I worked it out. *This* Akira must have been the father. The man who had been so in love with Hana that he gifted her both teahouses. I nodded encouragingly. I needn't have bothered. It was apparent from his expression that Hara's thoughts were roaming back in his past. "For months, I worked both yakuza, one against the other. I hoped that eventually I might destroy them both and take power for myself. I was an absolute fool.

"One day, my old master summoned me to his presence and confronted me with my actions. I denied everything, of course. He didn't believe me and said that the only way I could prove my loyalty was by the traditional way of cutting off my finger. I obeyed at once. I had no alternative. He was a clever man. He may not have believed me, but he knew that once I had been marked as having demonstrated my loyalty to another leader, I could never go back to Akira. He would have known instantly that I had been disloyal. So that was it. I had to stay with my yakuza, and he made it very clear that I was no more than a foot soldier in his organization.

"In any event, it all turned out for the best in the end. My old master was eventually defeated by Akira, and he was forced to slink back to Osaka. Both sides had taken hefty losses. We were lucky to escape before Akira could take his revenge on those of us who were still alive. I stayed with my master and gradually worked my way back up to be his trusted second in command. When I felt I had a chance, I took those men who were loyal to me and murdered the old man." He spoke so casually that it took a moment for me to realize what he had said. "I never looked back after that. Soon, I was wealthier than any noble in Osaka. But I never gambled again without thinking carefully first, Kamakiri. In time, I saw that there were men below me who wanted my place. I could have fought them, but why take the chance? I already had more money than I could spend in a lifetime. And by then, I was also owed a debt by many important men.

"One of them was the local magistrate, a samurai who

had fallen on hard times and who had had the sense to accept my presence. He told me that the Osaka daimyo had decided that the yakuza grip in the area had become so strong that they perceived us as a threat and were about to clear us out. That was enough for me. I sold all my assets quietly and told my friends I fancied a change of scenery. I was delighted to find that my letters of introduction from my high ranking acquaintances in Osaka opened many doors for me in society here in Edo." I kept my face fascinated even as I thought how delighted his "acquaintances" must have been to learn he was leaving Osaka. "I liked Edo when I was here as a young man, and I'm very pleased to find that the Floating World still suits me perfectly. I shall stay, I think. Edo society sees me as a rich and respectable man. What more could I want? Particularly now that I have the chance at such a lovely companion to support me in my failing years."

He leered at me, raising his eyebrows and smiling. I pretended to find his words amusing and giggled behind my fan. At the same time, my brain was flicking like the beads on an abacus, ordering all he had told me. Akira the elder had been denied his revenge. I knew the yakuza had their own twisted code of honor. I guessed shrewdly that Akira's son would be delighted to find that after all these years his father's enemy was suddenly within reach.

But first, I had to get away from him. I patted my lips with my finger, pretending to be bewildered.

"I'm honored by your regard for me, Hara-san. But my mind must be failing me this evening. I still don't understand. Why did you ask if I was a gambling woman?"

He laughed softly, clearly amused that I had chosen to pick on such a small comment.

"I am going to propose a wager, Kamakiri-chan. The

odds will be simple. If you win, then you leave my house as soon as the rain stops. I hope we will remain friends, but I will ask no more of you."

"And if I lose?" I asked.

"If you lose, then I keep you. You become my concubine for however long it takes me to tire of you. Isn't that generous of me? The odds are very much in your favor. You simply can't lose. If I win our wager, you will enjoy a life of luxury. Anything you ask for will be yours. And what do I ask in return? Nothing at all except what you already give to any man who takes your fancy. If I lose, you have gained a valuable diamond and we have had a pleasant evening together."

"That sounds very generous, Hara-san." I wrinkled my brow as if I was giving serious consideration to his ludicrous offer. "But can I trust you? How do I know you won't cheat?"

"You have my word, Kamakiri," Hara said pompously. "But if it reassures you, shall we play first just for fun? Or for something that matters not at all? That way, you can see for yourself that I don't cheat."

"That would be good," I replied. "What shall we play? Mahjong? I'm quite good at that."

"I'm sure you are. But it would take far too long. I know—what about paper-rock-scissors? It's impossible to cheat at that, and it's quick."

I wondered what he was up to. The childish game was pure chance, and I couldn't see how he could cheat. I was nodding my agreement before I remembered we had not agreed on the forfeit.

"And what are the stakes for this nonsense game?" I asked cautiously.

"When you were a child, did you play at statues?" I blinked, wary at Hara's apparent change of tack.

"Of course." I smiled.

"The yujo in the teahouses in the Floating World play a similar game with their patrons. They dance to music, which stops abruptly. Should one of the yujo be caught out and still move when the music stops, she is forced to pay a forfeit. She must take one item of clothing off. The patrons gamble on which girl will be naked first. I am proposing something very similar. Whichever of us loses a game will remove an item of clothing." He smirked. "Who knows? If we are equally skilled, we may both be almost naked before the end."

Kamakiri the oiran laughed with him. Keiko the onna-bugeisha searched for the meaning behind his words and decided he was simply a vain, rather stupid man.

"Oh, that would be fun!" I clapped my hands in pretended amusement. The rain was falling yet more heavily. I could hear it drumming on the roof. Hara's silly game would pass the time until it stopped.

We faced each other. Both of us had our palms pressed together. Hara counted one, two, three and we both made our shape. I had chosen scissors at random. Hara had gone for paper. He laughed at my triumph.

"Ah. You win. Scissors cut paper." Without any comment, he unfastened his and let it drop to the tatami. "Fortune is obviously with you."

Next time, Hara went for scissors, and I chose rock. I won again. He promptly took off his kimono, leaving him sitting in nothing but a silk loincloth and his zori.

I stared at his body in surprise. As I thought, he was running to fat. But there was still plenty of muscle there. But it was his skin that astonished me. From the wrists to just below his neck he was thickly tattooed. The tattoos ran down below his loincloth and ran out again below it on to his legs.

"I see you're admiring my needlework." Hara turned so I could see his back. I said nothing but stared silently. He chose to take my repulsion for admiration and smoothed both hands across his chest. "They are irezumi tattoos. A very old yakuza tradition." He pointed to his chest. "These are koi carp. The red one on the left represents my loyalty to my yakuza clan." He paused, and I wondered cynically which of his two masters he was referring to. "And this blue one is a symbol of masculinity."

He smiled at me. I widened my eyes in what I hoped he would interpret as admiration.

"They must have been very painful when they were done," I said dutifully.

"Oh, they were. This one in particular." He hunched his shoulders and half turned to show me the oni mask that covered most of his back. "That took a day and night to complete. But it was worth it. To have a demon whose favorite food is human flesh guarding my back is truly priceless. I rather like my snakes as well." He parted his legs to show me the thick serpents that coiled up each leg.

Partially hidden by the colorful tattoos were thick scars, whitened and made shiny by the passage of time. One ran across his left shoulder, bisecting his chest and dividing his nipple and appearing to cut his red koi neatly in half. Several more ran horizontally across his belly, creasing it. Three smaller ones had been slashed across his ribs on the right. My gaze followed their lines, interpreting the rhythm of the vicious knife fights that had caused them. They were ancient scars, yet still looked inflamed and painful. How much agony must they have caused when they were inflicted.

I tore my gaze away and managed to smile at him. He was preening, obviously proud of both his tattoos and the trophies of war he had collected. I managed to look suitably awed and bowed my head. Hara inclined his own head regally and held out his hands to signify he was ready to play again.

Next time, he went for paper against my rock.

"Ah! Luck is back with me." He wagged his finger at me playfully. I took off one of my zori and held it out, allowing it to drop deliberately. After that, I watched him very closely from beneath lowered eyes. He won the next time, and the other *zori* followed the first. I laughed, pretending an amusement I was far from feeling. Hara laughed with me, leaning toward me. His forehead was prickled with sweat and his mouth was open. He was obviously excited by our game. I tossed my head and glanced at his loincloth. As I had guessed, he was aroused. The front of his loincloth was poking out from the pressure of his tree. I felt the atmosphere tighten and I tensed with it.

"Well, it seems to me as if we're quite evenly matched." Hara's voice was throaty. "One more game for fun, and then shall we get down to it? The next game will be for real. If I win, you agree to become my concubine. If I lose, you walk away and that will be the end of it." He wiggled his eyebrows at me, a grotesque expression from a fat man wearing nothing but a loincloth.

I laughed flirtatiously, but behind the amusement, my mind was ice. He was cheating. But how, I had no idea. I watched as he held his palms out, clasped together. I noticed he held them rather low, and an idea came to me. This time, I watched his hands, not his face.

And there the answer was. Hara might not be young, but his reactions were pin-sharp. There was a hesitation so slight that if I had not been trained to look for the unexpected I would never have seen it. He waited for my hands to begin to make my chosen shape before he responded. It was absurdly simple, but completely effective.

This time he made sure he lost, of course. I swallowed nausea as he laughed delightedly and rose to his knees to tug off his loincloth. His tree wagged at me in apparent delight at finding freedom. He put his finger on the end of it and bounced it at me, grinning happily.

"Ready, Kamakiri? As you can see, I certainly am!"

I said nothing and held my hands out. I hesitated, frowning thoughtfully as if I was doing my best to second guess Hara's reaction. He waited, watching my hands rather than my face. I made my mind up and started to form scissors. As I expected, Hara immediately reacted with a bunched fist for a rock. But his own eagerness was his downfall. He was quick, but I was quicker. Instead of forming scissors, I clasped my fingers together and held my palm out flat. Paper. Paper wraps rock.

I had won.

I put my fingers to my lips as if in amazement at my victory. I watched his expression move from baffled surprise to absolute fury. I tensed. I would allow him to make the first move and then catch him off balance. It was an excellent thing that he was naked. A naked woman is a distraction to a man. A naked man loses too much of his dignity to be anything but a target for a warrior woman.

My every sense was tuned and alert for him to make his move, and I was quite disappointed when I heard the sound of the door being opened behind me.

"I am so sorry, master." The servant who had let me in earlier stood in the doorway. His smug expression faded to amazed disbelief as he regarded the naked Hara. "I...I barred the door by mistake," he muttered. "I was waiting for the rain to stop to come back…" He trailed off miserably. Hara's face was creased with fury. I felt almost sorry for the servant.

I stood and hooked my feet into my zori. "Thank you for a most entertaining evening, Hara-san," I said smoothly. "I found our little games most amusing, but I believe that now it's time I took my leave of you."

The servant jumped aside as I passed him. The palanquin was still outside. The rain had penetrated the curtains and the cushions inside were damp, but I made myself as comfortable as I could. I heard Hara's voice barking an order, and a moment later the palanquin was lifted and we moved off. I guessed his dignity had been so affronted by both his failure and the unexpected entry of his servant that —for tonight at least—he wanted me to go, and quickly.

I also guessed it wouldn't last. As soon as his anger was forgotten, he would be back, more eager than ever. That was the nature of the man; he wanted what he could not ever attain. All the treasures in his house, all his ostentatious display of wealth, and—most especially—his talk of having samurai and daimyo at his beck and call explained everything to me. This yakuza trash wanted nothing more than to be the equal of his betters, even as he knew it would never happen. That was why he had been willing to bid what was no doubt an outrageous amount to buy me from Hana. By possessing a samurai lady, he would have gloated in getting his revenge on the whole class of those who sneered at his ambition to be one of them. And his interest in Kamakiri the *oiran*? That was obvious. He perceived me as the very best of my type. Just as his works of art were both priceless and beautiful, so he thought of Kamakiri. To add spice to the dish, he would no doubt know that I was also pursued by men who *were* nobles.

Then I remembered Hara's casual remark that he had murdered his old master for his own gain and decided not to waste my pity on him. The wheel of Hara's karma had begun to turn, and now I knew exactly the direction it was going to go in.

TWENTY-FIVE

> If I choose to walk
> On ice, then first I must make
> Sure how thick it is

I decided we would stop our nightly walks, at least for a while. My assignation with Hara had been more successful than I could have hoped. If it looked as if I had disappeared, I guessed gleefully that it would drive him mad, wondering if I had accepted an offer from another man.

I was not short of offers. The notes—each one passionate and laden with promises of lavish presents in exchange for my favor—continued to pour in. Niko used them for practicing her reading, and we snickered together over them.

"Do they know how stupid they are?" she asked. "They all promise you heaven on earth and seem to think they're the only one you might even consider. Are all men so silly?"

"No, just the ones who are so foolish they think they're the answer to a woman's prayers," I said cheerfully.

"That seems to be the last of them." Niko shredded the mound of paper into small pieces and added it to the pile already laid at the bottom of the charcoal-burner, ready to help light it. "Best place for that lot."

I nodded absently. My head was full of plans for the way forward. Hara's future was already decided. I had gotten the better of him once—or rather twice, even if he did not know it. I knew his failure this time would only whet his appetite. He was safe for the moment, but I thought that he would be a dangerous man to have as an enemy. He would be... removed. And soon.

One man down, two to go.

I had heard no word of Ikeda—the man who had wanted to use Hana's virgin offering to cure his hideous disease—in the Floating World. That surprised me, as I thought his grotesque appearance would make him well known. Niko made inquiries for me, but also came up empty-handed. Very well. I would put him aside for the moment.

The louche youth Sato was far easier to track down. I had guessed that a man who so obviously thought himself deeply iki—that unique Floating World word for a man who combined all the virtues of sophistication, wit, and originality—would be well-known and well-connected in the Floating World.

My brother, Isamu, unusually for a samurai, had been accepted by the Floating World—especially the yujo and geisha—as supremely iki. My heart contracted as I remembered him. The irony of the fact that I could avenge the wrongs done to me but never the murder of my brother and father made me feel sick.

Suddenly, a storm of contradictory thoughts had me clutching my head as if I could force them to be silent. Our own peasants had risen up and murdered my menfolk. But they had been driven to it by desperation when their crops had failed. Father had more than enough rice stored to enable all the villagers to eat and sow for next year's harvest, but he was too mean to part with a single grain at a price they could afford. Had he, then, invited his own death? And what of Lord Akafumu, who had happily told me that he had ensured revenge for my father and brother's deaths by having every one of the remaining men in the village rounded up and executed and their women sold into slavery. Should I have been grateful to him for that instead of destroying him? I closed my eyes in despair. Niko's voice offered an unexpected kindness.

"Kamakiri," she said timidly, "don't be so distressed. Whatever happens is the will of the gods. We can only hope to carry out their wishes."

I took a deep breath and smiled shakily. "And how do you know what I am thinking about?" I asked.

Niko touched my face with a single finger. "You're crying," she said simply. "I've never seen you cry before."

I wiped my cheeks with the back of my hand and found to my astonishment that she was right. Niko was staring at me with such a worried expression that I managed to laugh.

"Memories," I said briefly. "Now, tell me if you know anything about a young man called Sato."

Niko knew everything that went on in the Floating World. She would surely know Sato. He had to be wealthy; he had been interested enough in me to want to spend a great deal of money to purchase me. I was surprised he had shown no interest at all in the new and very popular oiran Kamakiri. Surely a man who considered himself to be supremely iki would want to be linked with me. Niko giggled when she heard his name.

"Oh, him. The boy with no kintama." She made an obscene gesture with her hand, as if she was cupping a man's testicles. I should have reprimanded her rudeness, but I was too interested to bother. "I wouldn't think he'd be interested in an oiran. He's not that way inclined."

"Ah. You mean he's nanshuko." Amongst the samurai classes, it was common for an older man to take a younger male lover. It was called wakashudo—the way of youth. But most samurai, no matter how enamored they were with their wakashu, also took a wife and concubines. For a man to be nanshuko was different. In that case, he was interested only in his own sex. I remembered Sato scrabbling at my buttocks when I was masquerading as Jun, the young girl who could have been taken for a wakashu with her samurai top-knot and slender body. And Hana had known her man all too well. I remembered that she had whispered to Sato that I had fled my noble home to escape to the Floating World with my female lover who had left me for a man. I had no doubt that my ambivalent sexuality had intrigued Sato.

No wonder he had shown no interest in the sumptuous oiran Kamakiri. I frowned, wondering if Niko's words meant that Sato was out of my reach. Niko was still smiling, and my spirits rose as she passed on the gossip about Sato.

"He is nanshuko, but not always." She waggled her hand from side to side in an ambivalent gesture. "Everybody in the Floating World knows about Sato and his nasty habits. Generally, he sticks to the kagema." I nodded. Even I had heard of the male prostitutes of the Floating World. "When he wants a change, his reputation is so bad he has problems. The yujo hate him, and not even the owners of the cheapest lattice brothels will let him in anymore. He's too fond of hurting the girls. He has to take himself off to the children's brothels instead and buy young girls. I've heard he's not welcome in most of those places anymore because he doesn't care how badly he marks the little girls, and if he hurts then too obviously, it destroys their value. Even most of the kagema don't like him because he enjoys hurting them too much as well.

"It's not just that he's too rough," Niko explained cheerfully. "I mean, the kagema are used to that sort of thing. It's his attitude as well. He thinks if he pays enough, it's his right to do exactly as he likes. I heard—" She dropped her voice to a confidential whisper. "—that he hurt one poor kagema so badly the poor thing nearly died. This particular kagema was a favorite of his. Sato used to visit him often, and the silly man had actually fallen in love with him. He was so infatuated with Sato that he took anything he wanted to inflict and actually showed off his bruises. He seemed to think they were proof of how much Sato cared for him."

She was silent and we both shook our heads in disbelief at the powers of deception that love could arouse.

"Anyway, Sato must have gotten bored with just beating this kagema, and one day he used a wakizashi samurai sword instead of his tree and the kagema was cut so badly he nearly bled to death."

"No!" I exclaimed. Niko nodded.

"I believe it's true," she said. "It was the gossip of the Floating World at the time. Mind you, once he recovered, the kagema got his revenge. I heard he went and got an audience with Sato's father and actually had the courage to whip his kimono aside and show the old man the scars his son had inflicted. The father must have given him a great deal of money to keep him quiet, as he disappeared from the Floating World altogether after that. Of course, Sato's father wouldn't have known we all knew about it already.

"After that, Sato stayed away from the Floating World for months and months. When he came back, he went straight back to a kagema. He boasted that he'd convinced his father he'd reformed, and that the old man must have believed him as he was arranging a marriage for him. Sato seemed to think that was really funny. I heard he made a joke of it to the extent of saying he hoped his future wife wasn't a virgin because if she were, she'd stay that way forever after he married her."

"Really?" I breathed. "What is Sato, then? I mean, does he come from a noble family?"

"No. His father's a civil servant."

"You're certain he's not samurai?" I was surprised. Virtually all high-ranking civil servants came from samurai clans.

"I'm sure," she insisted. "His father's the first assistant to a governor of one of the domains just outside Edo. I think Kamakura. Anyway, I'm certain Sato's father isn't noble. I've heard his family is wealthy and well connected, but not samurai or daimyo. But that doesn't stop Sato from taking lovers from influential families. There's no accounting for taste! Anyway, the latest gossip is that Sato's father has convinced himself that his only son will settle down once he's married to a suitable girl and will give him grandchildren. He's dreaming. All Sato wants to do is enjoy himself amongst the kagema and those children's brothels that are still willing to take his money."

Niko made us tea, and I sat and sipped my cup with great enjoyment. After a while, I asked Niko if she would be all right if I left her on her own for a few days.

"I think it might be as well for you to move back into the

Jokan-Ji house until I come back," I added. "You'll be safe there."

She looked at me with her head on one side. "If you say so. Planning on going on a trip outside Edo, are you?" I shrugged. Niko sighed theatrically, obviously not at all fooled. "I'll be fine. I've got Matsuo to protect me, and Aisha to go to if I have any problems."

"Good. Before I leave, there's somebody that I must go and visit," I added.

Niko gasped in horror when I told her who we were going to see.

TWENTY-SIX

> What matters in life
> Is not what you have achieved,
> But that which remains

I had decided on my journey back from Hara's residence that I needed to talk to Akira, Hana's yakuza. And if I was about to leave Edo, then I should do it now. It fitted in perfectly with my plans. Nobody except Niko would know where I was, and Niko herself would be safe, hidden in the temple house. I couldn't imagine that anything could go wrong with my scheme, but if the gods turned their faces against me and something were to go wrong, then my enemies could suspect all they liked, but they wouldn't be able to find me, and Niko would be safe.

Niko walked behind me, but close enough to hiss directions. We caused our usual stir. I had become used to people turning to stare as I passed by, and now I simply ignored them.

"Here." Niko inclined her head. I had been deep in my thoughts and looked around startled. We had stopped at the head of a short cul-de-sac. There was only one house in it, a large, single-story building almost hidden behind a high, stone wall. The sturdy wooden gate set in the wall reminded me very much of our family estate. I looked at our destination curiously. Of course, I should have anticipated that the head of the most powerful yakuza clan in Edo would take great care of his safety. I supposed that the house hidden behind the wall would be every bit as vulgar as Hara's opulent home.

Niko jangled the bell beside the gate. I had expected to be kept waiting, but we were not. The gate swung open before the noise of the bell ceased. I glanced at Niko and shrugged. Once we were inside, the gate closed behind us immediately. I glanced around, expecting to see a servant, but there was nobody.

"Is it magic, do you think?" Niko asked fearfully.

I shook my head. "Of course not," I said firmly. "It's just some sort of clever mechanism. No doubt meant to impress visitors."

Although I didn't say it, I *was* impressed. I was even more impressed by my first sight of Akira's house. Unlike the immaculate exterior of Hara's home, the wood here had been allowed to mellow to a natural silver color and the roof tiles were mottled with lichen. The effect was harmonious and very pleasing to the eye.

A garden ran around the front and sides of the house. That also surprised me. Every garden I had ever seen had been planted on Zen principles. They might contain a few carefully pruned shrubs and—if they were large enough—small trees, all set on carefully raked gravel and interspersed with smooth rocks or boulders or possibly interesting driftwood pieces. Akira's garden laughed in the face of Zen. It was a mad riot of color. Azaleas entwined with hibiscus. Maple and cherry blossom trees lived next to each other. Camellias nudged dwarf bamboos. It should have looked a mess, but the combination of so many colors and varied scents was a delight to my senses.

I took a deep breath and found that I was remarkably relaxed.

"Should I ring?" Niko was clearly on edge. Her eyes darted around as if she expected us to be surrounded by armed men at any moment.

"Of course." The bell's sound seemed very loud in the peace of the garden. It suddenly occurred to me that although we were in the very heart of the Floating World, there was no noise at all, apart from birds singing in the garden. Was Akira so very feared that the people of the Floating World avoided his house?

The tranquility was broken abruptly by a loud, high pitched scream. Niko wailed in fear, and I grabbed her arm to stop her from turning and running. The howl was repeated as the shoji door slid back.

The interior of the house was too dark for me to see a great deal. I assumed a servant had opened the door, but before I could speak, a man's voice came out of the shade. A deep, very attractive voice that carried a clear undertone of amusement.

"Kamakiri-san, I am honored by your visit. Welcome to my home."

The high-pitched howl was repeated. It sounded like a woman being tortured. I felt Niko shaking with terror and I touched her arm reassuringly. I had heard that unearthly screech before, and I knew there was no danger in it for us. Dreadful as the sound was, it came from no human throat. It was a dog, a shiba inu. Soji, my sister's future husband, had kept two shiba inu bitches, both loyal and intelligent dogs. And they had always greeted guests with this unearthly howl. It had delighted me when Soji had commented that I was the only person—apart from him, of course—that his dogs would allow to pet them.

"My girls may be small, but they are fierce," he had said complacently. "They are terribly aggressive toward strangers, and fussy about who they like. You're honored," he had complimented me.

Remembering my old friends, I spoke calmly. "Good day, Akira-san. As you can see, my dog has accompanied us. Will he be safe with your shiba inu?"

"Undoubtedly. My bitch is always delighted to be in the company of large dogs. I think it amuses her to bully them. Will you come inside?" he replied courteously.

"It will be my pleasure," I replied. And I meant it.

Niko followed so closely behind me that she nearly trod on my kimono. She flinched back as Akira's dog barreled into the room. The creature stopped dead at the sight of us and then advanced cautiously and sniffed at Matsuo with interest. I bent and offered my hand to her for inspection.

"What's she called?" I asked as the dog abandoned Matsuo and licked my hand.

"Marika." Akira sounded surprised. I stroked the dog's head and she pushed her muzzle into my hand.

"Jasmine. A good name for her. She's as white as jasmine and just as beautiful," I said approvingly.

"I'm astonished," Akira commented. "Shiba inu are the most loyal of dogs and always intolerant of strangers. Yet you have her at your feet."

"I like animals." I smiled. "And fortunately, they like me."

"So I see," he said approvingly. "You will take tea with me, Kamakiri-san."

It was a statement rather than a question. My usual reaction to such high-handedness would have been to refuse, simply to teach him a lesson. But there was something about Akira that intrigued me and instead I smiled.

"That would be lovely."

Akira clapped his hands without taking his gaze away from my face. A young servant girl appeared immediately. I was very pleased that he was courteous to her.

"Ami, prepare tea for us, please. Niko, will you go with Ami? I'll call you when your mistress is ready to go."

Niko bowed and scurried after Ami without a second look. I got the distinct impression that she was deeply relieved to have been dismissed from his presence.

Akira stood aside and held his arm out in a gesture that invited me to pass into the next room.

As I walked past him, I said casually, "How did you know who we were?"

"I've been expecting you," he said simply. "In fact, I'm surprised it's taken you so long to come see me."

TWENTY-SEVEN

Should I be content
With touching no more than the
Moon's pale reflection?

*A*kira no doubt expected his words to amaze me. Thanks to Niko, they did not.

She had commented several times that she had expected a visit from one or other of the Floating World yakuza eager to offer us their protection.

"By which you mean they want tea money from me," I said wryly. "Not much point in them asking for that. I haven't taken any patrons."

"Yes, but they don't know that," Niko pointed out shrewdly. "All they'll see is a beautiful new oiran who's creating a tremendous stir. They'll expect you to be earning lots of money, and they'll want their share."

As not one of the yakuza had come forward to offer to safeguard me, I had shrugged off Niko's warnings. Now, I understood.

"I've been expecting a visit from one of your...

colleagues," I said carefully. "Do I have you to thank for their neglect?"

"You do," he said simply. "I was beginning to wonder when you would find it curious that you had been ignored. In fact, if you hadn't come to see me, I was beginning to think I would have to go to you."

"I see." I smiled, ordering my thoughts. This wasn't about tea money; Akira was too rich and powerful to concern himself with the earnings from a single *oiran*. I was puzzled. He appeared to be totally unlike the gangster I had expected to find, but even so, he could have no idea why I had really come to see him. So, what *did* he think I was here for?

We were both silent as we waited for the tea. It was a comfortable sort of silence. The quiet that exists between very old friends who have no need to speak just for the sake of it. I stared around the room with interest. At the same time, I noticed Akira was staring at me with equal interest.

My inspection finally complete, I brought my attention back to my host. After my experience with Hara, I had expected Akira's home to be similarly vulgar. I could not have been more wrong. Certainly, everything I could see was the very best of its kind. But the furniture was sparse, and there was no decoration at all apart from an obviously very old and equally very beautiful scroll in the *tokonoma* alcove. The room was elegant in its simplicity, and at the same time extremely comfortable. This was a room meant not for show, but for living in.

"You approve of my humble home?" Akira asked. I felt he really wanted to know my answer, and I nodded quickly.

"Yes," I said simply. "It's beautiful."

Akira was looking at me intently. Even if I had not known of his reputation, I would have understood instinctively that he was a dangerous man. He had the air of a man who was used to being obeyed—instantly. And something more. I stared straight into his eyes, and the word "power" sang in my mind. That was it, exactly. Akira had power. And I didn't doubt for a moment that he was completely ruthless in the way he used that power. And, I admitted, he was also a remarkably attractive man.

His eyes were the unusual, very light grey color that is held to show when a spirit has much water in its being. Others might find him intimidating, probably terrifying if that was how he chose to present himself, but to me, he was courteous and friendly. Almost gentle. His character was obviously as fluid as the water that composed his inner spirit. His nose was long and straight, his cheekbones as high as my own. His lips were rather full; I was suddenly sure that Akira would know how to kiss a woman properly. Kiss and give her other pleasures even greater.

I wondered cynically how many women had looked at Akira and thought exactly the same thing. Just as well that I had no intention of standing in line to await his attention. Besides, I was here purely on business. I reminded myself briskly that my thoughts were entirely inappropriate. I was a samurai; he was nothing but a low-life yakuza. Under normal circumstances, we would never even have spoken.

Ami came in with our tea, and I took my cup from her with a murmur of thanks.

"I am very glad you are here, Kamakiri-chan." The endearment fell so naturally from his lips that it took me a moment to notice it. If any other man had been so familiar after so slight an acquaintance, they would have felt the cutting edge of my tongue. I was annoyed with myself for accepting it and would have corrected Akira firmly if his next words hadn't surprised me into silence. "I owe you a very great apology."

I was startled. This was not what I had expected. I inclined my head and raised my eyebrows in surprise.

"How can that be so, Akira-san?" I was too polite; my response sounded artificial. "I don't believe we have met before, so how could you have offended me?"

"No, we haven't met. If we had, I would surely have remembered you." Was the yakuza flirting with me? I watched the small muscles of his face and saw none of the tell-tale tightness I would have expected if he was trying very hard to impress me. I was wary. Even more so when he went on. "But I know of you. From Hana."

He paused, looking to see my reaction. I kept a stone face, counting my racing heartbeats until they began to slow. When I was ready, I spoke carefully.

"Hana," I said softly. "Yes. It is partly because of her that I came to see you today. But you said you owed me an apology. Tell me why."

"I have been out of Edo for some time," he said, apparently irrelevantly. "I had business elsewhere that detained me for longer than I expected. When I got back, I found that Hana had been attracting even more attention than usual. The Floating World loves gossip, particularly when it involves any sort of scandal about the noble classes."

He stopped and sipped his tea, looking at me over the top of his cup.

"Ah, I see." I was amazed, and I also felt very foolish. I thought I had been so very clever, slipping away from Hana unnoticed, and now it appeared everybody was talking about it! In the future, I would remember that and be even more careful. "And you believed this bit of nonsense?" I said lightly.

"I thought the rumors were exaggerated at first. Anybody who knows Hana also knows how very clever and ruthless she is. But the gossip persisted, and in the end, I asked Hana if it was true. I have never seen her as angry as she was when I spoke to her then. She was very reluctant to tell me about it. When I got the whole story from her, I was even angrier than she was. I told her she had been a fool. That even if she had succeeded, she would have put herself in jeopardy as your family would never rest until they had taken revenge on her. That you were samurai, not some woman she had plucked from the streets.

"That is one of the reasons I am so pleased that you came to see me today. It gives me the opportunity to ask your forgiveness for Hana's actions, and to apologize on her behalf. Hana's an extraordinary woman, and one of the few ever to be successful in a man's world. Because of that, she sometimes forgets that there are limits, even for her."

"I have no family," I said stonily. Although I heard everything Akira had said, only the mention of my family really mattered to me. I was bewildered by the sudden access of grief that threatened to overwhelm me. I had not cried for my brother or father since I had found them dead. I had no idea why my emotions threatened to betray me now, but I felt it would be deeply inappropriate to show my grief to this stranger. "I am the last of my line, and that line is samurai. Hana mistook me for nothing more than a spoiled noblewoman. I am not. I'm as much a warrior as my father and brother were. You have no need to apologize for Hana. She saved my life. If she had not kept me prisoner, I would have died fighting at the side of my men."

Akira surprised me when he spoke. "I understand that. I only wish I had returned earlier. If I had, I could have spared you much pain. Things would have been very different if I had been here when Hana took you."

The arrogance of his words was beyond my understanding.

"You think so?" I said incredulously. "You think you could have saved my father and my brother? I doubt it."

"Of course I could," he said calmly. "You have no idea how much power I have. If I had been here, I would have heard of how desperate your peasants were."

"And would you have done anything about it?" I jeered. "Why should you? I would have thought that you would have been amused to think that a high and mighty samurai family was in danger from their own peasants."

"If I had met you, then I would have kept you and your family safe from danger," he insisted. "Whatever it took, I would have done it. As it was, it would have been simple. I would have given the peasants enough rice to feed them and to allow them to plant for next year. They would have paid me back—with interest, of course—when times were better. But there should have been no need for my help. What was your father thinking of, letting them starve?"

I took a deep breath, trying to control my anger. This yakuza dared to question my noble father's actions?

"You did not know my father," I grated. "He did what he thought was right. We did not need any help from the likes of you and would never have accepted it if it were offered. My father and brother were samurai. I am samurai. It's impossible for you to understand what that means."

The words were a calculated insult. I might just as well have called him a riverbed beggar to his face. When he started to laugh, I was bewildered.

"I apologize again, Kamakiri-chan," he said with exaggerated politeness. "Of course the honorable samurai would never have accepted help from a mere yakuza. And naturally, a warrior woman such as you doesn't need my help either."

I put my cup down carefully—it was made of very fine porcelain so transparent that I could see the tea inside, and even in the depth of my fury I had no wish to break such a lovely thing—and sprang to my feet. A second later, my hand dealt Akira a smart smack across his face.

I wear only one ring. It is rather heavy for my hand, being a large and ornate shakudo piece that Emiko became bored with and passed on to me. I realized I must have caught Akira's lip with it as a spurt of blood splashed across his cheek. It must have hurt him, but his expression of amusement didn't waver. I knew I should apologize, but I was determined not to.

"Kamakiri-san," he said politely, "I must apologize to you once again. To have aroused such anger in an honorable samurai must have involved the most terrible discourtesy on my behalf. But of course, a mere yakuza dog such as me would never understand how to speak to a noble with the necessary courtesy."

I was horrified as he bowed deeply, his hands clasped humbly in front of his chest. Of course he had no idea how deeply he had insulted my father's memory. How could he? As he had said himself, he was nothing but a yakuza. I was deeply ashamed; I should have made allowances for him.

And then he raised his head and I saw the laughter in his eyes. I stared at him in disbelief as I realized that this low-life gangster had outwitted me. Suddenly, I saw the funny side of it and I began to laugh myself. No polite giggle, this, but rather a full-throated shout of amusement. Akira joined in with me.

"We are far more alike than you want to think,

Kamakiri," he said finally. "We both know exactly what we want, and we would do anything to get it."

His words sobered me instantly. He was right, and I knew it. But could I put aside centuries of tradition? Throw away everything I had been taught was right and acknowledge him as my equal?

"I'm sorry," I said finally.

Akira nodded and stared at me. I felt as if he was looking straight into my mind.

"So am I," he said gently.

I paused and then spoke quickly, recalling what had brought me here. "I will be leaving Edo very shortly, and I will be gone for some time. That's why I came to see you today. I wonder, do you remember a man from Osaka who came to Edo to work for your father? I think you must have been very young at the time, so perhaps you don't recollect him."

Akira's face was wiped clean of laughter abruptly. His eyes narrowed and I saw the man that the Floating World feared. Unexpectedly, I found myself grateful that I had no reason to be afraid of him.

"I remember such a man very well. He betrayed my father. These things are not forgotten. What do you know about him?" I noticed Akira's voice had changed. Suddenly, he was intensely focused on my words.

"I have no idea what he called himself then, but I believe he's back in the Floating World. He calls himself Hara-san now. He appears to be a rich and successful merchant who trades with the gaijin."

"I know him." Akira paused, ordering his thoughts. "Or at least, I know of him. The man who betrayed my father called himself Iwo. How do you know it's the same man?"

"He boasted to me about his past," I explained.

Akira shrugged. "As would any man who wanted to impress the lovely oiran," he said politely. "If he is yakuza, he would have irezumi tattoos. Did Kamakiri the oiran see such tattoos?"

I was deeply grateful for the tactful way he had phrased the question. I nodded. "He had two carp on his chest. A red one on his left breast and a blue on his right. Here." I reached forward and touched Akira's chest, right and left. My fingers tingled. "On his back, he had a large oni mask. Snakes on both legs." I had a sudden, inexplicable urge to justify myself. "He insisted we play rock/paper/scissors, with an item of clothing being removed for each forfeit. I beat him," I added.

"That is Iwo. He had the carp tattooed here in the Floating World in honor of my father. The carp were his mark. I thank you for giving him to me after all these years."

The air sizzled with his anger. I felt a pang of pity for Hara, and then I remembered how he had tried to buy me. Not once, but twice. How he had been prepared to cheat and lie to keep me. The man had no honor. He deserved all he got.

"It's my pleasure," I said. And I meant it. Akira was looking at me intently.

"Hana told me that there were three men finally left in the bidding for you. I assume Iwo was one of them. And the other two? What about them?" he demanded bluntly.

"I believe that one will be dealt with very quickly. The other is proving more difficult, but I assure you he will be found and dealt with."

"I hardly dare offer my help again, Kamakiri. But should you need me, then I am here."

His face was serious. I smiled my thanks as I stood up.

"As I said, I will be leaving the Floating World for a

while. Thank you for your hospitality, Akira-san." His name tasted pleasant in my mouth. "Should I find I need your help to finish matters, then I will be pleased to accept your offer."

"I'll be here," he said briefly. I was about to call for Niko, but he put his hand on my arm in a gesture that said "wait." "Now I am even more indebted to you, Kamakiri-chan. Not only have you given me my father's enemy, but you have also given me the chance to right the wrongs inflicted on you by Hana." He paused delicately. Once again, he had surprised me. This yakuza had far more subtlety than I had expected. I answered the unspoken question behind his words.

"Hana did what she felt she had to do." I frowned as I searched for the right words to explain to him. "I have already forgotten Hana's actions."

I would seek no revenge on Hana, but neither would I explain why. Would Akira be puzzled if I told him that had I been in Hana's place I would probably have taken the same chances? The gods had dictated that our paths in life should be very different. But I saw the same determination in Hana as I knew to be in my own soul. It would be too much to say I admired her, but I admitted to myself that I understood her. Besides, the wrongs that the samurai had visited on her family made me deeply uncomfortable.

I had become lost in my thoughts. Akira's voice recalled me to the present.

"Thank you. By the way," he said casually, "I wonder if you have ever come across your namesake? A blind anma who is also called Kamakiri?"

"I believe I have heard of her," I said carefully. "I understand she is very skilled."

"Yes. I heard that as well," Akira said delicately. "She

seems to have disappeared from the Floating World. That's all to the good. Rumors are circulating that Lord Akafumu's family want to see her very urgently."

My lips felt parched. I licked them with a tongue that almost equally dry. My voice was scratchy when I spoke.

"Really? Is Lord Akafumu in need of her services?"

"No, not now. I have heard that the anma was treating him for his pains and that he was very pleased with her. Unfortunately, his family is now insisting that she's a witch and that she was in the pay of Akafumu's enemies. They claim that she gave him something that caused him to lose his wits and then disappeared. Ever since she vanished, it's said that he wants nothing but an opium pipe and can't live without it. He cannot make any decisions. He isn't even able to say what he wants to eat. I have been told that unless he is roused and taken by the hand like a child, he doesn't even notice when he needs to pass water, among other things."

"How strange! Surely an anma cures pain, not inflicts it?" I said innocently.

"Oh, I'm sure it's just a coincidence," Akira said. "Nothing to do with the anma at all. But unfortunately, Akafumu's eldest son decided to petition the shogun to inherit his father's title and estates on the grounds that his father is no longer capable of managing them. But the eldest son is not a great favorite with the shogun. Some trifling matter of a concubine, I believe.

"In any event, the shogun in his great wisdom has agreed that Akafumu should be put aside and has also decided that the estate should not pass to the eldest son. As the next son is very young, and his other brothers even younger, the shogun has decided that the title and estate should revert to the shogunate, at least until the younger son is of an age to inherit. But who knows what will happen before then. In any event, it would be very bad for the anma if Akafumu's eldest son found her."

He pursed his lips and nodded wisely. My heart was beating in a slow drum roll. I felt triumph, but there was a dreadful bitterness mixed with it. I had done this terrible thing to a once noble lord. He had surely deserved it; still, a small voice deep inside my mind nagged and soured my pleasure.

"Probably it's as well that the anma has disappeared," I said neutrally. "If the gossip is true, that is."

"Oh, I'm sure it is. The Floating World hears everything. And this has caused a great stir. Not just amongst the ordinary people, either. I believe that even many nobles are unhappy about Akafumu's recent behavior regarding a certain samurai lady." He paused and I raised my eyebrows in polite question.

"Really? And what would that be?" I asked. My voice trembled with eagerness; I hoped he had not noticed.

"I've heard it said that Akafumu was too greedy. The samurai lady petitioned him to allow her to keep her family estate when her men were murdered by insurgents." I closed my eyes with remembered pain. Akira paused and waited until I was looking at him before he continued. When he spoke, his voice was very gentle. "She was refused, of course. Akafumu insisted she marry the man her father had already selected for her. All well and good. But Akafumu should have gone further. Her new husband should have inherited her father's estate. It's said that as the samurai lady was of slightly higher caste than he was, he was willing to adopt the Hakuseki family name."

I let out my pent up breath in a gasp of disappointment. Was that all? Even if Tadatomo had taken my family name, it would only have postponed the inevitable. He had no male children. Was it at all likely at his advanced age that he could have fathered a boy? It was clutching at reeds to hope for it.

"I see," I said dully. "I hadn't heard that."

"I thought not," Akira said quietly. "In that case, I don't suppose you heard the rest of the tale, either. Tadatomo was not only willing to take the Hakuseki name, he was happy to join both his estate and the larger Hakuseki lands together. What's more, he was so delighted by his sudden good fortune that he told Akafumu that he would be happy to adopt a boy from within his own family to ensure that the Hakuseki name was carried on. Not being a noble samurai, I don't understand such things. But I believe that would be the traditional way to deal with the situation."

My mouth opened and closed but no words came out. The boy child would not be mine, of course, but was that the important thing? Of course it wasn't. The thing I had fought for, the thing I had humbled myself before Akafumu for, was that our great family name would survive. And now it appeared that I had thrown it all away by my own actions. All I had to do was wait and everything would have been well again. Instead, I had condemned Akafumu to a living death. Destroyed a great noble for nothing. I felt sick with horror.

My voice was an unlovely croak when I managed to speak. "Akafumu was willing to do that?"

"Oh, no. That was the trouble. Quite correctly, Tadatomo petitioned Akafumu with his plans. But Akafumu turned him down. Apparently, he said that he felt it was better for the Hakuseki title to revert to him at once. He used the civil unrest as an excuse, saying it was essential that the peasants shouldn't be given any more time to rebel. Tadatomo was turned away empty-handed. And of course, if there was no land or no title involved, he was no longer interested in marrying the samurai lady. Oddly enough, she's disappeared as well. Many think she committed suicide in despair."

Akira was smiling gently. Relief filled me in a rush.

"The general opinion is that Akafumu deserved all he's got. He's always been an arrogant, selfish man who cared for nothing but his own comfort. But this was too much. Many say it's simply the gods punishing him for his pride. And if they chose to use a poor, blind anma to be their instrument, then so be it."

"Thank you. If the rumors about Lord Akafumu are true, I think you're right. He got no more than he deserved." My voice was bitter, and I went on quickly, hoping to distract him. "In any event, I am delighted we have met at last, Akira-san. Thank you for your hospitality."

"It was my pleasure to meet you, Kamakiri-san." He was equally polite. "Will you be gone for long?"

"I don't know. It depends on how things go." I shrugged and smiled.

"Then take care. I look forward to seeing you when you return."

I called for Niko and Matsuo and walked away. I had no need to look back to know that Akira was watching us.

TWENTY-EIGHT

> Why do you ask my
> Opinion when you know I
> Change my mind each hour?

"Do I really have to go back to stay in the temple house?" Niko was sulky. "I like it here, in the center of things. Why can't I come with you? Who's going to look after you if I'm not with you?"

"I'll look after myself," I said patiently. "I need you to stay here to care for Matsuo. Besides, if word comes from Yo, you must be here to take the message."

Niko brightened immediately. "I can do that. Will he be back soon?" She glanced sideways at me. "I can't imagine what he'd say if he knew you'd been to see that dreadful yakuza Akira."

"Didn't you like Akira?" Why, I wondered, should it matter to me whether Niko had liked him or not?

"No. I don't like him at all," she said firmly. "He frightened me. You haven't been here long enough to hear about his reputation. He's ruthless. Anybody who gets in his way just disappears. Or worse," she added darkly.

"Well, he didn't frighten me," I said firmly. "And anyway, it's nothing to do with Yo who I choose to visit."

"Isn't it?" She was glaring at me disapprovingly and I changed the subject quickly.

"Go to the temple house. Go for your lessons and stay out of the Floating World as much as you can. I shouldn't be gone for more than ten days or so."

She pouted sulkily. I was surprised and touched when she hugged me fiercely before I went.

"Listen, Niko," I said impulsively. "If you have any trouble, anything at all, get word to Akira. He'll help you, I promise."

We stared at each other and she nodded finally.

"I will. But I hope I don't have to."

I smiled reassuringly. I was surprised by my own certainty. I barely knew the man, yet here I was assuring Niko that the most feared yakuza in the whole of Edo would take the time to solve her problems. At the same time, I knew I was right. I sighed. If only Akira weren't a yakuza. If only the burden of my samurai tradition wasn't so heavy on my shoulders. I had found him deeply attractive, and I felt instinctively that he in his turn had found me enticing. But there could be nothing between us. It was impossible.

He was a man of no caste at all. He was outside society, a gangster who made his living by preying on those who were weaker than he was. Everything he did was the exact opposite of what the code of bushido taught. Then I reminded myself sharply that I was no longer in a position to call any man my inferior. Just like Akira, I had no position in society. The knowledge was almost frightening. Trying to reassure myself, I spoke my thoughts out loud.

"I have no lord. No master. I am a ronin. I do what I like."

A beggar glanced at me and I threw him a coin.

"Thank you, master. May the gods smile on you," he whined.

His innocent response was reassuring. I was happy now that I had left Kamakiri the woman behind me. In her place strutted a perfumed and painted *kagema* youth.

I had chosen the quietest hour to make my escape. Truly, the Floating World never slept. But this time—just after the midday meal—was the moment when life was at its lowest ebb. I had pulled my hair up into what was almost a samurai topknot. It had grown longer since it had amused my brother to take me to the Floating World disguised as his young, male lover, but I found if I relaxed the knot, it still worked. I thought it looked slightly feminine, but as I was now Jun, the supplicant kagema, that was no bad thing. I wore only a little light makeup, but I had dabbed on enough heavy, spicy perfume to make me sneeze. I was satisfied that my kimono was plain enough to be worn by either a man or a woman. Tied tightly, it hid my breasts.

More importantly than anything else, as I walked, I became neither male nor female. I walked firmly, with long steps. But my head was held down almost timidly. By the time I arrived at the livery stables to rent a horse, I was not at all surprised when the stable hand gave me a salacious grin and demanded to know if my boyfriend knew where I was?

The journey to Kamakura was uneventful. I broke my journey overnight twice at simple ryokan. At both, the innkeeper looked at me suspiciously and demanded money in advance. When I arrived at my destination, I looked around the city with interest and decided I liked it. It was bustling, the streets thronged with people. Not as busy as the Floating World, but still lively. I knew my disguise was perfect when a couple of yujo looked at me briefly and then turned away, giggling to each other. Even better, a well-dressed man came up to my side and tried to grab my hand, rubbing his thigh against me lasciviously. I growled a few words in a rough Edo accent and he scurried off, throwing me an angry glance.

A few coins earned me directions to the governor's residence. A few more bought me an audience with Sato's father.

He kept me waiting.

He was writing when I was finally allowed to enter his presence, pausing to nod to himself as if he was gathering his thoughts. I waited patiently, my shoulders hunched, my whole body deeply humble. Finally satisfied that he had kept me waiting long enough, he raised his head and stared at me. I was sure I saw a flicker of worry cross his face quickly, and I exulted silently.

"Well? Who are you? What do you want? Hurry up. I'm a busy man. I haven't got time to waste on the likes of you." To emphasize his words, he glanced at his unfinished scroll as he spoke, as if he was eager to get back to his work.

"Lord, I am so sorry to trouble you," I whined. "I would never have come here if it wasn't terribly important. It's about your son, lord. Sato-san."

His face was stone. I glanced at him once and then lowered my eyes. I felt the fear spreading out from him.

"My son? What about him?" Sato senior grated. "What is he to you that brings you here?"

"I know him well, my lord. In fact, I love him!" I threw myself to my knees as I spoke, kowtowing deeply. "And he loves me. I know he does. He told me he did!"

I waited for three heartbeats, knowing that this was the critical moment. If I were going to be thrown out, then it would be now. But Sato was silent. When he finally spoke, I heard the horror beneath his curt words.

"What nonsense is this? My son isn't even here. He's in Edo."

"That's where I come from, lord. Edo. The Floating World. I've been…very good friends with your son for a long time." I spoke archly, allowing myself a small, satisfied smile. "We love each other, lord. He promised me that we would always be together. He said that he would arrange for me to be adopted into your family so we would never be parted. He told me he would bring me here and introduce me to you. But he keeps putting it off, the naughty boy. That's why I've come here today, to ask you if the arrangements have been made yet."

The silence that fell when I stopped talking was terrible. Sato's face had turned the color of a ripe plum. His eyes bulged so far from their sockets that I thought they were going to pop out. I could hear his breath rasp in his throat. I admired him when he kept his composure and spoke with barely a tremor in his voice.

"You are mistaken. Whatever your name is, this all nonsense. Or is it your idea of a joke? If it is, you'll be very sorry you came here."

"Jun, lord. My name is Jun. How could I joke about something as serious as this? Surely, your son must have spoken of me."

"Certainly not," Sato snapped. "He's never mentioned you. Besides, if you really knew him well you would know that he's betrothed. He is to be married in the new year."

"To me, lord! He's to be married to me!" I wailed. "Not officially, of course. But once you've adopted me into your family, we'll be together for always. He promised me that, and I believe him. After all, we live together as husband and wife in the Floating World. You can ask anybody. Everybody knows about us."

Sato put his hand to his chest as though he was suppressing pain. I watched him carefully, worried his heart might be failing him. After all, I had no quarrel with him. His voice was strong when he spoke, and I sighed softly with relief.

"Does my son know you are here?" I knew then that I had won. I shook my head vigorously.

"No, lord. I wanted it to be a surprise for him when I go back and give him the good news that all is arranged."

"It will undoubtedly be a surprise," Sato said dryly. "You are a *kagema*, I suppose." I pretended to be hurt and widened my eyes piteously.

"I have to earn a living somehow, master," I whimpered. "But I assure you, once I am adopted into your illustrious family, there will be no man in my life other than your son. We will be together forever." I clutched my hands in front of me in supplication and smiled fawningly. "Sato-chan told me that you are a rich man. That being the case, I will never have any need to work for a living again. I will belong solely to dear Sato-chan and we will be endlessly happy together."

Sato's lips were pressed so tightly together that they had almost disappeared.

"You will leave me now, Jun." He spoke my name as if it left a nasty taste in his mouth. I pursed my lips in a pout, as if I was deeply hurt. "When you get back to the Floating World, you will give Sato a message. You will tell him that I no longer have a son. He is not welcome here. If he tries to see me, he will be turned away. He is dead to me. Do you understand that?"

"But what will he—we—do for money if you don't give him an allowance?" I wailed. I paused as if something had occurred to me and added craftily, "Sato-chan is a gentleman. He has no trade, no way of earning his living. If you cut him off, he'll have to become a kagema just like me. Surely you don't want that to happen to your only son?"

"I have no son," Sato repeated stonily. "You may tell your lover that I intend to adopt his cousin, Abe. From this moment on, Abe will be the only son I have."

"Lord, I cannot tell him that! He will be furious with me." I clawed at my face, dragging my skin upward. It was a gesture I remembered Emiko, my sister, using many times. It had never failed to soften my father, even when he had been very angry with her. As I expected, the femininity of my action infuriated Sato still further.

"You will tell him! Tell him that his bride will marry Abe. Tell him I want nothing more to do with him, ever. Get back to that place, and I hope you are both very happy together. I don't care what either of you have to do to earn a living. Sato's going to get not so much as a copper coin from me."

I hurled myself forward and wrapped my arms around his legs, wailing loudly.

"Lord, no! You cannot do this to your only son!" I knew I was taking a risk, but I had to be certain he wouldn't change his mind. "Please, forgive him. Only say that you will take him back and I will disappear from his life forever. Once I am gone, I know he will be happy to marry the girl you have chosen for him. I will be happy to do this in my turn, as long as I know that he will be secure."

"Sato is a lucky man to have such a devoted...friend," the lord said drily. "I hope he remembers that when you give him my message. Nothing you—or he—can say will make me change my mind. He is no longer my son. He can do what he likes with his life, but I will not allow him to stain my family's name. Now get out of here and go back to Edo as fast as you can. Tell Sato that he has no father and no family. Tell him that if he comes here, the servants have orders to beat him from my door. Get away from me."

I let go of his robes and sat back. So convincing had been my act that I felt tears flowing down my face.

"He is mine, then?" I gulped. "You will not try and force him to marry this woman?"

Sato stared at me, his lips curling with disgust. "I have no idea who you are talking about. Get out. And if I see you anywhere near here again, I will set the dogs on to you."

I scrambled to my feet, sobbing loudly. Sato picked up his brush and returned to his scroll as if he couldn't see me. I hiccupped for breath as I backed out of his presence.

The tears turned to smiles as soon as I was outside Sato's compound. I had no doubt that he had meant every word. He had forgiven his errant son once, when the unfortunate kagema Sato had hurt so badly had come to see him. My visit must have been the final insult; Sato had taken his father's love for granted once too often. He had made a fool of the old man for the last time. His fate was sealed.

I smiled with pleasure.

"Oh, there you are, my pretty one." I had thought myself alone, and I had been deep in the pleasure of knowing that my revenge on Sato was complete. It had been so very easy! The voice startled me. I glanced around and saw the man who had accosted me earlier. Only now, he was not alone. Two burly men accompanied him. One had a staff in his hand, although I doubted he needed it for support. The other was wearing a sword, and his hand flirted with the hilt. I had seen men like this in the Floating World. Men who were not quite tough enough to be taken on by the yakuza, so instead hired themselves out to anybody who wanted their services. For protection. Or—brave men that they were!—to wait in dark alleyways and ambush men who were to be taught a lesson.

And now these two big, brutal men were being used to frighten the life out of a poor, helpless kagema.

My hands flew to my mouth and I gasped with fear. "Oh, sir. I hardly expected to meet with you again. And I see you have brought some friends with you!" I fluttered my eyelashes shamelessly. The two hired thugs turned and grinned at each other.

"This is the *man* you were looking for, sir?" one of them asked. "Want us to teach him a lesson for being rude to you?"

"I don't think that will be necessary," their employer said loftily. "And if he needs a lesson, I'm sure I can administer it myself perfectly well. But he seems to be a feisty little thing. I would be obliged if you could just escort him back to my home for me. One does so dislike the thought of making a scene in the street."

I smiled. There must have been something unexpected in my expression, as the thug who was closest to me glanced at his companion warily.

"I'm afraid I really can't spare the time," I said sweetly. The man who thought he was obtaining the services of a delectable new kagema raised his eyes to the heavens. He lifted a languid hand and flicked it at the two thugs.

"Enough of this nonsense. Just get hold of him and bring him along."

They were fools, these brutes. Instead of coming at me together, the man with the staff closed in on his own. I tripped him before he could touch me. His staff flew out of his hand and I caught it swiftly, bringing the butt around and smacking it hard just below his chest. Not hard enough to break any ribs—after all, he was only following orders—but enough to knock the breath out of his body. He lay wheezing on the cobbles, his face a bewildered mask of shock and pain.

"Ready?" I raised my eyebrows at the man with the sword. He goggled at me and I became impatient. I flicked the staff at him, hitting him a stinging blow on the side of his neck. It obviously infuriated him. He drew the sword and lunged at me clumsily. I feinted and then darted back within reach and smashed the staff on his wrist. I heard the bone snap. The sword fell from his hand and he stood back, howling in pain. I flipped the sword up and into my hand with the tip of the staff. The man backed away, quickly followed by his panting colleague. Both of them ran away without a backward look.

Everything had happened so very quickly that their employer was still standing, gaping. He backed away as I walked toward him until he hit a wall and could go no further. I put the sword point against the base of his throat and leaned gently until I saw a bead of blood on his skin.

"Please don't hurt me!" he yelped. "Take my purse. Just let me go!"

"What? Just like you were going to let me go?" I said coldly. I heard an odd noise. When I looked down, I saw with revulsion that he was so terrified he had wet himself. His urine puddled around his feet.

"Please," he whispered.

I was suddenly disgusted. I curled my lip and lowered the sword. "Get away from me. And in the future, take care who you try and bully."

"Thank you. Thank you," he babbled. He was so

relieved he actually bowed before he scuttled off down the street after his henchmen. I hoped they would be annoyed with him when they finally met.

The staff felt familiar in my hand. It wasn't as comfortable as the staff Kamakiri the anma had used, but still, I enjoyed the feel of it. I would keep it. I left the sword where it was. It was a crudely made weapon and had no place in my hand.

I turned and sauntered toward the livery stable. This was a pleasant enough town, but the enchantment of the Floating World was beckoning me back.

TWENTY-NINE

A bright moon casts a
Shadow like the noon sun. Day
And night become one

Niko wasn't in the temple house. Neither was Matsuo. I was immediately anxious. I called out, and when there was no answer, I searched to see if she had left me a message. I was annoyed with myself as I remembered that her writing skills would hardly have gotten to the stage where she could have done that.

I tried to reassure myself that she had simply gotten bored and decided to ignore my instructions and go back to Kamakiri's house. But something felt wrong here. I stood very still, looking around the house.

It had the indefinable air of emptiness that comes when a house has been uninhabited for days rather than hours. There was no smell of cooking. I went into the kitchen and touched the kettle. It was cold, and the fire ashes were white and powdery. Fear began to prickle my skin.

I shook it off. No need to be apprehensive. Obviously,

my first thought had been correct. Niko had become bored with the relative quiet of the temple house. She had missed the excitement of the center of the Floating World. I was about to leave when I paused, wondering if I should change. I was still dressed as Jun the kagema. I hesitated for a moment and then shrugged to myself. I would change when I got home. Jun could stay for the present.

Kamakiri's home was as empty of life as the temple house. The blood pounded in my temples, drowning out rational thought as I walked through, calling as if I truly thought Niko was here, hiding to play tricks on me. The only voice that answered me was Matsuo's howl, coming from the small walled-in garden to the rear of the house. For a moment, I was relieved. Surely, if Matsuo was here, Niko couldn't be far away. I walked through quickly and slid the shoji back. Matsuo trailed in with his head down. His tail was wagging, but his whole body was low, as if he expected me to scold him. I rubbed his ears gently.

"Matsuo, what happened? Where's Niko?" I asked pointlessly. He whined at me and walked out to the garden, returning to stare at me pleadingly when I didn't follow immediately.

At first, I thought there was nothing amiss. Then Matsuo ran over to the wall and scraped frantically at the base of it. I followed. When I looked carefully, I saw that a particularly beautiful rhododendron shrub had some of its twigs broken off on both sides. The sap had stopped bleeding, and I guessed the damage had been done at least a day ago. A red flower had been trodden beneath somebody's foot. It looked like a smear of blood on the earth. I bent down and fingered the gravel.

There were the faintest impressions still there. Footsteps, two sets, I thought. Somebody had run heavily across the gravel, not caring if they disturbed it. The foot trail led to the house shoji, and parallel prints went back again. I felt sick with fear as I glanced down and saw that the shoji was torn. Matsuo held his paw up and I nodded soberly.

"You tore that trying to get back inside, didn't you? How did they lure you into the garden, Matsuo? Did somebody come over the wall and make plenty of noise? Was that it? And of course, as soon as Niko let you out to investigate, whoever it was climbed back over the wall. And while you were occupied out here, another somebody slid the front shoji open and let themselves in. They must have been quick to get through the house and fasten you in the garden. Were there two of them? Or more than that?"

Matsuo whined pitifully. I stroked his head gently, trying to reassure him it wasn't his fault. It was all down to me. Somebody had come to my house, no doubt searching for me. When they had failed to find me, they had taken their revenge on my poor Niko. I clenched my teeth, fury and guilt making nausea rise in my throat.

Who had been here? I forced my brain to function through the storm of emotion that tried to distract me. Lord Akafumu's family? Had they somehow associated Kamakiri the oiran with Kamakiri the blind anma? No. Surely this had nothing to do with Akafumu. Hadn't Akira told me the family was looking for Kamakiri the anma? And not Sato's father either. To him, I was Jun the kagema. Anyway, he had not even known I had existed until a few days ago. Hara? Had he decided to take Niko to use as leverage to force me to give in to his demands? It was possible, but I doubted it. As far as he was aware, Niko was simply my maid, a no one. He could have no idea how very fond I was of my younger sister. No, not Hara.

Hana, perhaps? Hana was said to know everything that

went on in Edo. She hated me, and I guessed she would take an interest in anything I did. Akira may well have told her that I had resurrected myself as Kamakiri the oiran, if only to warn her to keep away from me.

To make matters worse, her beloved Akira had scolded her about her treatment of me. And he also found me deeply attractive. Surely resentment and jealousy together were enough to make her want revenge?

I wanted it to be Hana. She would be easily dealt with. All I had to do was go to Akira and tell him she had taken Niko from me. I was certain that he would side with me and ensure that Niko was returned at once, safe and sound. I relaxed. I would go to Akira immediately.

My relief lasted only a brief moment. Matsuo was growling, deep in his throat, and pawing at Niko's futon. I saw at once that it had been slept on, but not shaken out and remade. That was so unlike Niko, who liked everything neat and tidy. She would be annoyed that I had found it in such a state. A rush of affection for my younger sister at this small thing made me pull back the kakebuton to straighten it.

Immediately, Matsuo darted forward and grabbed something in his teeth. The way he held his lips peeled back from it made me certain he found it distasteful. I held my hand out for it, and he dropped the item in my palm.

A doran—a man's tobacco pouch. The leather was soft from much use, feeling almost like human skin. It was ornamented with deer being hunted by dogs, the pattern much worn. I grimaced as I touched it. Hanging from it by a cord was an ivory kiseruzutsu, the pipe still inside.

I closed my eyes, running my finger over the carving on the kiseruzutsu. I was sure I had seen this before, but my memory denied me. I shook it angrily as if I could make it speak by my action. But the memory of where I had seen it last still eluded me.

I slid it into my obi. No matter. I would forget about it for the moment. The memory would come to me, all the sooner if I stopped worrying about it. I clicked my fingers at Matsuo and he was at my side at once.

"Good boy," I murmured. "Come on. We're going to Jokan-Ji Temple to see Aisha. There's still a chance that Niko might be there. I'd better check before I dash off on a fool's errand to hone a bull's horn."

I could not deny the evidence. Undoubtedly my house had been entered by strangers, but surely it was possible that my clever, courageous Niko might have eluded them? And if she had, she would have made straight for the safety of the temple.

The kannushi seemed calm, as always. If my appearance surprised him, he gave no sign of it. Yet I sensed the agitation beneath his measured walk and polite bow. My gut tensed with renewed fear.

"I am pleased to see you back safely, Keiko," he said courteously. "Come and drink tea with me."

Matsuo and I followed him into his private apartment. Politeness demanded that I waited until tea was served and the first sip taken before I could speak. A few moments, but they took the toll of years on me.

"Aisha, is Niko here?" I blurted the words with no courtesy at all. "I asked her to stay in the temple house, but she wasn't there when I got back. When I found she wasn't in Kamakiri the oiran's house either, I was deeply worried. Have you seen her?"

Aisha scratched his chin with a long fingernail. It sounded like dry sticks being rubbed.

"No," he said finally. "She isn't here. We expected her

yesterday for her lessons. She's a good girl. She's been here every day that you've been gone. When she didn't arrive by yesterday afternoon, I sent one of my monks to the temple house to look for her. I was worried she might be ill. He said that he called out, and when there was no answer, he came back."

"The monk didn't look inside the house?" I interrupted. Aisha shook his head and sighed heavily.

"I am getting old, child. And I think my wits must be leaving me. My monk said everything seemed peaceful enough, so I decided that Niko-chan had just decided to play truant from her lessons. I thought she might have gone back to your house in the center of the Floating World to make sure all was well there. Besides, yesterday was a great festival, and I was taken up with preparations for it. Ah, what am I saying? I was at fault. I should have gone to both houses myself and looked inside. When Niko did not come to us again this morning, I decided that I would go and look for her myself. But obviously I am already too late. I am deeply sorry."

I stared at him in mute horror. I wanted to get to my feet and run out of the temple and start combing the streets for my younger sister. I had no idea where to start looking, but it didn't matter. My body demanded that I do something. Now. I was just about to get to my feet when Aisha shook his head. Such was the authority of the kannushi that I sat back down abruptly.

"No, child. That is not the way. You can do nothing until you know which direction you need to go in."

He held his hands out to me, palms up. I was perplexed. I heard what he said, but it gave me no comfort at all. Couldn't he understand that I had to act? That every moment I stayed was time lost?

Aisha stared at me silently. Slowly, I began to understand. He was right; I would waste my time running about with no idea where I should go, what I should do. At this moment, it was my mind that needed to be exercised, not my body. And Aisha was offering to help me. Together, our thoughts would be focused. He could help me gain the insight I needed.

I placed my palms gently against his. Gradually, our surroundings faded. Aisha's gaze held my eyes on his face. My breathing slowed, my heartbeat slackened to a murmur. Our minds joined, and I felt a sense of immense awe as I understood how much this old man had experienced. More than I could begin to comprehend.

There was no sense of time passing, nor was there a sudden revelation. I began to sense that Niko was no longer in the Floating World. I sensed that she was terrified and frantic with worry. For a moment, fury savaged my meditation and I lost both my link with Aisha and Niko. I willed my spirit to be calm, and I found my inner serenity again.

I opened my eyes and felt the kiseruzutsu pressing into my waist.

I knew where I had seen it before. I knew who had taken Niko. I knew why she had been taken. My poor Niko, who was barely more than a child. A child I had promised to care for. I had failed her, and now it was my duty to find her, and it had to be quick.

Aisha took his hands away from me and I felt an odd sensation as if I had suddenly lost something very precious. He had no need to speak. We both knew that I needed help. A different kind of help than Aisha could give me.

"Thank you." I bowed deeply to the old kannushi. "I'm sorry, but I must go."

"Of course," Aisha said at once. His face was ashen, so

white I could see the blood pulsing softly through the veins in his forehead. I was grieved that I had brought such trouble on the old man. "Please, be very careful. Even with Akira at your side, you'll face great danger."

"Yes. I know. But I have to get to Niko as soon as I possibly can."

I was almost out of the room before I realized that I had not told him where I was going. When I turned back to ask him how he knew, he seemed to have fallen asleep. I closed the shoji very carefully so I did not disturb his dreams. I hoped they would not be nightmares.

I walked through the seething streets, blind and deaf to all those around me. Matsuo peeled back his lips from his teeth and snarled at a man who put his hand out to delay me. The man jumped back and hurled curses at both of us. I barely heard him. Somebody had dared to steal Niko from me. And that same somebody was going to suffer for it. This was nothing to do with the code of bushido. Even less was it a matter of my personal revenge. My younger sister had been taken. I had to find her before it was too late. And when I found her and had her safe at my side, I would show neither pity nor mercy to the monster I knew intended to destroy her to save his own wretched life.

Tears ran down my face as I walked. They stung, and I was bitterly pleased to feel the pain. My heart felt as if it was bursting with fear and anger.

I thrust my way blindly through the hampering crowd, ignoring the howls of protest as I used my staff to push anybody aside who got in my way. It seemed as if I would never reach Akira's home.

THANK YOU!

Thank you for reading *Mantis*. I hope you enjoyed it! Don't forget to read the next book in this series, *Chameleon*.

Subscribe to my mailing list so you never miss a new release.
https://indiamillar.com/contact-me/

CHAMELEON

https://books2read.com/u/4A719N

Keiko's revenge on her enemies is almost complete. Like her namesake, the chameleon, she has changed herself to attract and entrap the men she seeks. Now, just one man remains unpunished. But before she can complete her vengeance, karma destroys her plans cruelly. Niko—her adopted younger sister—has been kidnapped. Keiko is sure she knows who is behind the abduction, but she cannot act alone to get Niko back. She is forced to turn to the most unlikely ally to help her—Akira, the most feared yakuza in Edo.

Karma forces Keiko to change her colors to get what she wants. She has become as adaptable as the chameleon. But first and last, she is still a warrior woman of the samurai.

WILD IRIS: DAUGHTER OF THE YAKUZA
BOOK 1

https://books2read.com/wildiris

In a world built on lies, one woman's quest for truth and freedom begins.

Life is never easy for a rebel, especially one determined to forge her own path in a society that demands conformity. Ayame has always felt at odds with her place in the world, her spirit yearning for freedom. Her parents' latest decree—to marry her off to a repulsive suitor—becomes the final straw, pushing her to the brink of despair.

In a desperate bid for autonomy, Ayame turns to her new friend in Kyoto's infamous pleasure quarter. Amid the vibrant chaos and shadowy corners of this sleazy district, she makes a startling discovery: her entire life has been built on a foundation of lies.

The truth about her origins, hidden from her for so long, emerges, revealing that her past is not what it seems.

Determined to break free from the shackles of her fabricated existence, Ayame embarks on a perilous journey back to her unknown beginnings. As she delves deeper into the mysteries of her past, she must navigate a treacherous path filled with unexpected allies and dangerous enemies. Along the way, Ayame discovers a strength she never knew she possessed and learns that true freedom comes not just from escaping one's circumstances, but from embracing one's true self.

ABOUT THE AUTHOR

 With a literary journey spanning more than a dozen captivating novels set in historical Japan and a collection of evocative haikus, India Millar has embarked on a diverse career. Her professional odyssey commenced amidst the machinery of British Gas's heavy industry, eventually culminating within the hallowed halls of the British Library, where the tapestry of knowledge and storytelling merged seamlessly.

Now, India finds herself in the idyllic embrace of early retirement on the enchanting Costa Blanca. As she continues to explore the realms of history and poetry, India remains deeply grateful for the winding path that has led her to this peaceful and creative haven. Each word written, each page turned, is a testament to the enduring passion for storytelling that continues to shape her life's narrative.

Learn more about India and her books and sign up for her mailing list at https://indiamillar.com/.

ABOUT THE PUBLISHER

*VISIT OUR WEBSITE
TO SEE ALL OF OUR HIGH QUALITY BOOKS:*

http://www.redempresspublishing.com

Quality trade paperbacks, downloads, audio books, and books in foreign languages in genres such as historical, romance, mystery, and fantasy.

Printed in Dunstable, United Kingdom